THE Authentics

THE Authentics

Abdi Nazemian

BALZER + BRAY
An Imprint of HarperCollins*Publishers*

Balzer + Bray is an imprint of HarperCollins Publishers.

Typography by Michelle Taormina

17 18 19 20 21   PC/LSCH   10 9 8 7 6 5 4 3 2 1

❖

First Edition

This book is for my children, Evie and Rumi.
There is nothing more authentic I can think of
in this world than my love for you.

Chapter One

WHEN YOU LOOK UP AT the sky in Los Angeles, all you see is a strange film of smog, like the whole city is filtered through the lens of your dirtiest sunglasses. You can't see any stars. And if you're really unlucky, there's a blimp up there writing the words "Happy Birthday, Heidi!!!!!!!!!!!!!!!!" in the sky in pink. Yes, with sixteen exclamation points, one for every year of my former best friend Heidi Javadi's life.

I was at the rented mansion hosting Heidi's sweet sixteen party, wishing I was anywhere else. Seriously, I would rather have been dissecting a bat or listening to my mother lecture me about how there's nothing shameful about Spanx.

Caroline led Joy, Kurt, and me inside. I turned my gaze down from the sky toward the mansion the Javadis rented for Heidi's party. Beautiful cocktail waitresses in pink dresses stood at the entrance of the event, holding pink champagne for the grown-ups and pink "Heidi-tinis" for us, welcoming us to this very opulent version of hell.

"You guys know this is exactly what Iran was like before the revolution, right?" I asked.

"Obviously," Kurt said. "Everyone knows all of Iran was painted pink until those mullahs stepped in."

"And Heidi's name was permanently emblazoned over the skyline of Tehran," I added.

Caroline laughed, slapping me on the shoulder a little too hard. Caroline did everything in her life with a little too much passion. She was the most outspoken member of our group of friends. If someone was leading the way, it was usually Caroline.

Kurt, Joy, and Caroline had been their own little posse since junior high. I joined the crew when high school began, so I was still the newbie. But I was the one who had dubbed us the Authentics, because my new friends were the first people I'd met more concerned with being who they were than with who others wanted them to be. We weren't the coolest kids in school, or the most popular, but we were the realest. At least that's what we thought.

"Wow," Caroline said, looking at the pinkstravaganza around us. "Is this the most Persian party in the history of parties?"

"It may be super-Persian," I said, "but it has nothing to do with being Iranian."

"Semantics," Caroline said. Being my friend, she knew that

Persian and *Iranian* were terms the same exact community of people used to describe themselves. Persians felt pride in their ancient empire and shame about the current regime of their homeland, while Iranians believed in accuracy over pride and shame. "This is who you are, Daria. Embrace your truth. You do you."

"*You do you* is a really gross expression," Kurt said. "It's trying to be about self-empowerment, but doesn't it sound like it's about masturbation?"

"Ew," Joy said. "Seriously. I do not want to picture you *doing* yourself, Kurt. And can we stop? This is actually Daria's culture, so can we all be a little less judgy?"

Joy got it since her parents were from Nigeria, which is nothing like Iran, but which is still somewhere *different*. She got that living in one world in your home and in a completely different world outside your home was like being two puzzle pieces that didn't really fit together.

We found a cocktail waitress holding a pink tray of Heiditinis, and grabbed some.

Caroline gazed around the room. Pink balloons, pink disco balls, pink tablecloths, pink cupcakes. "This is color fascism," she announced drily.

"Or tint totalitarianism," Kurt said, and Caroline high-fived him.

But I was still stuck on Iranian stereotypes. "I mean, my culture basically invented poetry, math, and rice," I said. "But all people seem to care about is that some of us have tacky taste, wear too much cologne, and build really ugly McMansions."

"Hey," Kurt said. "At least you have a culture. The only culture in my house growing up was homemade yogurt." Kurt's mom was an actress or therapist (depending on what day you asked her), and she was all about growing her own vegetables and fermenting kombucha.

Kurt had a point, but I hated that most people who heard the words *Persian*, *fifteen*, and *Beverly Hills* would immediately assume I was a spoiled Persian princess. They would've thought I was one of those girls who pouted until her father hired One Direction to perform at her sweet sixteen party. For the record, I liked One Direction . . . when I was nine.

The girl you're imagining—the beautiful Persian princess—that's Heidi, who stood in a circle with her Persian posse, aka the Nose Jobs. Heidi looked up at me and smiled. Her just-whitened teeth were perfect. She was wearing a skintight pink leopard-print dress. Her hair looked like it was straightened on an ironing board, and it had pink highlights for the occasion. Basically, she looked like a cross between Kylie Jenner and Hello Kitty, and by the way, she was the kind of girl who would've taken that as a compliment.

Heidi gave me a small wave with her left hand, and I noticed how perfect her manicure was. She had turned into our mothers, and I had turned into a chunky girl with dirty fingernails. I gave Heidi an awkward wave with my left hand, and then I quickly tried to hide my hands in my pockets. But the poufy pink dress I wished I weren't wearing didn't have pockets, so the gesture just felt weird and unfortunate. I knew better than to bother walking over to Heidi, and she didn't come over either. It was hard to imagine that Heidi and I used to be best friends, but that was a long time ago. Now she was beautiful and popular, and I was, well, authentic.

Heidi's mother, basically a grown-up version of Heidi, approached her and whisked her off to another room, no doubt to greet some elderly Persians. Respecting your elders is a really big thing for us.

As the Authentics and I did a lap around the room, I realized this was the first time my two disparate worlds—high school and Tehrangeles—had been brought together. To my left were the drama kids. To my right were my father's golf buddies. To my left was our high school soccer team. To my right were my mother's rummy ladies. And then I saw my parents gliding toward me, looking sophisticated as ever. We had arrived separately, since I'd gotten ready at Joy's house.

"There you are," Baba said. "You look beautiful."

He was lying. I looked fat and pimply, though the dress Joy had picked out for me was cool in a throwback kind of way.

"Thanks, Baba," I said.

"Hello, kids," my mom said as she took in our colorful outfits. Caroline was wearing a pink bow tie with a vintage white

5

polyester suit. Kurt was wearing a pink checkered shirt, white pants, and his signature fedora. Joy wanted to be a designer, so she'd picked all our outfits, but obviously hers looked best, a fuchsia disco dress she found on Melrose that she swore once belonged to Bianca Jagger. Joy was good at dressing us, but an expert at dressing herself. True confession: I had to Google Bianca Jagger, but I didn't tell Joy. She took her style icons *very* seriously.

"It's wonderful to see you all," Sheila said to my friends. My mother liked me to call her Sheila, probably because it allowed her to pretend she was my older sister.

She was lying too. I mean, my mother liked the Authentics all right, but she wished I were still best friends with Heidi. She *got* Heidi, and she had no idea what to do with the Authentics. Maybe it's because my mother valued being fabulous way more than being real. If my mother still believed in the Persian *Empire*, then she also believed she was its Cookie.

"Did you see the aquarium of pink goldfish in the bathroom?" Sheila said. "They're so beautiful."

We all laughed.

"What's so funny?" Sheila asked. "I thought it was clever."

"Beauty is in the pinkeye of the beholder," I said, and my mother gave me that look she gave me when she thought I must be an alien she birthed.

"LOL," Caroline said. Caroline's goal in life was to skip college, move to New York, and become our generation's preeminent lesbian performance artist. In her last piece, she vowed to incorporate an internet acronym into every sentence she spoke. IMHO, it wasn't her strongest piece (that was definitely the one with the rats and the stilettos), but it did get people talking about communication and technology, and how we had all stopped really listening to each other.

Baba grabbed a pink meatball from a waiter's tray. "Is this meatball undercooked or color-treated?" he asked as he popped it into his mouth.

Sheila laughed and threw her hair back. She turned to me and asked, "So, any ideas for your party yet?"

"We've talked about this. I don't want some gross sweet sixteen party," I said. "I just want to invite my friends—*my real friends*—over to the house."

Perhaps sensing a tense mother-daughter moment, Caroline announced, "I think I'm gonna go try some pink fondue. The line doesn't look too bad right now." Joy and Kurt followed Caroline, and though I wanted to go with them, I stayed behind with my parents. Sometimes I felt like so much of my life was an obligation. There were so many things I *had* to do that it was hard to remember what I really *wanted* to do. But that's what I loved most about the Authentics. They were the first part of my life that hadn't been curated by my parents.

"Daria, please understand," my mother pleaded. "We can't throw a party without inviting the Ghorbanis, and the Palizis, and the . . ."

As Sheila continued rattling off the names of every Iranian family within a ten-mile radius of Beverly Hills, I caught Baba giving me a sympathetic glance. "Sheila *djoon*," Baba softly interrupted, "I think Daria already understands that you would like to invite the entire Persian community to her sweet sixteen."

"It would be rude not to," Sheila said, as if we had no choice in the matter.

"Yes, I understand," Baba said. "But since it's Daria's birthday, perhaps we can all compromise . . . and only invite *half* of the Persian community."

And to my surprise, my mother threw her hair back and laughed again. This was her physical cue that she was having a good time. She did it when she was dancing, watching reruns of *Seinfeld*, or winning a round of rummy. Her hair was her tell. Kurt, whose mother had instilled in him a very deep love for astrology, said it was because she was a Leo. He said Leos needed their manes brushed all the time. I think Kurt meant that Sheila needed to feel admired, and Baba had figured out exactly how to do that. As for me, I wasn't much of a mane brusher. I was the girl who'd chopped the hair off every Barbie doll I ever had.

"Well, I love parties," Sheila said. She wasn't lying. Sheila was always telling me to dress up more, go out more, put on more makeup, and have more fun. Sometimes, when I was in the library studying, I would tweet that I was having a dance party with friends just so Sheila would get off my back.

"So, Daria, if you don't want your sweet sixteen to be the party of the century," she continued, "then how about we focus on my forty-ninth birthday party next summer. I'd like everything to be lavender."

"Even the goldfish?" I cracked, and to my shock, Sheila laughed and threw her hair back. Had I brushed her mane without even meaning to?

"Okay, we'll throw you a lavender forty-ninth birthday," Baba said, with a smile my way. In truth, she was fifty-two, but we let her get away with shifting her age as she saw fit. "It'll be a party to remember," Baba said. "We'll paint the house lavender, and have lavender fondue, and lavender meatballs, of course."

Sheila laughed and slapped Baba's arm playfully. He pulled her close to him and gave her a kiss. And by *kiss*, I mean he *went for it*.

"You guys, get a room," I said. "Preferably soundproofed." Their passion was a cruel reminder that I had never even kissed anyone.

Luckily, a slide show began, diverting my parents' attention. The whole party *ooh*ed and *aah*ed as photos from Heidi's past appeared on-screen. There was baby Heidi, smiling a gap-toothed smile in her mother's arms. There was toddler Heidi, in ballet class, obviously. There was seven-year-old Heidi, randomly sitting on Kelly Ripa's lap. There was tween Heidi, riding a roller coaster with her father. There were Heidi and her new friends, looking airbrushed and blow-dried, posing on top of Heidi's dad's car like they were Bravo reality stars doing a Carl's Jr. commercial. And there was Heidi and me. We were twelve years old, lounging by her pool. Heidi, of course, looked adorable. I, on the other hand, looked frightening. My skin was covered in acne, my hair was frizzy, and I was wearing a too-tight bathing suit that made me look like a raspberry muffin.

All around us, the Persian parents commented on how cute Heidi looked and how beautiful she always was and how she looked just like her mother. I hated myself in that moment, because I wanted their approval as well. I wanted to be cute and beautiful and to look like my mother. The picture was up there for all of five seconds, but by the fourth second, I felt like I was being suffocated by it.

"Can we please leave?" I begged my parents in an urgent whisper.

"They haven't even cut the cake," my mother replied in a hushed tone. "It would be rude to—"

But I didn't wait for her to finish the sentence. Instead, I walked out, causing a few of the guests to turn their attention away from the slide show. My parents followed me outside, and I could feel my mother's annoyance radiating off her.

Once we were outside and alone, I turned to my mother ferociously. "You know who's rude, Sheila?" I asked. "*Heidi* is rude. She makes me feel awful."

"She's your friend," Sheila argued.

"If she's my friend, then the shah and the ayatollah were besties."

"Who is the shah in this situation?" Sheila asked.

"Obviously, she is," I said.

My mother rolled her eyes. If anyone was going to be the shah in this analogy, it would be her daughter.

"Maybe you're the queen," Sheila said.

"Fine," I said, "I'm the queen."

Sheila placed a hand on my shoulder and looked me in the eye. "Now you just need to believe it."

Chapter Two

THE LAST DAY OF CLASS before Christmas break at Beverly Hills High was always entertaining as kids tried to one-up each other with the trips their families were taking. As we waited for our English teacher, Mr. Farrell, to arrive, the competition began. Stella Burr told us she was going skiing in Aspen. Lance Summers said he was going to Romania to visit the set of a Socrates biopic that his dad was producing. Kimmy Kaplan was going to Israel to visit family. Betty Powell's parents were taking her to see her birth mother in concert in Las Vegas. But the winner of this game every year was, of course, Heidi, who announced that her family was going to spend the holidays with the king and queen of Jordan in their castle. When Heidi finished telling us about how she was going to have her own royal servant, she turned to me and asked, "And you, Daria? Any glamorous plans?"

I didn't answer. Heidi already knew my family was staying in Los Angeles. My brother, Amir, and his husband, Andrew, were expecting their first child, and we weren't going to miss the birth because we were on a trip to Jordan that we couldn't even afford. And by the way, Amir was twelve years older than me, so it's not like he was a gay teen dad, if that's even a thing.

Luckily, Mr. Farrell finally entered, his brow glistening with sweat. "Sorry I'm late, kids. There was an accident on the 405."

"You should always take surface streets, Mr. F," Heidi offered.

Mr. Farrell ignored her. "Before we begin, I'd like to congratulate Daria on writing this month's extra-credit MVP book report." Mr. Farrell gave me his megawatt smile. He was kind of a hunk. He used to play college basketball (hence his use of sports terminology when describing book reports) before an injury took him out of the game, so he was, like, the tallest English teacher in California. "Daria chose to write about a graphic novel that tells a coming-of-age story set against the backdrop of Iran's revolution, relating it to her own identity as an Iranian woman. Daria, with your permission, may I post the report online?"

"Um, sure," I said to Mr. Farrell, a little embarrassed by the attention. I had always been a good student, and I was usually proud of it. But I also knew that people often resented me for doing well, like somehow I was trying to make them look bad, which wasn't true at all.

Heidi raised her hand and spoke before Mr. Farrell called on her, which was pretty much the way most classes worked. Raising your hand was really just a warning that you were going to talk. "If Daria can write about a graphic novel," she said, "then how come I can't write about Betty and Veronica?"

"Random side note, but I was named after the comic book character," Betty said. "My mom and my birth mother bonded about their childhood Archie obsession."

"There's a difference between a graphic novel and a comic book," Mr. Farrell said, ignoring Betty.

"I don't see the distinction," Heidi said. "They're stories told in pictures."

Mr. Farrell, unwilling to take Heidi on in a public argument, finally shrugged and said, "I'll think about it, Heidi."

"Thanks," Heidi said, beaming. "That's all I'm asking for."

As Mr. Farrell turned his attention to his lesson plan, Heidi whispered to me, "Congrats, teacher's pet. Is that the most attention you've ever gotten from a man?"

A few students laughed, and Heidi smiled devilishly. I longed for the Heidi of BNJ, which, if you haven't figured it out yet, stands for Before Nose Job.

BNJ, Heidi was my friend, and ANJ, she turned into my enemy. It's as simple as that. Heidi came back after that summer a different person. She started high school dripping in bling and brands, and her face had noticeably changed. Gone was the beak nose that had made her so unique and so insecure. In its place was a perfect little button nose, with a straight ridge, and nostrils so small I wasn't sure how she breathed anymore. Once her nose went from a double black diamond to a bunny slope, Heidi swiftly took control of the Persian clique of students who drove BMWs, dressed in designer clothes, and left the smell of their perfume and cologne lingering a mile down the halls.

You might ask why I wasn't invited into this exclusive clique, especially when Heidi was my friend since birth. Well, for starters, there was the obvious fact that I didn't drive a BMW, dress in designer clothes, or wear perfume. But it wasn't just that. On the first day of high school, after Heidi ignored me to hang out with her new clique, I approached her privately in the bathroom.

"Hey," I said. Seriously, that's all I said.

"Don't make such a big deal out of it," she said.

"Big deal out of what?" I asked.

"I know you're Persian, but you just don't fit in with us, okay?"

"I, um, I just said hey."

"We're rich. We're fabulous. We're beautiful. Hanging out with us would just make you feel bad about yourself," she explained.

"Seriously?" I said. "You think a nose job makes you fabulous and beautiful?"

"I did not get a nose job!" she protested.

"Right," I said, my face burning. I wanted to tell her that if she was going to be the queen of a group of Persians, then why was she butchering her face to look less Persian? I wanted to tell her that her nose job was like cutting off a piece of her heritage. And that instead of sitting around reading fashion magazines, she and her friends should be reading the poetry of Omar Khayyam. I wanted to remind her that her nose was probably still growing, so she'd have to get another nose job soon. But all I said was, "Well, have fun with your fabulous friends. Bye."

Mr. Farrell took a plastic box out of a bag and held it up so we could all see it. Inside was an old potato, cut in half. "What do you guys think this is?"

"A rotten potato," Heidi said.

"Be more specific," Mr. Farrell said.

"It's fungus," Kurt said.

"You're right, Kurt. It's mold growing on a potato," Mr. Farrell said. "Now, what if I told you that if it wasn't for this potato, I wouldn't be your teacher? I probably wouldn't even be here in this country."

"I'd say that was a superpotato," Caroline said, and a few of us laughed.

"Maybe some of you know that in the nineteenth century, this fungus caused a potato famine in Ireland. Over the course of five years, half a million people left Ireland and came to the United States. Including one of my ancestors. So if this fungus had never infected this potato, I'd probably be living in Ireland."

"And you'd have a hot accent," Stella said, then immediately blushed. I mean, we all talked about how hot Mr. Farrell was, but not in front of him.

Heidi raised her hand. "Mr. Farrell, is this some kind of intro for some assignment you're going to give us about how we're all immigrants and we have to share our story with each other?"

"No, Heidi," Mr. Farrell deadpanned. "I brought a moldy potato to class because it's completely unrelated to your schoolwork. The most important part of my job as an educator is to waste your time." Mr. Farrell paused just long enough for Heidi to groan before continuing. "There's no right or wrong way to do this assignment. You just need to think about what brought you to this point in your life, to this country, and tell the class a story that illustrates that journey. Some of you might bring a piece of art you made. Some of you might bring some food you cooked. Some of you might play a piece of music that's significant."

"I'm sorry, but I thought this was an English class," Heidi said.

"You're right," Mr. Farrell said. "Which is why you'll be writing an essay in addition to making a presentation."

The class groaned, and then Lance said, "I'm Irish too. Can I just borrow that potato?"

Mr. Farrell ignored him. "This may seem like an easy assignment, but it's not. I want to see investigative work. I want to see emotional analysis. I want to see creative thinking. I want to see that you're thinking deeply about issues of genealogy, immigration, assimilation, identity. You'll all present your work in January. Have a great vacation."

The bell rang, and as I stood up to leave class, I was accosted by the Nose Jobs. "Daria," Heidi said. "Why did your mother do a save-the-date email for your sweet sixteen? Can she not afford stationery?"

Behind her, the Nose Jobs nodded and muttered in Farsi. Apparently, their families had all received a save-the-date email for my sweet sixteen party as well. I could feel my heart pounding in anger at my mother.

"Maybe she accidentally BCCed you," I said. "You know how hard it is to type with Persian nails."

On cue, the Nose Jobs all looked down at their manicured nails. "Whatever," Heidi said. "Our families are gonna make us come, so we'll see you there." Once again, the Nose Jobs muttered their agreement. I didn't say a word, because I knew she was right. "Hey, Daria," Heidi continued, "if you want, I'll do your makeup before the party. You don't want to be all zitty on your big night."

My face got red and hot. I hated her. I hated them. And I hated my mother most of all for forcing these people into my life. I grabbed my backpack and rushed away toward the cafeteria. But I'd lost my appetite, so I escaped the incoming horde and went outside. I searched for an isolated spot, and decided on the shade of an avocado tree.

I tried to distract myself from my anger by taking out a notebook and a pencil, and beginning a family tree. The truth was that I knew very little about my extended family. I placed myself in the center with a large circle around my name. Then I added in my brother, Amir, and his husband, Andrew, and my parents, Sheila and Pasha. On Baba's side, I added his brother, Abbas, who lived in Houston with his family, and then I added his parents. His father had died of a heart attack years earlier. I was never that close to him.

But Baba's mother, Maman Homa, was one of my favorite people. She lived in a nursing home not far from us. She used to live with us, but she had to be moved when she started forgetting things. My parents refused to ever use the word *Alzheimer's* in the house, so we just said she "forgot things," as if her condition were comparable to me forgetting my notebook on a school day. Watching her lose her memories was so painful, like this person I loved was disappearing before my very eyes. If it was that awful for me, I could only imagine how awful it was for Baba. But if it hurt, he never showed it.

I moved my pen toward Sheila's side of the family tree. I drew in a square for her sister, Lida, but then I realized I didn't know much else. I knew Lida took care of their mother in Iran, but I didn't even know her name. And I knew nothing about their father. I hadn't even seen a picture of him. Sheila didn't really talk about her past much. She was all about staying current.

The Authentics found me sitting alone by the avocado tree, and walked over. Lance Summers stopped Joy to talk. Kurt and Caroline sat down next to me.

"You okay?" Kurt asked.

"Oh, you heard that?" I asked, embarrassed by my public humiliation.

Caroline put a hand on my knee and squeezed it hard. "I tried to intervene, but Joy said you wouldn't want more attention drawn to a miserable situation."

"She was right," I said, looking up to Joy, who finished up her conversation and joined us.

"What was that about?" Caroline asked Joy.

"Nothing, really," Joy said. "He said his dad's producing a movie in the city this summer, and he thought I could intern for the costume designer or something."

"Jesus, can that guy talk about anything but his famous dad?" Caroline asked. "It's pathetic."

"It was kind of a nice offer," Joy said. "If my parents actually let me do it."

"Wait, do you think he likes you?" I asked, and immediately Joy blushed. "You should go for him. He's totally cute."

"Yeah, if self-involved bros who post selfies once a week with their dads' Oscars are your thing," Caroline said.

"Can we move on?" Joy asked. "A boyfriend is not in my life plan until junior year of college."

"Well, I think you guys would be cute together," I said. "But I guess I selfishly don't want any of you guys to date anyone. The Authentics come first, right?"

"Right," Joy said.

"Is he the kind of guy that girls want?" Kurt asked, looking at me. "'Cause I could be all douchey if that's what it takes." And then, imitating Lance, Kurt said, "Yo, ladies, my dad's doing a Rumi biopic starring Zac Efron. Wanna see a selfie of me and his abs?"

"That is disturbing 'cause it could actually happen," I said. "And no, that is not what girls want, Kurt."

When I first became one of the Authentics, Kurt did my chart and declared that we were each other's astro–soul mates, which was his very Kurt-like way of saying he had a crush on me. Caroline suspected that Kurt was gay, and using me as a beard crush. She based this on his lack of a girlfriend and his flamboyant style, but I disagreed with her. Personally, I always thought the most likely explanation for Kurt's crush was that he pitied me and was pretending to like me to boost my confidence. If I was right, Kurt was an even better friend than I had imagined.

"Okay, this is me officially changing the subject," Joy said. "What were you guys talking about before I got here?"

"I was about to offer to beat Heidi up on Daria's behalf," Caroline said. Joy raised her eyebrows at her. "What?"

"Thanks, Caroline," I said. "But let's stick with nonviolence for now."

"Don't let her get to you," Joy said.

"Heidi or my mother?" I asked.

"I was talking about Caroline," Joy said with a smile.

"Oh" was all I said. I knew Joy was trying to lighten the mood, but I just couldn't stop thinking about how I was very much letting both my mother *and* Heidi get to me.

"You know what Daria needs?" Kurt asked, and before anyone could answer, he yelled, "A group hug!"

He leaped on top of me, pinning me down on the grass. Caroline and Joy jumped on top of Kurt. We were one big mass now.

"Don't you wish you could pick your family members?" I asked, a little breathless from being smothered by the three of them. "Because honestly, I'd pick you guys."

"Speaking of family, what are you guys thinking of doing for the assignment?" Joy asked.

They all slid off me, and that's when I had an idea, and my eyes grew wide with excitement. "You guys," I said. "We should all buy those DNA kits and do genealogy testing like on that TV show. How fun would that be? And who knows, maybe we'd even find out that some of us are related."

"Do we have to give blood?" Joy asked. "Because needles give me traumatic flashbacks to my mother piercing my ears."

"Have you never seen an episode of *CSI*?" Caroline asked. "A single strand of hair is enough for DNA testing."

"I'm not pulling out my hair," Joy said, and before she could say another word, Caroline reached over and yanked a hair from her head. "Ow," Joy screamed. "You're insane."

"You know you love me," Caroline said.

"I do not love you right now," Joy responded, glaring at Caroline.

"Well, I think it's a genius idea," Kurt said. "Let's find out which one of us is descended from Jesus."

"Um, I don't think Jesus had kids in any universe that isn't *The Da Vinci Code*," Joy said.

"So we're doing this?" I asked, and they all nodded. "I mean, we probably won't find out anything all that interesting," I said. "But you never know."

I yanked a strand of hair from my head and held it in my hand. It was brown and stringy, with a little white tip at the end where it had been attached to my scalp. I stared at the strand of hair with fascination. It was so thin that when the sun hit it, you could barely see it at all. Could this really tell me all about my ancestry?

"You know you didn't have to pull that hair out of your head," Kurt said. He was holding his phone in his hand. "I just Googled the company that does the tests and they want a cheek swab."

With that, I let go of the strand of hair and watched it fly away.

Chapter Three

WHEN THE RESULTS OF MY DNA test arrived on Friday morning, I tore the heavy envelope open like a little kid on Christmas morning. The cover of the binder was white, and big block letters spelled out "THIS IS DARIA ESFANDYAR." I smiled. I had been trying to figure out who I was for a long time, and now here was a binder that thought it could answer the question for me.

The first few pages of the results were full of fun, seemingly trivial information that I pretty much already knew. Like it said I could digest lactose, which wasn't exactly a surprise since ice cream is my favorite thing in the entire world. And it said that I'm not among the small percentage of people who are insensitive to caffeine, which was definitely not a surprise since the one time I decided to emulate my parents and have an espresso after dinner, I couldn't sleep and ended up watching a marathon of *Hoarders* on TV. The next page of the test said I have a mutation of some gene with a lot of letters and numbers in it that basically enhanced the taste of bitter foods, which is probably why I love eating lemons and limes the way most people eat oranges.

And then I turned to a page with the heading "Ancestry." On the page was a large gray map with a bunch of areas colored in bright pink. My eyes went to the Middle East first, which was the area I expected to be highlighted, but then my gaze found the other highlighted area on the map, Mexico. I looked to the right, where there was a breakdown of the ancestry: 50 percent Middle Eastern and 50 percent Mexican, which was then traced back to Spanish and Aztec heritage.

My heart started to beat really fast. My head was pounding too, not just at my temples but everywhere, like my brain was working overtime to process this disorienting information.

If half of my ancestry was Middle Eastern and the other half was Mexican, that basically meant one of my parents wasn't really my parent. For a brief moment, I thought this explained everything. It explained why my mother and I were so different. It explained why she thought I was an alien child. But then it hit me that the much more likely scenario would've been for Sheila to be my mother. She was the one who was pregnant, right? Maybe she had an affair with some random man and hid it from Baba, and all these years he never even suspected that I wasn't really his flesh and blood. When I thought about Baba finding out the truth, my heart broke for him.

I Googled the company that did my test, and there were lots of really bad reviews for it all over the internet, including a case where they mixed up a bunch of people's results.

I slowly let out the breath I was holding. It was obviously a mistake.

Besides the drama of my mysterious DNA, I had enough to worry about leading into the holidays. My nanny, Lala, was leaving our house and going to live with my brother, Amir; his husband, Andrew; and their soon-to-be-born daughter. I know, it's weird that I was fifteen and had a nanny. It's not like she needed to take care of me anymore. But she had been living with us since I was born, and my parents promised her (and me) that she could keep her job as long as she wanted it. Lala was the one who watched *Pitch Perfect* with me fifty-three times while my parents were playing cards. She was the one who taught me how to make cupcakes. She was the one who taught me how to speak Spanish, and listened to me talk about the crush I had on Ebon Buchbinder in the fourth grade, and helped me sew my Halloween costumes. She was the one who listened to all my stories. Watching her pack up her room was so sad, and all that much harder given how pissed I was at Sheila for sending out a digital save-the-date to the sweet sixteen party I didn't want to have.

"How could you plan a party for me after we agreed not to have one?" I asked Sheila. We were both standing in Lala's room, which was almost entirely boxed up.

"I had a great idea for a venue, and they only had one date available. If I hadn't booked it, we could've lost it," Sheila argued.

"And how could you invite the Nose Jobs to my party when you know how awful they are to me?" I continued.

"That name is not nice," Sheila said, rubbing her perfect nose. And that's when it struck me that my mother *was* a Nose Job.

"Well, I'm not trying to be nice," I said. "I'm trying to be real."

Lala approached the heated scene gently. "Daria, don't speak to your mother like that."

I turned to Lala and told her in Spanish that my mother deserved it. Sheila hated it when Lala and I spoke Spanish because she couldn't understand us. She always said it was impolite to speak a language people didn't understand, but I knew this wasn't the real reason because she herself spoke Farsi in front of my friends, or Andrew, or Lala, all the time. The truth was that she hated feeling left out. She hated that Lala and I had a language of our own that she didn't have access to. But here's the funny thing: my mother, being an enigmatic and contradictory puzzle in human form, had *insisted* that Lala teach me Spanish. In fact, I remember Sheila admonishing Lala for speaking to me in English when I was a kid. "Spanish," Sheila would tell her. "It's important that she speaks Spanish."

I always thought my mother's insistence was strange since no one else in my family spoke Spanish. I figured Sheila insisted I speak Spanish because she wanted me to learn another language, but after reading those DNA test results, I wondered if there was another, deeper reason.

Lala's departure meant that my auntie Lida, who was visiting from Iran for the holidays, had a room to stay in. As much as I missed Lala, I did love having Auntie Lida in the house. Auntie Lida was like the anti-Sheila. It was sometimes hard to believe they were sisters, and I imagined that when Auntie Lida was growing up, she must've constantly looked at her older sister and thought, *I'm going to do the exact opposite of that.* Unlike my parents, Lida loved to talk about the past, and I thought she could help inspire my genealogy project. After all, she still lived in Tehran, among all the ruins and monuments of my history. But every time I tried to ask Lida about the past, Sheila would say it wasn't a good time. We had been busy showing Lida around Los Angeles, but my mom's avoidance was annoying.

Finally, we had a quiet morning on Friday. Sheila and Baba were teaching Auntie Lida and me how to play bridge. No one was into the game. Baba was distracted because he was waiting for a call about the environmental impact report on one of his properties. Sheila was annoyed because Auntie Lida didn't like card games as much as she did. And I was busy staring at my parents, trying to convince myself that they really *were* my parents.

Auntie Lida, exasperated by the game, threw her cards down and asked what else we could do. "Well," I said, my mind fixated on my ancestry, "we could finally talk about my school assignment."

"Of course," Lida said. "You want to know about your past, right?" I nodded. "I wish you had told me about the assignment earlier. Your grandfather painted a whole family tree that went back centuries. It was incredible. He did so much research, and he painted a miniature next to each name. There were dervishes and politicians and farmers. You have so many interesting people you're descended from. It's such a beautiful painting. Did you know your grandfather was an artist?"

"I think Sheila mentioned that once," I said. Then I turned to my mother. "Why don't we have any of his art here?"

"It was too difficult to ship the pieces from Iran," Sheila said. "And anyway, the mullahs destroyed most of them."

"Unfortunately, he didn't paint many pieces," Lida said. "He stopped when our brother died."

I turned to my mother, confused. "You had a brother, Sheila?"

Sheila looked away from me, nonchalant. "He died when he was very young."

"Like how young?" I asked.

"He was two months old," Lida explained.

"How did he die?" I couldn't believe this was the first time I was hearing about him. What else had they kept from me?

"People just died back then," Sheila said curtly. She stood up quickly. "I have an idea. Why don't we have a girls' trip to the salon? I'm sure Pasha is tired, and your highlights could use some freshening up, Lida."

Lida laughed. "My hair is gray, Sheila. And most of the time, it's covered by a chador, so I don't feel the need to freshen it up."

Sheila sighed dramatically. "I don't know why you insist on letting yourself go, Lida. You could still be beautiful. You could still find a nice husband."

Once again, Lida laughed. "You moved to America, and yet you think a woman is defined by beauty and marriage prospects. I stayed in Iran, and I think a woman is defined by her intelligence and independence. Interesting, isn't it?"

"Of course I think a woman's intelligence is important," Sheila said. "But an intelligent woman wouldn't let herself go like you have. And an intelligent woman would leave Iran. What is there left for you in that country?"

"It's my home," Lida declared.

"Iran isn't a home," Sheila said. "It's a prison. You do realize my son would be hanged in Iran, don't you?"

"I see you're a big gay rights activist now," Lida said. "I

remember you wanted to hang him yourself when he first came out to you."

I shot a judgmental gaze toward Sheila.

"I did not want to hang him." Sheila looked my way apologetically. "I just needed time to accept it, that's all. And now I have. And I'm glad we live in a country where he isn't considered a criminal for loving a nice Chinese boy, and where he can hire a surrogate to give birth to his child."

Baba finally inserted himself into the conversation. "Ladies, why does this have to happen every time you see each other? You're sisters. You love each other. Just enjoy your time together."

Sheila and Lida both sighed dramatically. Despite looking so different—Sheila with her cascading auburn hair and designer clothes, Lida with her loose gray hair and utilitarian outfit—their mannerisms quickly identified them as sisters. They had the same way of breathing out audibly when they were frustrated, the same way of rolling their eyes when they were annoyed, and the same way of tightening their lips when they were angry.

"I just don't know how two people who were raised side by side can see things so differently," Sheila said.

"I see a country I can't abandon," Lida said. "I see a mother who needs to be taken care of. What do you see?"

"I've told you a million times that you can send her to America. She can live with us!" Sheila exclaimed.

"Or she can stay in the nursing home with my mother," Baba added.

I noticed Auntie Lida grimace a little bit, so I said, "It's so nice there. Maman Homa loves it. Seriously."

"You know what," Sheila said. "I'll go see our lawyer tomorrow and ask him to get her a visa. Then you won't be able to blame me for not doing my share anymore."

"Our mother? Leave Tehran?" Lida laughed at the notion of it. Then she turned to me. "You know she very much wanted to come see you, but she's terrified of airplanes. Maybe someday you'll come to Iran."

"Not until they drop *The Islamic Republic of* from the name of their country," Sheila said. "Until then, I am a Persian, not an Iranian."

"You know not all Islamic people are bad, Sheila. We're Islamic."

"Speak for yourself," Sheila said. "I'm agnostic."

"But you're culturally Islamic," Lida shot back. "That's a fact."

"Islam isn't like Judaism. It's not a cultural thing," Sheila said. And then she sighed and added, "I wish we were Jewish." I had heard Sheila say this before. The majority of the Persians in Los Angeles were Jewish, and they had a strong sense of community that Sheila always felt just on the outside of. I remember asking Sheila when I was seven, "If you wish you were Jewish, why don't you convert?" She told me it doesn't work that way. I told her that Madonna converted to Judaism. But the subject was dropped.

"Well," Lida said, turning to me. "Let's keep talking about your assignment."

But Sheila cut her off. "I think you've said enough, Lida. I don't want this to get too depressing."

"Why is it depressing?" I asked. "I already know about your brother now."

Lida looked at Sheila sincerely. Her eyes swelled. "Oh, Sheila," she said. "You haven't told her, have you?"

"Told me what?" I asked as Sheila tensed.

"The past is the past," Sheila said.

"But it's a part of her," Lida said. "It's her history. It's her roots. It's not fair to hide it from her."

"It's not fair to burden her with it," Sheila said to Lida.

"But I want to be burdened," I said. "Please."

Sheila sat down next to me and placed a hand on my cheek. "Daria," she said, "it is a mother's job to shield her child from as much pain as she can."

"It's a mother's job to teach her daughter how to handle pain," Lida said.

Sheila rolled her eyes. Then looked at Baba, who shrugged. He was clearly staying out of this battle. Finally, Sheila said, "I haven't spoken to you about my father much."

"I know," I said.

"There's a reason I haven't. And a reason I can't bear to put his paintings on our wall. It's because . . ." Sheila trailed off. Her voice trembled and before she could continue, a tear fell down her cheek. It was the first time I had seen my mom cry, and it made my eyes well up too. I always thought my mother was impenetrable. Now she was breaking, and it made me feel unsettled, like the ground that had kept me stable for so long was shaking beneath my feet. "It's because . . ." But she still couldn't finish the sentence.

"It's because he was killed," Lida said. "They killed him."

The room fell silent. Lida took Sheila's hand in hers and squeezed it hard. Baba stood up and massaged Sheila's shoulders. I suppose I could've placed a hand somewhere on her body as well, but it didn't seem like she wanted to be ambushed just then. It seemed like she needed space. I guess I was right, because she pushed Lida and Baba away, ran into her bedroom, and shut the door behind her.

From behind the door, I could hear her screaming into a pillow. It was a trick of hers that she taught me the day that Amir first came out to her. She told me that it wasn't worth staying upset about anything for long, and that life was too short to spend on sadness. She told me that any time something upset her, she went into her room, put her head in a pillow, and screamed until she couldn't scream anymore. "When I'm done," she had said, "I let go of whatever I'm upset about. It's like it never happened." I always felt that there were two purposes to Sheila teaching me this trick. The first was to teach me how to cope with all the emotions inside me. The second was to tell me that I was to deal with those emotions quickly and privately, without ever airing them out publicly. And as much as I judged Sheila for being able to extinguish her emotions so effortlessly, I had somehow inherited this quality from her. I used the trick often, and it usually worked.

But this time, my mom was in her room longer than usual. Despite all my anger toward her about my stupid save-the-date, I felt real sadness for her. And compassion.

"She'll be all right," Baba said. "She just needs a minute."

"Who killed him?" It was all I could think of to ask.

"The Islamic fundamentalists," Baba said. "The revolutionaries. Whatever you want to call them."

Lida turned to me. "Your grandfather was a great man. When he quit painting, he became an art teacher. He insisted his daughters get an education. He was so good that he became the personal tutor for one of the shah's daughters."

"They killed him for wanting to educate women." It was Sheila again. She had emerged from her bedroom. "That's what your revolution did."

"It wasn't my revolution, Sheila. Yes, I believed in freedom of speech and freedom of expression. Yes, I protested against the shah. He wasn't perfect either, you know."

"Well, his replacement was worse," Sheila said.

"Yes, we can agree on that," Lida said. "But it's still our

home. And it's still a country worth fighting for."

I took a deep breath, but my breath was shallow, and it felt like I couldn't get enough air inside me. I struggled to take deeper breaths, but it only made me feel worse. Suddenly, I felt light-headed, and all these crazy thoughts filled my dazed brain. Like if Sheila was capable of hiding the fact that she had a brother from me, and of hiding the fact that her father was executed, then what else was she capable of hiding? Maybe the fact that Baba wasn't really my father?

In what seemed like a millisecond, all the compassion and sympathy I felt for my mother turned into resentment. I was convinced that Sheila had an affair with my biological father and never told a soul. It wasn't Lida who was the anti-Sheila anymore. It was me. I was so suspicious of her, and so mad. I wished I could have told her that there were so many gaps to my history that I felt like a piece of Swiss cheese or a piercing addict, full of holes. But I couldn't say any of that. All I could say was, "I'm sorry, Sheila. I can't imagine what losing your father must have been like."

Baba put a hand on each of my cheeks. He had been doing this my whole life, or at least as long as I could remember. I closed my eyes and swayed toward him. It was like we were dancing, and for a moment, I felt like I could almost make sense of the world. "And you won't ever have to imagine that, *aziz*," he said. Which should've been heartwarming, except my father was talking about his death, which didn't warm my heart at all. I was surrounded by three people who were supposed to be my flesh and blood, my family, and yet I felt completely alone.

Chapter Four

I THOUGHT I WOULD BE the last to arrive at the ice rink, but Kurt was the only one there. He had already put his ice skates on, and was skating in a zigzag through the middle of the rink as everyone else skated in a circle. I smiled at how quintessentially Kurt that was. He always did his own thing, never following the path laid out for him. I put on some skates and joined him on the ice.

"Hey you," I said.

"You hey," he replied.

We were standing, people skating around us, and we were surrounded by the skyscrapers of downtown Los Angeles, lit up in red and green for the holidays. That's when it suddenly struck me that despite being part of the same group of friends, Kurt and I hadn't really spent much time alone together. I mean, sure, there were some brief moments of solitude at parties, or in the hallways of school, but for the most part, Caroline and Joy were always there. In a group, Kurt was funny and confident, but alone with me, he seemed more shy.

"We're ice-skating in T-shirts!" I said. His was striped. Mine was emblazoned with the face of She-Reen, my favorite Iranian rapper, who we were all going to see in concert in a few days.

"Yeah," he said. Then he added, "You look really good."

"Oh, thanks," I said, blushing a little, grateful for the compliment. With all the ups and downs of the last twenty-four hours, I needed someone to make me feel good again. "Wanna skate?"

Kurt took my hand in his. If it weren't eighty degrees outside, we would've been wearing gloves, and the moment wouldn't have seemed as intimate. Our skin wouldn't have touched, and I wouldn't have felt how clammy his palm was, and how soft his fingers were, and how the edges of his nails were all jagged because he bit them all the time. It's weird how just by holding someone's hand, you can feel their heartbeat.

Kurt led me up the middle of the rink in his zigzag formation. Turns out zigzagging doesn't work as well with two people, and we almost immediately fell down and started laughing.

When the laughter stopped, Kurt looked at me intently.

"What?" I asked.

"Nothing," Kurt said. "I was thinking that it's fun to just hang out the two of us."

"Oh," I said.

"I'm sorry. Sometimes I can't keep my mouth shut," he continued. "It's because there's so much water in my chart."

I didn't know what to say, so I just stammered and said nothing.

"I'm sorry," he said. "I shouldn't have said anything. The Authentics come first."

"Right," I said, grateful for the save. "The Authentics come first."

I had to admit that tall, gangly Kurt was cute, with his mop of sandy-blond hair, always-crooked glasses, and unique ability to say things that were equal parts weird and sweet. But then I thought about how holding his hand didn't make my heart beat any faster. Maybe I was distracted by my test results, but it should have made me feel something, right?

Kurt stood up and held out his hand to me. "Maybe we should just skate in a circle?" he said.

"Sure," I said as he helped me back up on my feet.

"And maybe we should forget what I just said," he added.

"Okay," I said tentatively. "Is that okay with you?"

"It's okay with me," Kurt said.

We skated around in a circle, but this time we didn't hold hands. If we were having a moment, it was gone now, and we both stayed quiet, until Kurt noticed Caroline and Joy tying the laces of their skates on the bleachers in silence. Kurt skated over to them.

"Hey," he said. "How long have you guys been here?"

"Like ten seconds," Caroline said. "Did we miss something fun?"

"Nope," Kurt said. "We never have fun without you."

Caroline stood up and joined us on the rink. "I'm just warning you guys that I have only ice-skated once in my whole life. I will fall. Many times."

With that, Caroline skated off, and Kurt joined her.

I couldn't help but notice that Joy seemed a little down. It almost looked like she'd been crying. "Hey," I said. "Is everything okay?"

"Yeah, of course!" Joy said quickly.

"Okay," I said. "We could skip skating and go get an iced blended if you wanna talk or something."

"Thanks," Joy said, taking a breath. Then, after a long pause, she laughed and said, "Hey, did I ever tell you about the brief period in my early childhood when my parents thought I might become a professional figure skater?"

"Um, no!" I said.

Joy shrugged. "They turned it into such an obligation. I swear they thought I was going to the Olympics."

"I get it," I said. "My parents used to make me play tennis all the time. They called Heidi and me the Persian Williams sisters."

"That's disturbing," Joy said, finally smiling. "Wouldn't it be nice if parents would just let you be who you wanna be?"

"That'll never happen," I said. "They pretty much tell you who to be from the moment they name you."

"Well then, my parents really screwed me up when they named me Joy."

We both laughed. Her mood seemed to have lifted. That's when Caroline and Kurt came crashing into the wall. "Enough girl talk," Kurt said. "Get on the ice, because I have an important announcement to make." Once Joy and I joined them on the rink, Kurt continued. "Ladies of the Authentics, I know you guys have been waiting for me to come out, and now I'm going to do just that. The truth is that I am . . ." Kurt paused for a long time. We all skated in a circle together as he stretched out the moment, and then finally finished the sentence with the words, "A Neanderthal!"

We all laughed, and Caroline clapped her hands together. "That kind of explains everything!" Caroline exclaimed.

"At the very least, it establishes why I have such a big brain," Kurt said.

"And a big head," Joy added.

"In all honesty, I'm three-point-seven percent Neanderthal, but I looked it up, and that's bizarrely high for a modern human.

43

I mean, isn't that weird? I'm, like, not completely human. I am literally part of a different species."

"Well," I said, remembering biology class, "you're part subspecies of human."

"It's so cool," Kurt said. "And you know, Neanderthals lived in complex social groups, so maybe that explains why I fit so well in the Authentics."

"Are we a complex social group?" I asked.

"I mean, we're not *that* complex," Joy said. "My results were pretty boring. The only cool thing is that I have two percent ancestry from the Middle East, which I guess isn't that surprising since it's close to Africa, but I like that it kind of makes us sisters, Daria."

"Cool," I said with a smile, but I wasn't smiling inside. Secretly, I wished I had gotten results like hers. Why couldn't I have received confirmation that everything I believed to be true actually was true? Why was I the one who had to have my whole identity questioned by a stupid pie chart?

"What about you, Caroline?" Kurt asked. "Any big revelations in your results?"

"Not really," Caroline said. "My ancestry chart looks like a Eurail pass. Switzerland, Germany, Ireland, Italy, France, Poland. Oh, but there was one really weird detail. I have something called a warrior gene."

"Not surprising," Joy muttered.

"I think it just means I'm passionate," Caroline said, a little defensive. "Oh, and this is so random, but it said my earwax type is wet."

"My earwax type is wet too!" Kurt said, a little too loud. A few skaters looked over at us.

"You guys, can we not talk about earwax?" Joy said. "It's really vile."

"But what kind of earwax do you have?" Caroline asked as she tried to poke a finger into Joy's ear. Joy gracefully dodged Caroline's finger, causing Caroline to fall as Joy skated away.

Joy glided back toward Caroline and helped her up, before saying, "I have wet earwax too, okay?"

"Maybe the reason we're such good friends is because we all have wet earwax," Kurt said. "It's our secret bond."

I remembered that on my results, it said I had dry earwax. It was such a silly detail, but in that moment, it suddenly felt like a monumental difference between us. Once again, I was surrounded by people I loved, and I felt alone. Maybe that's what keeping a secret does to you, and perhaps if I'd just told them about my own results, I wouldn't have felt so isolated. But I just couldn't bring myself to say anything. Not until I knew more.

Chapter Five

I HAD TO KNOW MORE, so I accompanied my mother to our family lawyer's office at the Emerald Tower on Monday morning. The Emerald Tower was a nondescript office building from the 1960s. If you entered the Emerald Tower, you would immediately have been faced with a building directory, and if you weren't part of the tribe, you would most likely have found the names very difficult to pronounce: Alizadeh, Bahrampour, Darband, Davoudi, Esfandyar, Farrokhzadeh, Golsorkhi, Hakimi. I could go on, but you get the picture. Baba's office was on the sixth floor.

If the idea of an all-Persian office building in the middle of Los Angeles sounds strange to you, then you may not know that Persians like to pretend they live in prerevolutionary Iran even though they don't. It's like they don't want to face the fact that they were forced to leave their country.

My parents left Iran in 1979. They had just started dating when Baba's family decided they were going to flee. Sheila's family wanted to stay. That's when Baba proposed. I think it's a really romantic story, though sometimes I used to wonder whether they would have gotten married at all if there hadn't been a revolution in Iran.

Anyway, it doesn't matter because there *was* a revolution in Iran. See, before we had a revolution, Iran was a monarchy and we had a king who we called the shah. He wanted to make the country more modern—more like America, I guess. My parents loved the shah. Because of him, Sheila got to wear short skirts and see Bob Dylan and Dalida in concert in Tehran. But there were also people who didn't like the shah so much. Like Auntie Lida, who stayed in Iran. She once told me that the shah didn't believe in freedom of speech, that he killed people who spoke against him, and that he was a puppet of the CIA. At the time, I was too young to understand what she meant. But as I got older, I Googled my way through Iran's history and realized how complicated it all was. Like imagine if we had a terrible president and the people protested to get him to leave, and he did, but then he was replaced by an even worse president who told women they couldn't sing or show their ankles. That's pretty much what happened in Iran. Which I guess is why Persians in LA want to pretend they still live in 1970s

Iran. They feel like their real country was taken from them, and so they have tried to re-create it, in Westwood, of all places. How authentic is that?

When I was eleven, Baba took me on my first tour of the Emerald Tower.

"*Azizam*," he said. "You can do anything you want with your life. You can be anyone you want to be."

"I want to be Selena Gomez," I said, and he looked confused, 'cause he had no idea who that was.

Then Baba took me to visit all the men and women who rented office space in the building, many of whom I recognized from our parties. I met Dr. Alizadeh, the chiropractor. I met Mrs. Bahrampour, the esthetician. I met Mrs. Davoudi, the accountant. I met Mr. Farrokhzadeh, the lawyer. And of course I already knew our dentist, Dr. Majidi, and our doctor, Dr. Kalimi.

"You see, *aziz*," Baba said when our tour was over. "You can be a dentist, an accountant, a doctor, an esthetician. You can be anything you want."

"Can I be a nanny like Lala?" I asked. Baba frowned. Obviously, I had said something to upset him. "You said I could be anything I wanted."

"Yes. Of course," he said. "But you also want to make money."

"Does Lala not make money?" I asked.

"Of course she does. We pay her well," he assured me.

"Good," I said. "Then I can be like Lala when I grow up and make lots of money."

Baba finally nodded and told me that was fine. But of course I knew it wasn't. I wanted him to understand that being a nanny was just as valid a job for his daughter as being an accountant, chiropractor, or esthetician. I wanted him to get that Lala had a much more important job than cracking someone's back or squeezing someone's blackheads. I mean, she shaped my life, and wouldn't he rather I change someone's life than prepare their taxes?

When Sheila and I walked into Mr. Farrokhzadeh's office, he was walking briskly on his treadmill desk while typing. "Sheila!" he exclaimed, and then after a few pants, he added, "Daria!"

"Hello, Mr. Farrokhzadeh," I said. "Nice to see you."

"Who. Wants. Some. Tea?" he asked, taking a break between each word to catch his breath. His Stanford Law diploma stared at me from above his desk, along with a large framed oil painting of his wife and children.

"I'm fine," Sheila said.

"Me too. Thank you, Mr. Farrokhzadeh," I said.

"Please, call me Fred," he said.

FRED? His real name was Farhad. I hated when Iranians Americanized their names. It's like, could you be more ashamed of your culture? And it wasn't just Persians who were ashamed. Andrew's real name was Liang. When I called him on it, he said he changed it after he read a study that people with names that are foreign or hard to pronounce are less likely to get hired for jobs. I mean, the guy had a PhD in neurochemistry. I think he could get a job no matter how hard his name was to pronounce.

"So. You're. Here. To. Talk. About. Your. Mother?" Fred asked Sheila.

"She probably won't come to America. She hates it here. She's only visited once, and she said all the fruit tasted the same."

"She. Has. A. Point," Fred said.

"Farhad," Sheila said. "Will you please get off that silly treadmill and sit down? You can barely speak."

Fred jumped off the treadmill and had a seat. He took a deep breath. "My doctor recommended I get that thing. Apparently, sitting down is killing us."

"They say everything is killing us," Sheila said. "I say let's enjoy life and not worry about any of it."

"I agree," Farhad said. He looked over at me and smiled wide. "Daria, you are so big now!" I know he meant I had grown, but it kind of sounded like he was calling me fat. And then he reached over and pinched my left cheek. "I'm sorry. I can't help it. I still see a little girl when I see you. You know you vomited on me once."

"That's, um, gross," I said, forcing a smile. I kind of wanted to vomit on him again. It would've been better than having my cheeks pinched like a baby.

"Now I have to do the other cheek," he said, reaching for the right side of my face.

Before his hairy fingers could make contact with my face, I bolted up. "I think I'm gonna leave you two alone," I said.

"Great to see you," Farhad said. "I can't wait for your sweet sixteen. It's already in my calendar." *Of course it is.*

I glared at my mother as I left. Once I was out the door, I could hear Sheila say, "Like I said, the chances of my mother coming are very low. But let's get her a visa anyway. You never know. Perhaps in her old age, she'll decide to make peace with bland fruit. And even if she doesn't come, my sister won't be able to tell me I haven't offered to help."

I didn't hear Fred's response. By that point, I was back in the greeting area of his small office with a mission on my mind. If one of my parents wasn't my parent, there might be some kind of legal paperwork to prove it, and if there was legal paperwork to prove it, it would be somewhere in this office. Which meant I had to snoop.

Mina, Mr. Farrokhzadeh's intern, was sitting at the front desk, answering phones and reading a James Joyce book at the same time. That's the other thing about the Emerald Tower. Every Persian kid in town was expected to intern in one of the offices if they went to college in Los Angeles. I always thought this was a way for the Persian parents of Tehrangeles to keep a watchful eye on each other's kids while they were at their most rebellious age, and get some free labor while they're at it.

Mina looked up from her book just long enough to give me a barely audible "What's up, Daria?" She had her hair cut in a severe Cleopatra bob, and heavy black eyeliner on. Her whole look was very hipster–meets–ancient Egypt.

"Nothing," I said. "My mom's talking visas with Fred."

"I've told him a hundred times not to call himself Fred," she said.

"It sounds like he's a dad on some old sitcom," I added.

She laughed, which made me secretly proud. Mina was always so smart and cool. Of the Tehrangeles girls in the generation above mine, she was probably my second favorite after Goly Elghanyan, who was a professional snowboarder with a tattoo of Mossadegh on her shoulder. Goly was as cool as Iranians got.

"So, how's college?" I asked her, genuinely curious. I couldn't wait to go to college, as long as I could go to the same school as the Authentics, obviously. I couldn't imagine surviving a new school without them.

"The first year was rough," she said. "But now I get to take all my classes in my major, which is English. So basically I get to spend all my time reading, which is pretty much heaven."

That did sound like heaven. Though I was what Baba referred to as a well-rounded student, English had always been my favorite subject. I loved reading books and discussing them. I loved entering new worlds, imagining what it would be like to be different people, live in different places, make different choices. "How about this internship? Fun?"

Mina shrugged. "I mean . . . it's fine. My mom says English majors who want to make money need to go to law school, so here I am."

"Is it interesting or is it just, like, lots of filing?" I asked.

Mina pointed to a small room in the back. "See that room?" she said. "It's full of all his old files. I have literally spent most of the year organizing them all. They were a mess. You couldn't find anything. But I'm weird about organizing. I love it."

"You must be a Virgo," I said, remembering what Kurt had said about Virgos being superorganized.

"Impressive," she said. Then she put her book down and stood up. "Time for another cup of the grossest coffee known to woman," she said.

"I can watch the phones if you wanna walk to Starbucks," I said. "I'm pretty sure there's one down the street."

"Starbucks gets a B-minus," she said. "But there's this amazing coffee shop run by a Guatemalan psychic five minutes away. You don't mind?"

"Of course not," I said.

I gave her enough time to make it down the hall and into the elevator, and then I rushed into that room in the back. The filing cabinets were organized alphabetically by client name, and then within each client's file, she had separated the files into years. Most of the files dated back to 1979, the year Mr. Farrokhzadeh and most of his clients left Iran. I wondered how many secrets I would uncover if I had hours to spend in this room. Dozens at least. But I didn't have hours to spend. At most, I had ten minutes, and I would have to run back out into the waiting room if the phone rang because I couldn't have Fred wondering why no one was answering his phone.

I opened up cabinet after cabinet until I finally got to the *E*s and found our family file: Esfandyar. Like most of the other files, ours began in 1979, but I wasn't interested in that year. I was interested in the year I was born, so I went straight there.

I wondered whether there were security cameras in the office, and if there were, was it against the law to snoop in a lawyer's office? But then I figured my parents' file is like my file. We're all family, right? That's what Sheila must have told herself every time she checked my Twitter account, which was obviously meant for public but not parental consumption. Well, if she could poke around my social media, then I felt I could poke around in her legal files.

The first thing I found in the file for the year of my birth was an amendment to Baba's will, which I didn't read. I mean, I guess I was a little curious about it, but even the idea of reading it made me realize I would lose him someday, and I didn't want to think about that. Same goes for an amendment to Sheila's will, which was filed just after his. I preferred to think they were both immortal, or fantasize that by the time they got really old, doctors would have invented some way for them to stay alive forever.

I fingered through some boring documents, like life insurance policies, before I got to something strange. It was a contract between my parents and a woman named Encarnación Vargas. It was signed on February 19, my birthday. As I read the document, I became short of breath and dizzy again, and the words on the page grew blurrier and blurrier. But certain words—*adoption, no communication, birth mother, adoptive parents*—seemed to leap out at me. My head was spinning, and my ears were ringing, and then I realized the ringing was the phone outside. I stared at the last page of the contract. There were three signatures, and one blank space marked "birth father." That's what I felt like: a blank space.

Shocked and dazed, I quickly filed the contract back where it belonged, and ran to the front desk. "Mr. Farrokhzadeh's office," I said.

"It's Mina," the voice from the other line said. "I just realized I didn't offer to get you anything. Pick your poison."

"Oh," I uttered, barely audible. "I'm fine."

"I'm getting you a coconut chai latte. It's their specialty."

I hung up the phone and closed my eyes tight, wishing I could be somewhere else, or better yet someone else. And then it hit me. I *was* someone else, and that was the problem. With my eyes closed, all I saw was blackness. But then little white dots invaded the blackness, coming toward me like soldiers on a battlefield, and soon those dots were spelling words like *birth* and *adoption* and *communication* and *parents*, words that now felt like they were growing inside me.

"Daria, are you ready?" Sheila asked. I opened my eyes and looked up. There was my mother, hovering over me, looking as perfect and relaxed as ever, unaware that everything had changed and that her world had just spun off its axis.

"Sure, I'm ready," I said. But of course I wasn't ready for this. How could I have been? Nothing in my life had prepared me for this moment. I felt empty, like someone had taken a vacuum and sucked the *me* out of me, and left nothing but an empty shell with frizzy hair, bad skin, and a pug nose.

Chapter Six

I COULD HEAR THE *DING* of my phone. I knew it must be one of my friends. I never ignored their messages, but I just didn't know what to say to them. There were no words or emojis for how I was feeling. I was lying on my bed, with my face stuffed into my pillow, screaming as loud as I could for as long as I could. Usually, this trick of Sheila's worked, but this time it only made me more frustrated. *Ding*. Another message. I pushed my head deeper into the worn fabric of my pillowcase and screamed at a higher pitch, but it still didn't help. *Ding*. I grabbed a second pillow and smashed it above the back of my skull, so that I was encased by pillows. I grunted out as many strange, angry sounds as I could think of, but still felt awful.

I guess Sheila's trick worked when I was upset about little things, like a new zit, or not fitting into my favorite pair of jeans, or even having a fight with a former friend like Heidi, but it didn't do much after seeing a contract with my name and the word *adoption* and my parents' signatures on it in black ink. *Adoption*. They *adopted* me, which shouldn't have been a big deal. Betty Powell was adopted and no one cared, but then again it had never been hidden from her. My parents had lied to me. Everything felt wrong, like I had suddenly discovered the Earth was round after fifteen years of my selfish parents telling me it was really an octagon.

I finally glanced at my phone and read the text messages. It was Kurt.

Kurt: My mom is binge-watching Shahs of Sunset. Thought U would appreciate.

Kurt: Hope I didn't freak U out or anything yesterday.

Kurt: I'm assuming U R in the shower. If so, remember we R in a drought!!

I should've responded, but I just didn't have the energy to banter with Kurt about my complicated feelings about *Shahs of Sunset*, or about my even more complicated feelings about him. The truth was that all I could think about was my adoption, and there was only one person in the world I felt I could talk to about it. I picked up the phone and called my brother.

"Hey, Daria, your brother's in the shower," Andrew said. They always answered each other's phones and wore each other's clothes and drove each other's cars. That's just the kind of couple they were.

"Oh," I said. "Remind him we're in a drought."

"Amir, get out of the shower. We're in a drought. And your sister's on the phone," Andrew shouted. "So guess how long it took your brother and me to put together a crib?"

"Um, I don't know," I stammered.

"Eight hours and counting. You would think an MBA and a PhD could handle crib building, but nope. Oh, there he is, in all his glory," Andrew said, then quickly added, "Babe, dry yourself on the bath mat!"

"I love it when you turn into your mother," I could hear Amir say.

"Bye, Daria, see you soon," Andrew signed off.

"Hey," Amir said. "I miss you." I hadn't seen my brother in a few weeks. He had been so busy with baby prep: doctor's appointments with his surrogate, building a nursery, taking CPR classes, learning how to install a car seat. The list seemed endless, and the exhaustion was evident in his voice.

"Me too," I said.

"So what's up?" he asked.

I froze for a second, then finally I said, "What do you mean what's up? Can't I just be calling to see how you're doing? To see if my niece has been born yet?"

"Any day now," Amir said. "And when she's born, you'll know, 'cause Sheila will Instagram it within seconds."

I managed a smile. I closed my eyes, and willed myself to just tell him everything. "The truth is," I said, and then took another long pause. *Tell him*, I thought to myself, *just tell him*. But instead I said, "I'm just so annoyed at Sheila for sending out a save-the-date to my sweet sixteen . . ."

"Oh yeah, I got that," Amir said. "Listen, here's the tea. You've only got two years and change before you're out of the house. I know that's a lifetime in teenage years, but trust me, it's nothing. Just humor her, and it'll all be over soon."

"Right," I said. "Humor her. Thanks."

"I know it's not the best advice, but hang in there, okay?" he said.

I muttered a good-bye and hung up.

Two years and change? I didn't even know how I would make it through two more *days*. I caught sight of myself in the full-length mirror Sheila had insisted on putting in my room when I turned thirteen. I'm sure a full-length mirror made Sheila happy, since she always looked perfect with her silky auburn hair, smooth skin, honey-colored eyes, and slamming body. For me, it was an instrument of torture, a cruel reminder of how when it came to me and my mother, the pomegranate fell very far from the tree. And now that I knew why, the mirror seemed even more cruel than ever before. It felt like I was growing wider, and that the zits on my face were grower redder, and that the hair on my head was growing frizzier, all in a matter of seconds. Was it possible that my body was turning on me? That I was going through my own metamorphosis, like in that book I read for school where some guy wakes up as an insect? I wished I could turn into an insect. Then I could fly away, or sting my mother for lying to me, or both.

"What are you going to do, Daria?" I asked my reflection. I squinted my eyes at my own image, shocked that I had spoken to myself. I hated when people talked to themselves in movies and on TV shows. I always felt that no one did that in real life. But maybe I was wrong. Maybe I just didn't know what it felt like to want to talk so badly about something, and have no one in the world you felt safe to talk about it with. *Get some answers*, my reflection seemed to say back to me.

Answers. That's what I needed. There were so many questions swirling around in my head: Who was Encarnación Vargas? Was my brother adopted too? How did they choose me? And if this woman named Encarnación was my biological mother, was there a chance that Baba was still my biological father?

I built out a whole story that would allow me to keep Baba as my biological father. He had an affair with Encarnación but couldn't tell Sheila. So he orchestrated the adoption of the child that resulted from the affair, and left the space above "birth father" blank in the contract. He was the only one in the family who knew that I was his, and only his. I knew this sounded like the plot of one of those old Bette Davis movies my brother loved, but it's what I needed to believe.

There were so many more questions, but I knew that they wouldn't be answered by my parents. I knew that in order to get to the truth, I had to find Encarnación Vargas. I opened up my computer and went online.

I remembered a paragraph in the contract that said I could contact my birth mother via a lawyer when I was eighteen. Given the circumstances, I didn't feel I could wait another two years. I mean, society expects us to pick a college and a major and a career path by the time we're nineteen, but how are we supposed to do that if we can't even know who we are and where we come from until one year before?

I searched online for stories of people who went through similar experiences. One adopted girl started a whole Facebook page dedicated to finding her birth mother, which seemed like a decent idea, except Sheila stalked my social media and would inevitably find out. Instead, I tried searching Facebook, LinkedIn, Instagram, Twitter, Pinterest, YouTube, and Tumblr, desperately trying to virtually locate Encarnación Vargas. I found one Encarnación Vargas, but she was a teenager, so it couldn't have been her. The Encarnación Vargas I was looking for clearly did not have a very active social media profile. I tried the White Pages. There were two Encarnación Vargases, but one was the same teenager I found on Facebook. Immediately, I called the other, but the line had been disconnected.

There was a knock on my door. "Daria," Sheila called out softly. "I know you're upset about the save-the-date, but if you see this venue, you might get excited about the party. How about we go see it together?"

"I'm on the phone!" I yelled out.

"Oh, okay," Sheila said. "Well, we're all watching a great Italian singing competition. Come join us when you're done."

My mother gone, I typed Encarnación Vargas's name into Google and scrolled through page after page. I found a hair salon in Spain called La Encarnación. I found pages about Vargas girls, sexy pinups photographed by a Peruvian named Alberto Vargas in the 1940s. I found out that Encarnación is a religious name signifying the incarnation on Christmas Day. And then, finally, I clicked on an image from a *Los Angeles Times* article from seventeen years ago, less than two weeks before I was born. The article was about the Local clothing factory in downtown Los Angeles. At the time, Local was just a start-up company, but now they had stores all over California. They made clothes out of sustainable ingredients like hemp and recycled paper. There were two photos in the article. One was of two factory workers smiling side by side as they received massages at their sewing machines. The caption read: *Maria Tejeda and Encarnación Vargas enjoy one of the perks of the job.*

There she was: Encarnación Vargas. I felt myself starting to sweat.

I searched her face for some piece of myself. She did have my dark hair and my pug nose, but somehow it all sat better on her. She was, unlike me, beautiful. I read the article frantically for more information about her, but the article was all about Local's founder and CEO, Seth Nijensen, a scruffy hipster in corduroy and horn-rimmed glasses photographed standing triumphantly in the middle of the bustling factory. The article talked about how Seth gave his factory workers massages, organic lunches, and English lessons as part of the job. Nowhere in the article was there another mention of Encarnación Vargas.

I knew what I had to do. I threw on my shoes and marched out my door. On my way out, I could see Sheila, Baba, and Auntie Lida watching the Italian show on TV. "Where are you going?" Sheila said. "I thought we were going to see the venue."

I froze. I could feel my eyes welling with tears, and I willed those tears back inside. "I can't," I lied, my voice a little shaky. "I made plans with my friends." Before my parents could react, I rushed out the door and closed it behind me. I wanted to cry, but the tears were gone now, buried too deep to be released.

The Local factory was in downtown LA, which is where Angelenos live if they want to pretend they live in a mini-Manhattan. It's got skyscrapers, and homeless people, and lots of trendy restaurants, and subway stops. I got out of the bus and lurked outside the entrance of the factory, finally sneaking in behind an oblivious woman on her cell phone. Inside, rows of women sewed garments in neat rows. I pulled up the *Los Angeles Times* article on my phone and scanned the rows of women for anyone resembling Encarnación Vargas. Each woman looked like she could have been Encarnación Vargas's sister, or cousin, or aunt, or grandmother. But not a single one was her. One weathered lady caught my eye and gave me a half smile, revealing her crooked teeth. I approached her apprehensively. "Excuse me, do you happen to know Encarnación Vargas?" I asked.

The woman shrugged and said, "No good English."

"*Conoces a* Encarnación Vargas?" I asked, in the Spanish that Lala had taught me.

"Encarnación!" she said, and then went into a rapid Spanish monologue, most of which I understood, and the gist of which was, *Encarnación used to work at the factory but left many years ago.*

"Do you have her phone number?" I asked in Spanish. She didn't. "Or do you know where she lives?" The woman called out to her coworkers, asking if any of them knew where Encarnación lived now. A slew of answers came roaring back at us. Maybe she lived in Boyle Heights. Or West Adams. Or maybe she moved up north. Didn't she go back to Mexico? No, she went to Riverside. And then, as if under a sudden spell, the women stopped their chatter and all silently went back to work.

I turned around and found Seth Nijensen standing behind me, his hands in the pockets of his high-waisted corduroys, a loose-fitting T-shirt hanging on his lanky frame. He squinted at me through his horn-rimmed glasses, the hair of his beard bristling. "Can I help you?" he asked.

He was superintimidating, for an aging hipster.

"I, um, I'm looking for a woman named Encarnación Vargas," I said. "She used to work here."

"Why are you looking for her?" he asked.

"I just, um . . . am," was all I could think of to say.

"That's not very specific," he said, and then turned away from me.

I rushed after him, thrusting my phone at him. "She's the one on the right," I said, and then added, "I think. I guess she could be the one on the left."

"You've never met her?" he asked.

"Of course I have . . . ," I stammered. "I mean, not in person, but, like, I just . . . I need to find her, okay? Can you help me? Please?"

"Why?" he asked again.

"Because . . . ," I said. "Because . . ." And then I couldn't hold it in anymore. The tears I had willed back inside me came out in a torrential downpour, like I was a water balloon that just popped. The female workers all stared at me, probably wanting to comfort me, but too afraid to leave their posts in front of their boss.

Finally, awkwardly, Seth placed a hand on my shoulder. "Do you need a tissue?" he asked. I blubbered a yes, and he led me to his office.

Seth's glass-walled office overlooked the factory floor. From his perch, he could see everything that went on, like God watching us all from above. If God were a hipster, of course. I emptied his box of tissues, wiped my face, and blew my nose. "I'm sorry," I said. "You must think I'm crazy."

"So tell me why you're looking for a woman you've never met," he said, puzzled.

And then I realized something. "I *have* met her," I said. "The day I was born."

Seth nodded and looked at me intently. "Listen," he said. "I'd like to help you, but . . ."

"Please help me."

"Like I said, I'd like to, but I don't feel right giving out an employee's information. This is a sensitive situation."

"A sensitive situation?" I repeated. "I just found out I'm adopted. It's more than a *sensitive situation*. It's everything."

"Isn't there an agency you're supposed to go through?" he asked.

"I'm supposed to wait until I'm eighteen," I said. "The only other way to contact her would be through my parents, but they're the ones who lied to me about this for my entire life-time." He shifted uncomfortably in his chair. "If you found out you were adopted, wouldn't you want to find your biological mother?"

"Maybe," he said. "Don't you like your parents, though?"

Of course I liked them. But I was too angry with them right now to say so. "I'm an Iranian girl who just discovered that I was adopted," I said. "And you know what the worst part is? My friends and I call ourselves the Authentics because that's our thing. We're supposed to be *real*. And now I find out that I'm not even Iranian. I'm Mexican! Not that there's anything wrong with being Mexican."

"Some of your best friends are Mexican." He smiled ruefully.

"I'm proud of my heritage, okay? I love ancient Persian poets, and turmeric, and underground Iranian rap. So excuse me for wanting your help in locating my biological mother, but I would like to know who I really am, okay?"

"How old are you?" he asked.

"Um, fifteen," I said, not understanding the relevance of the question.

He stood up abruptly and shook my hand. "Listen, I have to go to a meeting."

"So that's it?" I asked.

"That's it," he said with a smile. "I'm sorry, but I don't feel comfortable giving out employee information. You don't have to rush out, though." I looked at him, confused. "Just do me a favor. Stay off my computer. It has confidential employment records. Okay?" He winked at me.

"Um, yeah," I said. Could he be saying what I thought he was saying?

"Hey, by the way, what size do you wear?" he asked.

"Medium, I guess," I said. "Depending on how much rice I eat."

He opened a closet door and filled a bag with clothes, then handed it to me. "There you go," he said.

"Thanks," I said as I sifted through the bag. There were jeans inside, and leggings, and three supersoft T-shirts, and a beautiful green V-neck sweater. "This is really cool."

"Don't thank me," he said with a smile. "I'm just acquiring a new customer."

With that, he left his office. His computer was on, and I searched his hard drive for any mention of Encarnación Vargas. There was no phone number for her, but there was a forwarding address. As I printed it, I looked out at the workers down below. A few of them were staring up at me, no doubt wondering what I was doing. I thought about what it would be like to run a company like this, to have a staff of workers waiting for your orders. Being in this office gave me the illusion of being in control, when in truth I had never felt more out of control.

Chapter Seven

I STOOD OUTSIDE ENCARNACIÓN VARGAS'S house for at least twenty minutes, just staring at it. I was trying to think through whether going inside was the right decision, but all the dogs barking up and down the block were making it hard for me to concentrate. It was like the dogs were annoyed with my indecision. The house was small, with chipping yellow paint, brown shingles on the roof, and grass that had seen better days. Strewn about the house were haphazardly placed Christmas lights, most of them clumped around the front door, on which hung a large, clearly homemade wreath made from twigs, apples, candy canes, and berries. On the lawn, a plastic Santa maneuvered his sleigh through the few sprigs of green grass, his plastic reindeer forging ahead to greener pastures. It wasn't glamorous, but it was a home. Down the block, a young couple were on their front porch, blasting old Motown music and dancing with each other. I took a breath and told myself it was now or never.

I walked toward the house and raised my fist to knock, but felt momentarily paralyzed by fear. All I could focus on was the fact that my fingers were shaking. I squeezed my fingers tighter, willing them to calm down. By the time my courage caught up with my nerves, I knocked so hard that a few twigs fell off the wreath. I quickly crouched down to pick them up when I heard his voice.

"Yo," he said. The first thing I saw was his sneakers: customized Nikes, purple and black, very shiny, with the word "Rico" emblazoned inside the Nike logo. Then I glanced up and took him in. His baggy jeans. His oversized T-shirt. His honey-colored skin, square jaw, and shaved head. The tattoos covering his thick arms. From down where I was, he looked to be at least six feet tall, and he hovered over me like a giant. A very sexy giant.

"Hello," I said. "I'm sorry. A few twigs fell from the wreath when I knocked." I stood back up, awkwardly staring at the twigs in my hand. "I'll put them back in. It'll be good as new. I'm sorry. I'm, um, looking for Mrs. Vargas, by the way. Is she here, maybe? She lives here, right?" I was nervous enough to be looking for Encarnación Vargas, and the hotness of the guy in front of me was not helping.

He reached for my hand and took the twigs away from me,

his skin brushing against mine. "I'll put them back," he said, and then flung them as far as he could. Most of them landed in Santa's sleigh.

"That's not very nice," I said. "Someone worked very hard on that wreath."

"That someone is in Mexico for the holidays and miraculously let me stay behind this time," he said. "And when that someone comes back home, Christmas season will be over and the wreath will end up in the Dumpster." He eyed me up and down with a mixture of fascination and disdain. "You're a good girl, aren't you?"

"Excuse me?"

"You're like one of those girls who always does the right thing. You always turn in your homework on time. You give up your seat on the bus for old people. You pick up your dog's shit even when no one's looking."

"I don't have a dog. But if I did, yes, of course I would do that."

"You don't have a dog? No wonder you're so uptight," he said with a smile. Was I imagining it or was he flirting with me?

"I'm not uptight."

"Sure you are. I mean, come on, you're visiting your teacher during the holidays. Who does that?"

"My teacher?"

"*Mrs.* Vargas?" So Encarnación Vargas was a teacher. "What

do you want? Extra credit for some Spanish verbs you conjugated in your spare time? Advice on your translation of a Neruda poem? Or are you just here to give her a reason to shame me for not going to college?"

"Yeah," I said. "I don't even know you, but I came all the way over here to shame you."

"Well, you've succeeded. I feel a deep sense of shame. I feel it in my bones. In fact, it's so bad that I think I need to dull this pain." He pulled a joint and a lighter out of his pocket, and sparked the paper, thick clouds of smoke exiting his mouth like smog. He held the joint out to me. "Want some?" he asked.

"No, thanks."

"Of course not. You've probably never smoked."

"That's not true," I lied.

He let out a puff of smoke as he stared me down. Awkwardly, I took out my phone.

"What are you doing?" he asked.

"Um, going back home," I said as I opened an app.

"Hey, wanna give me a ride to downtown LA? I can't deal with the bus, can't afford an Uber, and my parents won't let me drive their car. Punishment."

"For what?" I asked.

"I got arrested," he said. And then he added, "Once. It wasn't a big deal."

I probably should have been focused on the fact that I was

alone with someone who had been arrested. I don't think I'd ever even *met* someone who had been arrested. But what I couldn't stop thinking about is the fact that he used the words *my parents*. That's when it suddenly hit me that if Encarnación Vargas was *his* mother, and Encarnación Vargas was *my* mother, then me and the tall, jacked-up dude with the tattoos and the shaved head were . . . brother and sister? Ew, had I been flirting with my brother? I felt a sudden desire to scrub myself hard with the roughest loofah I could get my hands on.

I conjured up a mental microscope and analyzed each of his features with newfound fascination. His eyes were darker than mine. His nose was longer than mine. His body was taller, and thicker. His mouth was wider. But our skin tones were close enough, and our hair color matched. I was wondering whether we had the same father as well when he snapped his fingers in front of my eyes and yelled, "Yo. Take a picture and Snapchat that shit."

I came out of my reverie. "I'm sorry," I said. "I was just, um . . . thinking about something. How old are you?"

"Eighteen," he said.

It didn't make sense. He was two years older than I was. That would mean Encarnación had him *before* me. Why would she have kept him and given me up? I wanted to understand, but I didn't want to ask him. What if he didn't even know I existed? I couldn't betray the trust of my biological mother before even meeting her.

"And what's your name?" I asked.

"Lots of questions. Just tell me if I can hop in your ride or not."

"I'm not getting in a car with some dude whose name I don't know," I shot back.

"Said the girl who just called an Uber," he snapped.

"My parents don't let me use Uber," I said. "I use an app where all the drivers are female and background-checked."

"Wow," he said. "You *really* like rules."

"And I know the driver's name," I said, looking at my phone. "It's Joni, and she drives a black Prius. She looks very trustworthy." I held out the phone to him, showing him a picture of a smiling brunette.

"Point taken," he said with a smile. "I'm Enrique, but my friends call me Rico."

"Nice. Like Enrique Iglesias," I said.

"I am nothing like that douche."

"I'm gonna call you Iglesias." Was I flirting? No, I was just teasing him . . . like a brother.

"You are definitely not gonna call me Iglesias."

"Do you want a ride or not?"

He shrugged, accepting defeat. He ran into the house and emerged holding a large black suitcase.

"Um . . . am I taking you to the airport?" I asked.

"Nope. Just to downtown LA."

"Are you a . . ." I searched for the right words and finally came up with, "A dealer of narcotics?"

"No, ma'am, I am not a dealer of narcotics. I am a law-abiding citizen of these United States of America."

"Except you were arrested," I shot back.

"She pays attention," he said. "I like that in a woman."

"Are you talking *to* me or *about* me?" I asked.

"Both," he said, with a smile. "That's how I roll." He took one last hit of his joint, then put it out on the bottom of his sneaker. "So," he said. "Is the interrogation over, or do you wanna see my passport? I look real cute in my picture."

"How'd that happen?" I teased.

"Oh, you know, they used a real soft-focus lens."

A black Prius drove up, and Joni waved to us. "Follow me, Iglesias," I said, and then I asked Joni if she was okay making an extra stop.

Once we were both in the backseat headed toward downtown LA, he turned to me and asked, "So what's your name, anyway?"

"Daria," I said.

"Daria. I like it," he said. "A most resplendent name."

"Big word," I said.

"Hey, just because I'm not in college doesn't mean I'm dumb." He wasn't smiling when he said this. I had obviously hit a nerve.

"I'm sorry," I said. "I didn't mean it like that. My name means *ocean* in Farsi."

"I'm gonna call you Ocean," he said.

"You do that, Iglesias."

Finally, we pulled over in a bustling neighborhood just outside the garment district. Iglesias exited the car and took his suitcase out of the trunk. I followed him out. "It was nice to meet you," I said.

Iglesias shook my hand. "Hope it's not the last time."

I blushed a little, then couldn't help but ask, "So what's in the suitcase?"

"Why don't you come with me and find out?"

I knew my parents would start wondering where I was, but I couldn't resist the offer to spend more time with him. So I followed Iglesias as he zigzagged past crowds of people toward a historic art deco movie theater that had been converted into some kind of chaotic bazaar. Inside, people set up booths and sold shoes, and socks, and dolls, and Michael Jackson T-shirts, and Bibles, and churros, and stuffed animals. I remembered Auntie Lida describing the bazaar in Tehran to me. She said it was an endless swirl of vendors, each of them begging you to buy from them, the scent of leather and silver and baklava merging in the broiling air. I thought this was the closest I would get to Tehran's bazaar, since my parents would never let me visit Iran.

Iglesias said hello to almost every vendor in the makeshift mall, some of them high-fiving him as he walked inside. Then he finally reached a small area at the center of the former lobby, opened his suitcase, and began setting up the fake purses he had inside, gold Chanel and Fendi logos glimmering as they caught the light. As he pulled a beige clutch out of the suitcase, I had to laugh.

"What's so funny?" he said.

"Nothing," I said. "It's just . . . my mom has that bag."

"Yeah, maybe she bought it from me."

"Maybe she did," I said, knowing full well that she bought it in Beverly Hills, and not wanting to reveal this for some reason.

"So now you know my secret," he said. "Disappointed?"

"I mean, I'm not gonna lie, it would've been more exciting if you were a money launderer, but I'm okay with the fact that you sell fake handbags."

"Hey, they're not fake," he said.

"Oh, come on," I said, grabbing a Chanel clutch and inspecting it. "This is clearly made out of some kind of PVC. And the diamond stitching isn't even consistent throughout. And the stamp says 'Made in Paris.'"

"Because it was made in Paris," he asserted.

"Chanel bags never say 'Made in Paris,'" I said. "They say 'Made in France' or 'Made in Italy.'"

"Anything else?" he asked.

I held the bag up and inspected it further. I thought back to my first trip to the Chanel store with Sheila. She told me that a girl's first Chanel bag was a rite of passage to womanhood.

She explained the intricacies of the bags to me, showing me the detail in the stitching, explaining everything that made the bag so special. "When you graduate from college," she told me, "I will buy you your first Chanel bag. And then you will be a woman. And I will be so happy, and so sad."

I handed the bag back to Iglesias. "The hardware is all wrong. Chanel bags have hardware that is either all silver or all gold, but not both."

"Whoa," he said. "Thank you. I'll get on that."

"So you make these too? Or you just sell them?"

"I work for the dude who makes them. But I draw the designs."

"Oh, cool, so you're a designer? That's what my friend Joy wants to do."

"I'm an artist," he said proudly. "And in case you're wondering, that's what I got arrested for. I'm not a drug dealer or a thief. I just like to make walls more beautiful with paint. Not that my parents see it that way. All they see is that I have a record now."

"Well, a lot of artists get arrested, right?" I asked, wanting to make him feel better. "Maybe it's a badge of honor."

He shrugged. He obviously didn't love talking about it. "So how do you know so much about bags?" he asked. "You make 'em too?"

"Um, no," I said. "I do not make fakes."

"Hey, they might not be 'Made in France,' but they're not

fake," he said. "They're right here in front of you. You can touch them. You can hold them. You can see them. What's more real than that?" He smiled, and his eyes zeroed in on mine. Yeah, he was definitely flirting.

On my way home, I got a text from Joy. The Authentics were going to Kurt's favorite vegan pastry shop. I stood across the street, watching my friends inside, eating and laughing.

I had every intention of running in, ordering a vegan brownie, and telling my friends *everything*. But I didn't know where, or how, I would begin. How would I tell them that I was adopted? How would I confess to them, especially Kurt, that I had finally met a cute guy who seemed to like me, and he might just be my brother? And how could I reveal that my parents had lied to me for so long, knowing how harshly my friends—especially Caroline—would judge them? Though it was messed up, I wanted to protect my parents from the judgment I knew they deserved.

I had never kept a secret from the Authentics, but that moment seemed like the time to start. Instead of going in, I texted Joy.

Me: Hey, I can't make it. Have some extra rice cream 4 me.

And then I texted Kurt.

Me: Sorry I've been MIA. We R all good.

Me: Tell your mom that she should watch a Kiarostami movie for every Shahs of Sunset episode she watches. For balance!

Iglesias was wrong, I thought to myself. I was standing right in front of them, but in that moment, I was definitely a fake.

I couldn't take my mind off Iglesias that night, and apparently he was thinking about me too. I was sitting at dinner with my parents, Amir, Andrew, and Auntie Lida when my phone *ding*ed.

"Daria," Baba said. "No phones at the dinner table."

"Is it one of your friends, the Authorities?" Lida asked.

"The Authentics," Sheila corrected with a laugh. Then she added, "It's her father and I who are the Authorities."

Amir gave me a sympathetic smile and mouthed the words *two more years* to me.

"Let me just put the phone on silent," I said. But when I looked at my phone, I quickly realized it wasn't one of the Authentics texting me. It was a new Snapchat message from Iglesias, who I had followed before we said good-bye. "I'm sorry," I said, grabbing my phone and turning it so no one but me could see it. "I'll put the phone away after this."

I opened up Snapchat and a picture of Iglesias popped up. In the picture, he was holding up a Chanel bag in front of his bare torso. I noticed the bag had far superior stitching than the ones I had seen. This guy worked fast. *Like what you see, Ocean?* the text read. Before I could even process the hotness of his muscular shoulders, the photo disappeared. I quickly texted him back, *I hope you're talking about the bag, because I do not need to see this much of you, okay.* I immediately felt bad and wanted to say something else, but Baba was glaring at me, so I put the phone away.

"Is everything okay?" Lida asked.

"Fine," I said. What was I supposed to say? *No, my biological brother, who you probably don't even know exists, is sexting me right now.*

These were the topics that were discussed during our family dinner: my sweet sixteen party, the good news from Baba's environmental impact report, the state of women's fashion in Tehran, the fact that Amir and Andrew finally succeeded in putting a crib together, and my sweet sixteen party again.

I participated in a grand total of zero of those conversations. I was thinking about Iglesias, and how I wanted to see that picture of him again, and about how rude I was to him, and about how if there was one person in the word I could talk to about what was going on, he was the best choice.

The next morning, while Sheila and Auntie Lida went to Pilates, I decided to go see Iglesias again. I could see his face harden as I approached his booth at the bazaar. He was in the middle of a sale to a man. When the man walked away, I approached Iglesias apprehensively. "Congratulations on the sale," I said. He just cocked his head, willfully ignoring me. "Do you think that man's girlfriend or wife will ever know he bought her a fake?"

"Why are you so obsessed with calling these fake?" he asked, annoyed.

"Look, I'm sorry," I said. "You're probably mad at me 'cause of my super-rude Snapchat reply, but there was a reason—"

"I'm not mad at you," he said, interrupting me. "Damn, you think everything's about you, huh? I can't just be in a shitty mood because of something else."

"Of course you can. But still, I want to apologize. I was really rude to you when you, um, sent me that, um, you know, picture of yourself."

"You don't need to make a thing out of it, okay? I thought you were into me, and you weren't into me. End of story. If you wanna buy a bag, go ahead. Otherwise, we don't really need to talk about it."

"But that's the thing," I said. "It's not the end of the story." I fidgeted with a hangnail on my index finger, yanking it until a drop of blood appeared at the periphery of my fingernail.

"So you *are* into me?" he said, with a half smile.

"No!" I yelled a little too loud. "I mean, I don't mean it like that. I do think you're cute or not even cute, more like hot, honestly, but I can't think you're hot, or cute! That's the thing." I took a deep breath. "Okay, I'm going to explain now."

"I get it," he said. "You have a boyfriend."

"No!" Now I was blushing. "You're going to think I'm totally crazy."

"Oh, I already think that."

I looked around the bazaar, wanting to look anywhere but into his eyes. I caught sight of a seven-year-old boy holding his baby sister in his arms, feeding her a bottle of milk. Somehow that little boy, taking such good care of a baby, gave me strength in that moment. "Here's the thing," I said, still stalling. "The thing is that . . ." He looked at me impatiently. Finally, I just blurted it out. "The thing is that I'm your sister."

He laughed so hard that his eyes began to tear up. "You are a trip to Mars," he said.

"I'm not joking, Enrique."

He stopped laughing. I guess he must have known I was serious since I used his real name. "I don't get it," he said.

"I didn't come to the house because Encarnación Vargas is my teacher. I came because she's my mother." He stared at me, slack-jawed, so I continued, "I just found out, and I wanted to see her. And I didn't mean to lie to you, but I thought I should talk to her first in case you didn't know about me. Did you know about me?" He shook his head side to side, his mouth still wide-open. "And I would've waited to tell you.

But then you sent me that picture, and I realized I had to tell you, because you're my brother, so you can't flirt like that again. And I just want you to know that you have great shoulders. I just reacted that way because you're my brother, okay?" I took a deep breath. "Will you please say something?"

"This is a lot to take in," he said.

"Well, yeah. I get it. I mean . . . you were two when your mom gave me away. I guess she couldn't handle another kid."

"Oh, she's not my mom. I didn't even meet her till I was seven."

"Wait, what?" A wave of relief coursed through me. If she wasn't his mother, then he wasn't my brother. I kicked myself inside a little for making such a huge assumption, and I wondered how many of my other assumptions were wrong.

"She's my stepmother. She met my dad when I was seven. I mean, she feels like my mom, though. I call her Mom." He was rambling now, as nervous as I was only moments ago.

"Okay, I just need to say this out loud now," I said. "You are *not* my brother."

"Right," he said, putting it all together. "I'm not your brother at all. Not even your half brother. I am not in any way a brother to you."

"Whew," I said. "This has been a really bad week, but this is good news. You and I are not related."

A big smile came across his face. "So I guess that means I can do this," he said as he leaned over to kiss me.

His lips had almost reached mine when I put my hands on his shoulders and pushed him away. "Whoa."

"What?" he said.

"First of all, you might not be my blood brother, but you're like my second stepbrother twice removed, so there's still some residual weirdness. And . . ." I stopped myself. I was about to say that I had never been kissed, and that my first kiss wasn't going to be in the middle of a bazaar in downtown LA. It was going to be perfect. But instead I just said, "And I had an everything bagel for breakfast. My breath stinks."

"I had pad thai," he said. "Mine's worse."

"Who has pad thai for breakfast?" I asked, laughing.

"Someone whose parents are out of town."

As his face leaned in toward mine again, I heard the sound of my name—"Daria!"—screeched out by a familiar voice. I turned my head just before Iglesias's lips met mine, and saw Heidi and her mother, standing side by side, both in designer outfits, their matching noses pointed straight at me accusatorily.

"Heidi. Um, Mrs. Javadi," I stammered. "This isn't what it looks like."

"Oh my God, you *actually* have a boyfriend," Heidi said, under her breath, but just loud enough for me to hear.

"Oh, I'm not her boyfriend," Iglesias said. "I'm her—"

I quickly cut Iglesias off. "He's my tutor. In Spanish. I found him online."

Iglesias laughed. "Craigslist," he said. "I offer immersion

tutoring. I take my students to authentic Mexican locations to practice. Tomorrow, we're driving to the border."

Mrs. Javadi looked horrified. Heidi shook her head. "Mommy, they're just joking. Obviously, they're together and Daria doesn't want us to tell her parents."

"Daria *djoon*," Mrs. Javadi said in Farsi. "Don't worry about anything. I won't tell your parents what I saw." She paused and then added softly, "You won't tell them you saw us here either?"

And that's when it hit me. Heidi and her mother were supposed to be yachting and shopping with the king and queen of Jordan. Instead, they were in downtown LA, standing in front of a booth that sells fake purses. "Holy F, you're broke," I said under my breath, but just loud enough for them to hear.

"We're not broke," Mrs. Javadi said, again in Farsi. "We just took it a little too far with Heidi's party."

I wanted to relish Heidi's demise, but instead I found myself genuinely sad for her. She'd concocted a fake vacation to impress us. That was just so depressing.

"I'm sure you're gonna tell the whole school that I'm not in Jordan," Heidi said. "I guess I deserve it."

"I won't. I promise."

Heidi rolled her eyes. "Right. Because you don't want us to tell your parents about your BF. Fine, it's a deal." Then Heidi looked at me with real curiosity. "You didn't really meet on Craigslist, did you?" she asked me with the genuine concern of an old friend. "Please be careful, Daria. There are creeps on there."

"Heidi," Mrs. Javadi said in Farsi. "We don't pry into our friends' personal lives."

"Of course not," Heidi said with a laugh. "But we *do* pry into our enemies' personal lives."

I laughed along with Heidi, first out of nervousness, and then because of the absurdity of the situation. The humor of the situation was lost on Mrs. Javadi.

"Okay, enough," Mrs. Javadi said in Farsi. "Let's go, Heidi." And then, switching to English, she turned to Iglesias and added, "It was a pleasure to meet you."

"Wait, aren't you ladies interested in buying a bag?" he asked.

"You sell fake bags. How cute," Heidi said snidely, back to being herself.

I immediately came to Iglesias's defense. "He doesn't just sell them. He designs them. He's an artist. You'll know his name someday."

"Whoa," Heidi said. "Chill."

Mrs. Javadi was checking out a fake Chanel that Iglesias had on display. She opened it up, inspecting it. Iglesias had quickly and meticulously fixed his mistakes. The stitching was perfect. The hardware matched. He had even forged a certificate of authenticity. Mrs. Javadi was clearly impressed, and so was I. She pulled out her wallet and paid for the purse in cash.

"Why not?" she said to Iglesias. "I like to support my daughter's friends . . . and enemies."

In Farsi, I asked, "Mrs. Javadi? If you're scaling back, why buy a fake bag? Why not just buy nothing?"

She placed her hand on mine and said, "Because, Daria *djoon*, as you and my daughter obviously know all too well, being Persian means you must always keep up appearances."

Chapter Eight

HERE'S THE THING ABOUT IRANIAN Americans and New Year's Eve. We totally celebrate it twice. First, we must celebrate Nowruz, the Persian New Year, and then we celebrate New Year's Eve eight months later. I guess the order could be reversed, depending on which calendar you subscribe to.

This year, we began New Year's Eve with dinner at our apartment, and then my entire family was escorting the Authentics to see She-Reen in concert. That was, obviously, not the way I had planned it. It wasn't like I wanted my parents next to me when I was at a concert, especially when I was so pissed at them, but my mother had insisted that we all go together. I tried to scare her off by reminding her that She-Reen was a militant, feminist, lesbian Muslim, but that somehow made my mom more excited, since she loved being cutting-edge.

For our New Year's Eve menu, Sheila, Lida, and Lala came together to create a spread that was decadent and eclectic: bruschetta, rice, eggplant stew, chiles rellenos, beet salad, and Lala's *tres leches* cake. Kurt monopolized the meal by doing my entire family's astrological charts. My mother's and father's charts especially fascinated him.

"You guys totally complete each other," he said.

"We do?" Sheila said with a laugh, as if it wasn't obvious that even after all these years, Baba was totally crazy about her.

"Totally," Kurt said. He found a pen and pad of paper and began to draw their charts. "Look, Mrs. Esfandyar, you're an Aries and all your planets are in the west. And Mr. Esfandyar, you're a Libra and all your planets are east. You guys are polar opposites."

"I don't think we're so different," Baba said.

"Oh no, you are," Kurt continued. "And you're practically born on each other's exact half birthday."

"Do you really believe in all this?" Amir asked.

"Oh, he really believes in all this," I muttered with a roll of my eyes.

"It's incredible that you found each other," Kurt said.

"I suppose it is," Sheila said. "It was either him or Abu Khorami."

"Wait, who is Abu Khorami?" I asked.

"Oh, just some Scorpio that your mother had a crush on when she was young," Auntie Lida said. That got a laugh from the whole table, but it still didn't stop Kurt, who couldn't tell that Auntie Lida was desperately trying to close the door on this topic.

"Oh, you're so lucky you didn't end up with a Scorpio," Kurt said. "That would've been all wrong for you. Good for a fling, but wrong for a marriage."

"You know that the only way to get him to shut up is to *tell* him to shut up," Caroline said before turning to Kurt and adding, "You know I love you. Now shut your mouth."

Thankfully, this conversation was interrupted by the arrival of Lala's *tres leches* cake, which was so insanely delicious that all anybody could talk about was how a cake could taste so good. As the whole table devoured the cake, I noticed how my mother took just one discreet bite from her piece and left the rest. That was so her. Every time we went to lunch or dinner, she would insist on ordering dessert, and then she would take one tiny bite and leave the rest of it sitting on the table. I mean, why bother?

"The cake is delicious, Amanda," Sheila said. It always jarred me when I heard someone use her real name. I had been calling her Lala since I was a kid because she always used to sing me this song that basically went *La-la-la-la-la* forever, endlessly, and so that's what I called her, and it just stuck. Sheila and Baba said that when I was a baby, they were so sick of hearing that *La-la-la-la-la* song that they sometimes wore earplugs around the house.

"So, what are you gonna name your daughter?" Joy asked Amir and Andrew.

"We don't know," Andrew said, though the look he gave Amir indicated perhaps a choice had been made that wasn't meant to be shared yet.

"We want to see her before we pick a name," Amir added.

"Did you paint her nursery all pink?" Caroline asked in a tone that made it clear she found that idea offensive.

"Yellow," Amir said.

"Aaaaaw," Joy said. "I'm so obsessed with babies. She's gonna have the tiniest little hands and feet. And baby knees. Oh my God, I'm obsessed with baby knees. We will totally babysit any time you need it."

"Who's *we*?" Caroline asked. "I'm no babysitter."

"I was referring to me and Daria," Joy said. "That's we, right, Daria?"

I would've agreed, but my mouth was full again. I had already scarfed down my own piece of cake and couldn't resist finishing the rest of Sheila's cake.

I could tell my family was scared as we approached the She-Reen concert. Outside the venue was the concert poster, which depicted She-Reen on a motorcycle, wearing a hijab, and giving the finger. "You know her name means *sweet* in Farsi," Sheila said. "But she doesn't look sweet at all. She looks very angry."

"She has a lot to be angry about," I said. "She had to leave Iran because she wasn't allowed to sing there. Persians just love to repress each other." I glared at my mother.

"Wait, women can't sing in Iran?" Joy asked.

"We can sing at private parties," Lida said. "Just not in public."

"How authentic is that?" I asked, this being our favorite rhetorical question.

"That's Iran," Lida explained. "Everything happens, but behind closed doors."

"Isn't that hard?" Caroline asked.

"Well, I'm not a singer," Lida said. Then she added, more seriously, "It can be hard. But there are so many positive things about life in Iran. The food. The community. The culture. We all feel like one people there. Here, I don't know, it feels different."

"Yeah, but isn't that a good thing?" I asked. "I mean, America is a melting pot. Everyone is welcome here."

"That's true," Lida said. "But still. Everyone feels disconnected from each other here."

"Don't listen to Lida," Sheila said. "She defends that horrible place. Of course people all feel like one there. They feel like one because they look like one, all the women in chadors, all the men with beards."

"It is just like you, Sheila, to focus on people's external appearance."

"Clothing is an expression of one's individuality," Sheila said, sounding very academic.

"True that," Joy said. Her outfit on this night—bright yellow leggings, a black-and-white geometric skirt, and a horizontal-striped top—was clearly an expression of something. Joy's parents were superstrict about what she wore. Joy called them her personal fashion police, and any time she wasn't with them, she used fashion as her own personal rebellion.

Outside the concert, the adults got special wristbands so they could drink. Sheila took in the crowd. These weren't the Persians she was familiar with from dinner parties and *dorehs*. These were self-identified Iranians, a different breed altogether. They were not all of the privileged class. They did not all leave Iran during the revolution in 1979. Many of them were fresh off the boat or, more accurately, fresh off Emirates Airlines. They wore black. They had tattoos. They were pissed off.

In this hotbed of young, angry energy, my family felt completely out of place. I couldn't decide who looked the strangest in this scene: Baba, his sweat stains turning his blue button-down into a swamp; Sheila, the gold on her bag catching the spotlights; or Amir and Andrew, in their matching Polo shirts and wedding rings.

"I need a glass of champagne to handle this," Sheila said.

By the time She-Reen took the stage, my mother was

mercifully tipsy. She-Reen emerged onstage wearing a chador, a tank top, short shorts, and biker boots. She looked totally badass. She immediately began one of her most popular songs, an awesome rap about the thirteenth imam. The audience sang along to the lyrics, including Joy, Caroline, and Kurt. I could see Sheila's expression of surprise as she saw my friends sing along.

"I think I'm going to incorporate some kind of Farsi into my next performance art piece," Caroline said.

"I hope you invite me. I love performance art," Sheila said.

I wondered if my mother would appreciate Caroline's kind of performance art. There was the time she wrapped her entire body (including her face) in masking tape and rolled across the basketball court in the middle of a game. And the time she stole a dead frog from biology class and serenaded it with "Someday My Prince Will Come" during a school meeting. And the time she dressed as a drag queen for Halloween. When people asked who she was, she said she was a lesbian woman pretending to be a gay man pretending to be a straight woman.

"Really?" Caroline said to my mom. "You know what it is?"

"Of course I do," Sheila said. "I once saw a wonderful performance artist in Paris. She force-fed herself until she vomited. It was very disturbing, but strangely compelling as well. I was sitting next to Catherine Deneuve, who said she thought it was a statement about foie gras."

Caroline whispered in my ear, "Your mother is so cool."

I nodded, because for all her flaws, I couldn't deny that Sheila was indeed cool. I had to admit that as mad as I was at my parents, there was something really great about having them there. I guess part of it was that it was really insane to watch them in this environment. There were so many crazy stories that we would laugh about forever. Like the moment when Baba grabbed Sheila's hand and they started doing the tango, and a whole circle of people formed around them. Seriously, they did the tango. At a rap concert. Or when She-Reen saw Amir and Andrew holding hands in the audience and started screaming that they would be executed in Iran, and got the crowd to sing, "Gays rule!" in Farsi. And the best part was that Sheila, Baba, and Auntie Lida were screaming it along with the rest of the crowd. I hadn't expected my parents to make the night more fun, but then I remembered how cool they could be. None of my friends' parents would've come to the show or danced the tango. But best of all, the reason my parents were there was that they refused to spend the night without me. No matter how many secrets they had kept from me, that was pretty awesome.

As we got closer to midnight, I asked my parents if I could sleep over at Joy's. Whenever we had a sleepover, it had to be at Joy's, since her parents wouldn't let her spend the night anywhere but home. My father turned his gaze toward Kurt.

"Don't worry, I won't be there," Kurt said. "Joy's parents are anti–coed sleepover."

"They don't trust me to have a boy in my room," Joy said.

"As if you would even do anything with a boy in your room," Caroline added.

Joy glared at Caroline as Sheila and Baba agreed to the sleepover. Unlike Joy's parents, they did trust me. One more cool thing about them.

A minute before midnight, She-Reen began a chant of "Iran. Number one. Iran. Number one." The whole audience chanted along with her, losing themselves in their communal rhythm. I watched them all bouncing up and down, chanting, carefree and lost. I should have been chanting too, but something stopped me. It hit me that I might no longer be Iranian, at least not fully.

Before I could think too hard about this, She-Reen stopped the chant and led a countdown to midnight in Farsi. When the clock struck midnight, cheers erupted, and everywhere there were hugs and kisses.

Amir kissed Andrew.

Sheila kissed Baba.

Caroline grabbed Joy and pulled her close, screaming, "Come here, you lesbian." Joy pushed her away playfully and said, "You're insane."

There was a moment when everyone was occupied with

each other, except for me and Kurt. We stood in front of each other for a few long seconds, both swaying awkwardly to the music. I got lost in his intelligent eyes, and the comfort of his familiar fedora. Everything about Iglesias felt scary and new, and everything about Kurt felt relaxed and easy. I thought maybe Kurt would try to kiss me, but he didn't. He just gave me a friendly hug and said, "Happy New Year, Daria. I have a feeling this is going to be your year."

"Is it in the stars?" I asked.

"I'm not sure," he said. "It's just a feeling I have."

I hugged him tight. He was so comfortable. And when I let go, I realized there was no such thing as comfort anymore.

And then my parents pulled me into a hug. I had hugged them every New Year's Eve before that, and every Persian New Year's as well. As they held me close, I was reminded of how much I still loved them, and how terrified I was of having to tell them that what they had done had changed me forever.

Chapter Nine

WE WERE PILED ONTO JOY'S bed, in the house she referred to as "Nigeria adjacent." Before entering the house, Joy had changed from her fabulous outfit into a far more conservative long dress and cardigan that she had stuffed into a neighbor's mailbox. Now Joy was perusing the website for her favorite vintage store, on the hunt for outfits for my sweet sixteen party. "I know you don't want to have the party," Joy said. "But if you have no choice, then at least let me dress you. Oh, wait, here it is!" Joy turned her laptop toward me and Caroline, revealing an image of a supersexy, body-hugging, floor-length zebra–print dress.

"Um, I am never wearing that," I said with a laugh.

"You would look stunning in it," Joy said.

"No, *you* would look stunning in it," I shot back. Fact: Joy would look stunning in anything.

"Whatever, I'm buying it as your early birthday present," Joy said as she closed her computer. "It's Halston!" I nodded, like I knew what that meant.

"So, what did your parents do tonight?" I asked.

Joy laughed. "I'm sure they spent it watching TV. They're in their forties, but they act like they're in their sixties."

"Whatever, at least they still enjoy each other's company," Caroline said. Caroline's parents were divorced, and pretty much only communicated with each other through her. "Seriously, you won the parent lottery, Daria."

"Every family has their issues," I said.

"Sure," Joy said. "But your family's issues are so minor compared to everyone else's. I mean, your parents are awesome, and your brother is having a gayby. What's cooler than that?"

"Oh my God, please don't say the word *gayby* in front of an actual gay person," Caroline said.

"I think I'm allowed to use the word *gayby* if I want to," Joy countered.

"Not unless you're a lesbian," Caroline said. "Are you?"

Joy giggled. "Um, no," she said. "And please don't even suggest that in my parents' house or they will somehow telepathically hear you."

"Fine," Caroline said. "Well, in that case, when you have a baby someday, I'm going to call it a straightby."

Joy laughed. "I give you permission to call my child a straightby when he or she is born. Someday. Far in the future. When my crazy parents allow a boy within a one-mile radius of me."

"Good," Caroline said. "I can't wait to attend your straight wedding."

"You guys," I said. "My parents have real issues too."

"We've moved on, Daria," Caroline said. "Let's keep making fun of Joy's straightby."

"But I haven't moved on," I said. Joy and Caroline turned to me, surprised. Suddenly, my face felt like a furnace. I wanted to tell them the truth, but I was so nervous.

"I have something to tell you," I said, and my voice cracked.

"Oh God, are your parents getting a divorce?" Caroline asked. "Because I know how it feels."

"No." I shook my head. "It's just . . . I don't know who I am anymore, you guys."

They stared at me expectantly. I didn't know where to start, so I started from the beginning, with the DNA test results and the lawyer's office. Then I told them about visiting Seth Nijensen in the Local factory, and about meeting Enrique, and about how I called him Iglesias. The only part of the story I didn't tell was the part about Heidi and her family lying about their vacations and buying fake purses. I guess I didn't feel that was my secret to tell. When I finished, they both sat in front of me with their mouths hanging open.

"You guys," I said when I finished the tale, "I'm so sorry I lied to you. I wanted to tell you sooner."

Joy put an arm around me and pulled me into a hug.

"*You're* sorry?" Caroline asked, incredulous. "It's your parents who should be sorry. They *lied* to you. For years. There's nothing shameful about adoption, and they've made you feel that there is."

I gulped down hard. I knew Caroline would zero in on my parents' guilt, and I didn't blame her. She was righteous, but she was also right.

Joy turned to Caroline. "Let's focus on Daria right now," she said. Then she looked at me gently. "We love you. So much."

"Of course I love you," Caroline said. "Which is why I want you to know how pissed I am your parents did this to you."

"I get it," I said. "I'm pissed too, okay? But Persians are decades behind when it comes to issues like this."

"Issues like what?" Caroline barked. "Adoption? Sexuality? Why are you defending them?"

"Caroline, enough!" Joy rarely raised her voice, so it shocked Caroline into shutting up. "We're totally here for you, Daria," Joy continued. "Whatever you need. We just want you to be okay."

I lingered in the hug as long as I could, and when we all separated, I said, "I'm fine. I mean . . . I'm confused. And a little scared. And . . ." My lips quivered, and finally I admitted, "I feel like somebody ripped me in half." A few tears fell from my eyes.

"You're the same Daria you've always been," Caroline said.

"That's right," Joy echoed. "Nothing has changed."

"Yeah," I whispered. "I mean, I know that's what you're supposed to tell me, and I appreciate it. But the thing is, everything has changed. I can't look at my parents the same way. I'm so angry at them."

I was about to tell them my theory that Baba was still my father, and had had an affair with Encarnación Vargas, but I stopped myself. It made sense in my head, but I knew that the moment I verbalized it, I would realize how nuts it was.

Caroline was about to speak, but Joy nervously stopped her. "Let's not say anything else," Joy said. "Let's just be here. We're here for you."

We didn't speak for a long time. They had known me long enough to just sit with me in silence. To my surprise, I felt a little better after telling them about it all. I was still stressed and confused, but somehow not quite as alone.

Finally, I broke the silence by saying, "I really want you guys to meet Iglesias."

"Your brother?" Joy asked.

"He's not my brother!" I protested, too vehemently.

"I'm kind of confused," Caroline said. "Now that you know

there's nothing incest-y about him, are you into him again?"

"I don't know," I said, with a growing smile that was giving me away. "He told me to text him when the show was done. He said he'd be out with friends."

"Let's go meet him," Caroline said.

"My parents will kill me!" Joy protested.

"We'll be superquiet. They won't find out," Caroline said. "Come on, it's New Year's Eve. Let's go make some trouble. We're hormonal, ripe, fecund teenagers."

"Ew, the word *fecund* is gross," Joy said.

"Fecund, fecund, fecund," Caroline said. "That's what you are, whether your parents like it or not."

"Ew," Joy said. "I am not fecund."

"Really," Caroline said. "How authentic is that?"

"It's very authentic," Joy said, annoyed.

"Daria has a crush on her biological mother's stepson," Caroline continued. "This. Is. Huge. Can we just live a little?"

"If I live a little," Joy said, "then my parents will make me die a lot."

"I'll go with you, then," Caroline said to me. And then she turned to Joy. "Is that okay?"

Joy shrugged. "Sure, I think my parents are out by now. Just please don't wake them up."

"Cool," Caroline said. "Then text your man, Daria. We're about to hit the streets."

I texted Iglesias and asked what he was up to. He texted me back a street address in downtown LA, and told us to join him soon.

Caroline and I took a cab to the address Iglesias gave me. I laid my head on her shoulder in the backseat. I couldn't believe I was going out past midnight, without my parents' permission. But they had broken my trust, so I was breaking theirs. I guess maybe that's what happens when you keep one secret from your parents. It becomes easier to add another secret to the pile. Maybe this is what it was like for Sheila. Maybe she started with one small secret, and then added one atop the other until she had as many secrets as she had shoes.

The driver drove past skid row and stopped at a run-down street in the arts district. The street was virtually empty, except for two guys toward the end of it, spray-painting a wall. I immediately recognized one of the guys as Iglesias. I led Caroline toward him. Iglesias and his friend didn't hear us, so they just kept spray-painting. Iglesias was spray-painting the face of the *Mona Lisa* on the wall. He had done a pretty good job of reproducing her.

"Should I give her a nose ring?" he asked his friend, who was busy drawing some kind of robotic spider creature.

"Nah, give her a septum piercing," his friend said. "That'd be dope."

Iglesias took a can of black spray paint and gave Mona Lisa

a septum piercing, then signed his work in red spray paint with the name Rico.

"Bravo," I said as I clapped my hands, wanting to alert him that I was standing right behind him.

"Hey, the tide has rolled in," he said, a wide smile overtaking his face. "I can't believe you came, Ocean."

"I mean . . . this is basically the worst thing I've ever done, and if my parents found out I was here, they would put out a hit on me, but yeah, I'm here. This is my friend Caroline."

Iglesias shook Caroline's hand, then put his arm around his friend, a lanky white kid with a wisp of a beard, and an outfit that looked like it belonged in a 1980s hip-hop video. "This is my buddy Stuey," Iglesias said.

Stuey approached Caroline with his arms outstretched. "I'm a hugger," he said.

"And I'm a lesbian," Caroline said. "So back off."

"Whoa," Stuey said. "I was just saying hello. But if you're a little nicer, maybe I'll set you up with my hot sister."

"Thanks," Caroline said, "but I don't need to be set up."

Caroline so needs to be set up, I thought to myself. She was the only out lesbian in our whole school, and she was vehemently opposed to online dating. "A handshake will suffice," she said, as she put her hand out for Stuey, who put his hand in hers. Caroline squeezed his hand tight, then moved on to Iglesias. As she kept Iglesias's hand in hers for an uncomfortably long time, she looked him dead in the eyes and said, "Look, Daria told me everything. And she's one of my best friends. And she's not tough like me, okay?"

"I'm tough," I said.

"Oh please, your idea of hardship before this week was getting a zit."

"That is not true," I said, my gaze fixed on Iglesias. "Remember that time I had ants in my bedroom?"

"Whatever," Caroline said. "The point is that Daria's going through a lot right now. And you, Iglesias or Enrique or Rico or whatever your name is, better not be playing some game with her right now."

"I'm not playing a game," Iglesias said, trying to wriggle his hand out from Caroline's.

"You need to understand something," Caroline continued. "Daria's mission right now is to meet her birth mother. You are just a stepping-stone on that mission. And you'd better not screw up her mission."

"How would I do that?"

"Oh, I don't know. Maybe you break her heart and she doesn't want to see you again, so she never goes through with meeting her birth mother just to avoid you."

"She would have to like me for me to break her heart," Iglesias said.

"Exactly," I said. "And I don't like him." I glared at Caroline. I loved her for trying to protect me. But she was revealing way too much.

Taking the hint, Caroline finally let go of Iglesias's hand. "Okay, now that we've gotten that out of the way, let's have some fun. Somebody pass me a can of spray paint, and it had best not be pink."

Stuey tossed Caroline a can of green paint. Caroline moved toward an untouched patch of wall and pointed the can at the wall. Stuey told her to hold on and pulled a pair of gloves out of his bag for her. "You don't want that toxic crap all over your hands," he said. Caroline put the gloves on, and began painting the wall in bursts of green. She was having a blast.

Suddenly, I became dizzy, and grabbed on to Iglesias's arm. "I'm sorry," I said. "I just got a random head rush. I don't usually stay up this late."

Iglesias laughed. "Living on the edge, Ocean." Then he took my arm and led me a few feet away from Caroline and Stuey. "It's the chemicals in the spray paint. Makes you a little high."

"Oh," I said. "So you're trying to get me high, huh?"

Iglesias took a deep breath and then exhaled loudly. "Nothing like the smell of spray paint in the morning."

"It's nighttime," I said.

"There's a line from a movie about the smell of napalm in the morning," he said. "It was an attempt at a joke."

I didn't laugh. Neither did he. We sat in silence for a few breaths, my heart beating fast. I couldn't tell what was making me so nervous. Was it sitting so close to Iglesias that I could hear him breathe? Was it breaking the rules that I had followed so dutifully for fifteen years? Or was it the smell of spray paint in the nighttime?

"Sorry about Caroline," I finally said, breaking the silence. "She can be a little intense, but she's really sweet once you get to know her. She's like Persian rice."

"Is Persian rice a pissed-off lesbian?" he asked.

"No." I laughed. "It's hard on the outside and soft on the inside."

"Well, she's got your back," he said. "I like that."

"Yeah, she's a real friend." There was a long pause. "How about you and Stuey?"

"We met last year," he said. "He's been real good to me. Like a mentor, kind of."

"What's he mentoring you in?"

"He's a legendary tagger. You've probably seen his tags. He goes by Koffin."

"I know you're speaking English, but I don't really get what you're saying."

"A tagger's a street artist. Your tag is your name, or your symbol, or whatever. His is Koffin. He used to paint coffins everywhere, with different shit inside them. Like he would make a coffin and inside he would write *war* or *AIDS* or *hate* or shit like that. You've never seen his stuff?" I shook my head. "See, that's what sucks. We make art. We make beauty. And the city arrests us, and then cleans it up like we're defacing shit. You know who's defacing shit? The developers who tear down our awesome old buildings and replace them with ugly stucco crap."

Baba was a developer, and I knew that he didn't tear down beautiful things and replace them with ugly ones. In fact, it was usually the opposite. But it mattered to me that Iglesias like me, so I kept my mouth shut and changed the subject. "What's your tag name?" I asked.

He laughed. "It's not my tag name. Just my tag. It used to be Karne, like *meat* in Spanish with a *K*, but I hated that, so then I changed it to Hoopla, but I thought that sucked too, and now I'm just Rico, but I don't know . . ."

"Sounds like you have an identity crisis," I said.

"Yeah," he said. "Who doesn't?"

I laughed. That was certainly very true. Iglesias took his yellow glove off, and placed my hand in his, locking his fingers into mine. "Is this cool?" he asked. "I don't want your friend over there to come beat me up." We both looked up at Caroline, who was getting a lesson in tagging from Stuey. She had obviously warmed up to him.

My hand felt great in his. I thought back to Kurt and me holding hands at the ice rink. It felt nothing like this. With Iglesias, it was like every inch of my fingers and my palm was filled with nerve endings that were shooting energy through my body, making me feel more alive than I had ever felt. Now I understood why people said you glowed when you were in love. It was because all these nerve endings were lighting up your body from inside. I felt like I was iridescent.

I wanted to tell Iglesias that holding my hand was more than cool. I wanted to tell him that it felt fantastic, that it felt like a lunar eclipse happening within me. But all I said was, "Yeah, it's okay."

"Listen," he said. "My mom gets back next Saturday."

"Oh," I said. We had been living in our own fantasy world, and this brought me back down to earth. On Saturday, my birth mother was coming back, and I would meet her. The thought of it filled me with a mixture of dread and excitement.

"If you want, I'll introduce you," he said. And then, as if there were any question who we were talking about, he added, "My mom."

"Can you call her your stepmom? It would be so much less creepy," I said. "You call her your stepmother, and I'll call her my birth mother. Deal?"

"Deal," he said.

"Okay. Thank you," I said. "Do you think she'll be happy to see me?"

Iglesias squeezed my hand. "I don't know," he said. "I guess maybe she'll be happy and sad at the same time."

"Why would she be sad?" I asked.

"Not sad. But maybe a little guilty. 'Cause seeing you will remind her that she gave you up. And she'll see how awesome you are, and she'll feel guilty about giving up somebody so cool. And maybe that guilt will make her feel a little sad."

"So you think I'm awesome?" I asked, with a smile.

"Yeah," he said. "I think you're pretty awesome."

"So you think I'm pretty too?" I asked, and he laughed. "The thing is," I continued, "maybe I wouldn't be as awesome if she'd raised me. 'Cause obviously she wasn't ready. And I wouldn't be *me* if she had raised me, would I? So she can't think like that. She shouldn't feel guilty. I hope she doesn't feel guilty. I don't want to make her feel that way. I just want, I don't know, I want to know her."

"My mom died when I was a kid," he said quietly.

I felt my heart sink down into my stomach. I didn't know what to say, so I just stuck to the obvious. "I'm so sorry."

"Yeah, I was real young. I don't remember it. But it's not like my dad didn't talk about it almost every day. It was like his way of making sure I never joined a gang. 'You gonna join some gang like the one that killed your mother?'"

Now my heart sank even deeper. I wanted to hold him tight, to make his pain go away. "Oh my God, I'm so sorry." I couldn't think of anything else to say. All the other options seemed stupid.

Iglesias shrugged and then changed the mood with a smile. "I'm just telling you a sob story so you'll kiss me."

We looked into each other's eyes for a long beat. I was mesmerized by his ability to be so vulnerable and charming at the same time. Finally, I smiled back. "If you want to kiss me, you have to make it really special."

"Oh really?"

"Yeah, really," I said, and then, figuring this was a moment for honesty, I added, "Because I've never kissed a guy. Or a girl. And when I do, I want it to be a great story."

"This isn't a great story?"

"Not great enough," I said.

"So how come you've never kissed anyone?"

My face felt flush. Awkwardly, I said, "I don't know. No one's ever been interested in me, except maybe my friend Kurt."

"Maybe?"

I laughed. "I always thought he was just joking, but then we had this moment and I'm thinking maybe he does . . ."

"A moment? What kind of moment? Am I going to need to challenge him to a duel?"

"No," I said. "Nothing happened. Wait, what's your sign?"

"Don't change the subject," he said.

"I'm not," I persisted. "I was just thinking that when I finally tell Kurt about you, he'll have to do our charts. He's obsessed with astrology."

"Okay," he said. "Well, I'm a Libra."

I scrunched my face up, trying to remember if Libra was a good match for me.

"Uh-oh, you don't seem to like that. I'm changing my

birthday. I'm actually a Virgo." I must not have looked any more pleased, so he continued, "No, wait, I'm a Cancer. Better?"

I giggled. "You can change a lot of things about yourself, but not your birthday. Besides, there are lots of other factors, like your rising sign, and your moon sign. Kurt will explain it to you someday, when I tell him about you."

"So why haven't you just kissed Kurt?" he asked. "You seem pretty ballsy in every other department."

"That's kind of an offensive expression. What does having balls have to do with being courageous?"

"Point taken," he said, then quickly added, "And don't evade the question."

"What was the question again?" I asked.

"Why haven't you kissed Kurt?"

I didn't know what to say. The truth was that I wanted my first kiss to be truly special, and I never felt that magical pull toward Kurt as anything but a friend. And also, before this moment, I was always too afraid of what Baba would think. I was always too concerned with being his good girl. But I didn't want to say any of that. Instead I said, "I know it's not like what happened to your mom, but I just found out that my grandfather was killed during the Iranian Revolution, and my parents never told me."

"Wow, you really don't wanna answer my question," he said. And then he squeezed my hand tight. "Hey, at least they protected you from it. My dad talked about my mother getting shot every day. Like, 'Pass the carrots. Never forget your mother was gunned down, boy.' Didn't exactly make for an uplifting childhood. Your parents shielded you from their pain. Maybe that's a good thing."

"Isn't there a happy in-between place, where parents can tell their kids the truth, but not so often that it totally traumatizes them?"

"I don't know," he said. "All I know is that everything changed after my dad met Encarnación. She totally transformed him. He stopped talking about my mom all the time. I know he didn't forget her, but he just let go of all that anger. I guess meeting the right person can change your whole life."

"I guess it can," I said. And in the back of my mind, I was wondering if all this happened just so I could meet Iglesias. Maybe everything—the Iranian Revolution, my adoption, Iglesias's mother's death—happened because we were each other's *right person*, and were meant to be brought together.

"Look what I made!" Caroline screamed from down the street. We looked up at the wall, which Caroline had emblazoned with an image of some kind of blowfish, or amoeba.

"It's great," I said. "What is it?"

"It's a lava lamp," she said. "That's gonna be my tag. Lava. Because I erupt!"

"That's a dope tag," Stuey said. Caroline turned her attention back to the wall, on which she started spraying the letter *L*.

I looked back up at Iglesias's *Mona Lisa* painting. "So do

116

you always paint the *Mona Lisa*?" I asked.

"Nah," he said. "I just replicate famous paintings, then I change them. It's my thing. Like one time I did *Girl with a Pearl Earring*, but I gave her a big-ass hoop earring instead. And I did Warhol's Marilyn once, but I had pills coming out of her mouth."

I realized that by day, he copied other people's designs, and by night, he copied other people's art. "You ever make your own stuff?" I asked.

"This *is* my stuff." He had become defensive.

"Yeah, of course it is," I said. "But it's kind of an easy way out to copy other people's purses and other people's paintings, even if you add some new element to it. It's a lot harder to create something totally original, isn't it?"

"What're you saying? That you think I suck?" He pulled his hand away from mine. "Like birth mother, like birth daughter. She's always on me about my art too. Thinks I'll never make it. Thinks it'll just get me arrested again, and that I should go to college and be just like everyone else. I bet that's what you'll do."

"What? Go to college? Yeah, I'm going to college. My parents would kill me if I didn't."

"You always do what your parents tell you?" he asked.

"I'm here, aren't I?" That got him to soften a little bit. "There are colleges for artists, you know."

"I can learn more from Stuey than from some art teacher

who doesn't actually make any art."

"Okay," I said. "I guess all I'm trying to say is that maybe the reason you're not sure what your tag is has something to do with the fact that you're hiding behind other people's identities. And maybe it would be scary, and vulnerable, and liberating to just make something totally original."

He stood up, his face beet red and angry. He looked like a bull, and I thought he was going to charge at me, but instead he put his yellow gloves back on and started painting on the wall in front of us. He was painting a face again, and for a moment I thought it was going to be the *Mona Lisa*, or the *Girl with a Pearl Earring*, or Marilyn. But as the face took shape— big brown eyes, wide mouth with a large lower lip, thick black hair—I realized the face was mine, except he'd somehow made me look . . . pretty.

"I dub this the *Daria Lisa*," he said.

I walked close to the wall, breathing in the disorienting scent of chemicals emanating from the *Daria Lisa*. "She belongs in the Louvre," I said. "Or at the very least, LACMA."

Underneath the portrait, he painted a new tag: "Iglesias."

Chapter Ten

I WAS ON MY LAPTOP working on the essay portion of my genealogy assignment—by which I mean I was procrastinating by painting my toenails black—when my mother ran into my room and announced, "She's here. My granddaughter, your niece, she's here!" As I texted the Authentics the news, my mom screamed, "Get up, Daria! We have to go meet her."

We all rushed into Baba's car faster than I ever thought possible. Seriously, I think it was the first time my mother left the house without making sure her makeup and hair were perfect. Baba sped toward the hospital, and by some small miracle we didn't get pulled over.

When we arrived at the hospital, we ran through all the depressing wings toward maternity, which I guess is the only nondepressing wing of any hospital. It's like every inch of the place is about death, except for one section, which is about life. I couldn't believe that my niece was just born in this hospital. I hadn't even met her, and yet all I could think about was her: What would she be like? Would we end up being superclose? Would she see me as cool Aunt Daria or as weird Aunt Daria? What would she be like when she was my age?

When we got to the front desk of the maternity ward, Sheila told the nurse who we were. Then Amir emerged, with a big smile on his face. He was beaming.

"Hey," he said. "Are you guys ready to meet the newest member of our family?"

Sheila stood up quickly and gave Amir a hug. "Is she healthy? How much did she weigh? What's her name? You just texted us a picture with no information! What is wrong with you?"

Amir put his hand around Sheila's shoulder. He always handled her so well. "She's very healthy. She weighed seven pounds and three ounces. And her name is Rose."

"Rose?" Baba said. "That's not Iranian. Or Chinese."

"It's our flower," Amir said. "Every special occasion, Andrew gets me yellow roses, and I get him red roses."

I could see Sheila and Baba shift slightly with discomfort. Although they had accepted Andrew into our family, they were still unnerved when hearing about Amir and Andrew in romantic terms, or seeing public displays of affection.

"It's a beautiful name," Auntie Lida said. "Amir *djoon*, con-gratulations."

"Come on," Amir said. "Follow me. She wants to meet her family."

Amir led us to a small hospital room. Andrew was standing up, rocking his new child in his arms. Their surrogate, Maria, was in bed, her face flushed and tired.

"Congratulations, Andrew," Sheila said as she kissed Andrew on each cheek. And before he could thank her, she added, "Now give me that child!" Andrew handed Rose to Sheila, whose eyes welled up with tears as she looked at her granddaughter. "She's beautiful," Sheila said. "She's perfect. She's just perfect."

"Don't hog her," Baba said.

"You wait your turn," Sheila said, turning her back playfully. With her free hand, she snapped a photo of Rose's adorable, scrunched-up little face.

Baba sat down, dutifully waiting his turn. "How are you, Maria? Was our little Rose nice to you?"

"Oh, she was fine," Maria said. "We had our moments, Rose and me. There was a good thirty minutes when she didn't wanna come out. But then she did. I'm just so happy she's healthy."

"You were so good to us, Maria," Amir said. "I seriously don't know how to thank you."

"You don't need to thank me," Maria said. "I'm so happy for you guys. Kids are the greatest blessing there is."

"Are you sure you don't want to hold her once?" Andrew asked.

"I don't know if I should," Maria said. I knew from the way Maria said it that she was afraid she wouldn't want to let her go. Amir had already told me how he and Andrew had asked Maria to pump breast milk for their daughter, and how Maria had said no. Maria said that once she gave birth, she wanted to have some separation from the experience so she didn't become too attached. "Maybe I can just hold her for a second," she said.

I could tell my mom didn't want to let her go, but that she knew she had to. After all, Sheila would get to hold this child for the rest of her life, and Maria would probably only see her on special occasions. My mother placed Rose in Maria's arms, and I watched as Maria's eyes welled with tears. "You're so lucky, little girl," she said. "You have two of the best daddies in the world. They love you so much. They wanted you so much. And don't think you're gonna get rid of me, 'cause I'm gonna drive down for all your birthday parties, and I'm gonna introduce you to my daughter, and I will always remember the time we spent together, okay?" Rose cooed in Maria's arms.

I knew that Rose wasn't Maria's child. I knew Amir and Andrew were her parents. And yet Rose spent nine months in Maria's womb, listening to the rhythms of Maria's voice. That must have counted for something. There must have been something about Maria that comforted her. Would I feel the same way when I met Encarnación?

"Daria, you should hold her next," Andrew said.

"Me?" I asked. "I don't know how to."

"It's easy," Amir said. "Just be sure to support her neck."

I was scared to hold her. She looked so fragile, so totally breakable. I looked to Maria, who seemed blissful holding Rose. "Is it okay if I hold her now?" I asked.

Maria smiled. "Of course it is." I reached down and gently lifted her up out of Maria's arms. Maria placed my hand under Rose's neck. "There you go," she said. Then she guided my other arm under her body, like I was scooping her. "You're a natural."

"I don't know," I said. I looked down at Rose, who was gazing up at me. "Can she see me? Babies can't see far away, can they?"

"She can see you," Amir said.

"Oh my God," I said. "She's so cute. Hello, Rose. I'm your aunt. Which is crazy, 'cause I'm way too young to be an aunt. But I guess there are no rules anymore, right? You have gay dads, and a teenage aunt. You're like a reality show waiting to happen." I locked eyes with Rose, and it was like there was no one in the world but the two of us. She made everything else in the room, and in the world, feel blurry and unimportant.

"There are definitely no rules anymore," Maria said.

Lida looked down at Maria and said, "It must be hard, saying good-bye to her." Sheila glared at Lida, obviously unhappy that Lida would bring up this delicate point.

"It's hard, but I prepared for it," Maria said. "I always knew she wasn't really mine."

That statement snapped me out of my reverie. *I always knew she wasn't really mine.* Was that how my birth mother felt when I was born? Or was it different? Did she feel that I was hers, and gave me up because she couldn't afford to keep me? I was stuck on that word: *mine.* Everyone belongs to someone, and I wanted to know who I really belonged to.

When I turned my gaze back to Rose, I realized she had fallen asleep in my arms. Then I looked up and saw the Authentics were standing outside the room, quietly, not wanting to disturb the moment. I waved them into the room, and after congratulating Amir and Andrew, they all stared in awe at the little creature asleep in my arms.

"Oh, Daria," Joy said. "She's the cutest thing I've ever seen."

"How does it feel?" Caroline asked.

"I don't know," I said. "Surreal."

"Well, she's really lucky to have a supercool aunt," Kurt said.

I smiled, and we all stared at her in silence for a moment.

"I think this is the first time I feel kind of old," Joy said.

We all laughed, and that's when Sheila grabbed her phone, snapped a photo of us, and immediately posted it to Instagram. Seconds after my mother posted the photo, my parents' phones started ringing with congratulations from every Persian in Los Angeles.

✳ ✳ ✳

Later that day, after Rose was finally released to go home, we took her to Amir and Andrew's house, where Lala was waiting for us. The house smelled the way our house used to smell, which reminded me of how much I missed Lala. The mixture of her perfume and her Persian-Mexican fusion cooking in the kitchen was like the smell of home to me. Lala immediately scooped Rose up into her arms and cooed at her. She told Rose that she would be her Lala, and that she would teach her Spanish and play with her, just as she had played with me. Lala looked up at me and said, "It feels like yesterday that I was holding you in my arms, Daria."

"Well," Sheila said, "it feels like the day before yesterday, maybe."

"She looks just like you did, Daria," Lala went on.

"Except a little more Asian," Andrew joked.

"She looks just like her grandmother," Baba said.

My mother blushed. "She's much prettier than me," she said. "Just look at those perfect little lips." Baba said Sheila had perfect lips as well. Then Sheila said that Rose had Baba's eyes. And for a moment, they were lost in a haze of comparing Rose to each other with pride.

I suddenly realized that they never had this moment when I was born, because I didn't look anything like them, and even if I did, they knew it was merely coincidence rather than biology that was responsible for it. Even if my crazy theory about Baba still being my birth father was true, he wouldn't have been able to verbalize any of it. I felt like I didn't truly belong. I remembered going to Saint Martin as a kid with my parents, and Sheila explaining to me that we were technically in France, even though the island was so far away from it. That's what I felt like listening to my parents talk about how much Rose looked like them. I felt like an isolated island.

We spent the rest of the day settling Rose into her new room. I was surprised when I walked in and saw that it was pink. Hadn't they told us it was yellow? As if he could read my mind, Amir said, "Of course it's pink. Don't tell your militant friend Caroline, please. I didn't want some lecture about how we're abusing our child with gender stereotypes." The room was really cute. There was a beautiful white crib in the corner of the room, and above it was a decal of a caterpillar in every color of the rainbow. "The caterpillar is our little shout-out to the rainbow flag," Amir said.

"As if a pink room isn't gay enough," Andrew added.

"What's the rainbow flag?" Sheila asked.

"It's the gay flag," Amir explained. "You should come to a pride parade someday. You'll see hundreds of them, along with drag queens, and men in leather jockstraps."

"Maybe I will someday," she said, though of course we all knew Sheila would never attend an event that included men in leather jockstraps.

Above the crib was a mobile, pink-and-white fairies swinging away. "That was your mobile when you were a kid," Lala said.

"You kept it all these years?" I asked Sheila.

"Well, Lala kept it," Sheila said. "She's far more sentimental than I am."

"I think it's nice to pass things down from generation to generation," Lala said. And then she pointed out all the things in the room that had once been mine, from ragged stuffed animals to crayon-marked board books to a tiny wooden chair. I barely had a memory of any of the objects, even though I must have spent years of my life playing with them. "This was your favorite," Lala said, grabbing a stuffed dog and handing it to me.

"It was?" I asked, searching its plastic eyes for some sign of recognition.

"Oh, Woof went everywhere with you until you were four."

"*Everywhere*," Sheila concurred. "That thing came to every doctor's appointment, every trip to the park, every vacation. Woof was a part of the family."

"Wow," I said. "Well, Woof, I'm sorry I've forgotten you. And thanks for being a friend to me in my early years."

"Come, Daria, help me get her milk ready," Lala said. I followed Lala into the kitchen, where she picked up a box of formula, and handed it to me. "Use the scooper and mix some in the bottle with water." I did as she instructed.

"How is Roberto?" I asked. Lala's son still lived in Mexico, and because she was undocumented, she never got to see him, which was so unfair. She talked about him all the time, though, and I had met him on Skype. Roberto was married, but his wife was having trouble having a baby, which broke Lala's heart. She always said that when she had a grandchild, she would move back to Mexico for good.

"He's fine," Lala said. "They're moving to Mexico City. He says there's more work there."

"Do you miss Mexico?" I asked.

"Of course I do. But, luckily, I have a community here. When I go to my church, or to a friend's daughter's quinceañera, I feel like I'm in Mexico."

"I guess you're right. It's like how I feel like I'm in Iran when I go to the Emerald Tower." She nodded, and then I said, "Sheila didn't breastfeed me, did she?"

"Your mother didn't breastfeed *either* of her children, and many of her Persian friends didn't either," Lala said, eyeing me curiously.

"Of course. I was just curious."

"How are you, Daria?"

I could tell Lala knew something was up. She had some kind of sixth sense when it came to sniffing out any angst in me, which is maybe why I had avoided seeing her that week. "I'm fine," I said, too strongly. "I miss you, though."

"I miss you more," she said. "But now you can come see me and your niece together. And I'll teach you everything about raising a child. Changing diapers and swaddling and soothing."

"You know I'm not gonna have a kid any time soon, right?"

Lala laughed. "Yes, I know that. But trust me, the sooner you learn these things, the better. No matter how much or how early you prepare, you will never really be ready to be a parent. Parenting is life's most beautiful and most difficult challenge."

Chapter Eleven

THE FIRST DAY BACK AT school was eventful, to say the least. The day started with me telling Kurt the story of the adoption, except I left out the part about Iglesias. I just didn't want to risk hurting him.

"My mom always says that God doesn't give you more than you can handle," Kurt said. "I hate when she says that, but I also think I believe it."

"I thought she wasn't religious," I said.

"She's *spiritual*," he explained. "She believes in the universe, karma, reincarnation, and kundalini yoga. Anyway, my point is, you can handle this. And if you ever feel like you can't, well, that's what your friends are for, right?"

I gave Kurt a big hug and whispered a thank-you in his ear.

In English class, Mr. Farrell announced that every class would begin with one student presenting their genealogy assignment. This way, by the end of the month, we would know each other better, and appreciate the diversity of our peers. Mr. Farrell said he would pick a name out of a hat each day, and that person would present. He already had our names in a plastic cowboy hat—"my son's Halloween costume," he said—and he reached in and picked one. I silently prayed it wasn't me. I hadn't even thought about what I would present to the class when my time came. "Drumroll, please . . . ," Mr. Farrell said. "The first person to tell us about their fascinating genealogy is none other than the talented, the brave, the one and only . . . ," Mr. Farrell opened up the slip of paper and read the name. "Who's ready for some Persian history?" he asked. Uh-oh, the field had been significantly narrowed, and I was still in contention. "Heidi Javadi, you're it," he said. The Nose Jobs all began to hoot and holler for Heidi, who stood up, annoyed to go first but lapping up the attention she was getting.

"Of course it would be me," she said. "I know you rigged this, Mr. Farrell. I bet every slip of paper says my name." I didn't know the textbook definition of narcissist, but I was pretty sure that Heidi was it. Heidi used the dry-erase board to spell her name in huge, pink block letters. "Okay, listen up, people, 'cause I don't like to repeat myself. As most of you know, I'm Heidi Javadi, and I'm about to tell you the story of how I became me." Heidi told us all about how her father was an oil tycoon. Then she went deeper into her background, and suddenly she went to her desk, pulled a crown out of her bag, and placed it on her head. I am not kidding. "So, friends, classmates, and subjects, it turns out I am not *only* the queen of the Persian Inversions." Oh please, their name was the Nose Jobs. "That's right, I am a direct descendant of Cyrus the Great, the original king of Persia. OG."

For the next ten minutes, Heidi went on and on about Cyrus the Great, and how her lineage could be traced back to him. She talked about how Cyrus founded the Persian Empire, and how he'd conquered nomadic tribes just like she'd conquered high school. Finally, Mr. Farrell cut her off and reminded her that the class still had to discuss other work. That's when Heidi took her crown off and handed it to Mr. Farrell. "I'd like to donate this to the school," she said, with not a trace of irony. Heidi handed her essay to Mr. Farrell and sat down.

As expected, Heidi got a standing ovation from the Nose Jobs. It was an epic performance, maybe not worthy of an Oscar, but definitely a Persian People's Choice Award.

At lunch, as I carried my tray covered in that day's mock-healthy food—organic mac and cheese, fruit yogurt, banana chips—Heidi stopped me dead in my tracks, carrying her own tray, with nothing but some cottage cheese on it. "Hey," she said. "Why don't we have lunch outside? It's so nice out."

Heidi asking to have lunch with me was highly unusual, and I wondered if this was some kind of trap. "It's LA," I said as I debated whether engaging with her was a good idea. "It's perpetually nice out, which makes it not so nice in the grand scheme of things, because there is no light without dark, no cold without hot, no—"

"I got it," Heidi said. "I guess you don't want to lunch with a queen." She gave me a crooked smile, and when I realized she was actually making fun of herself, I couldn't help but consent.

I gave a shrug to the Authentics, who were visibly perplexed that I was exiting the dining room with my former best friend.

Heidi sat down underneath a big fig tree, and I joined her. Above our heads, a herd of giant squirrels chomped away on the figs. I was tempted to pull a piece of fruit from the tree, but was stopped by the squirrel poop that probably coated the figs. "So," Heidi said. "How's your man? He was cute, BTW. Well done."

"Thanks. He's fine," I said, wondering what she really wanted.

"Don't sound too excited," she said. "Look, make him take you out on nice dates before you put out, okay? Like make him take you to the pier, and ride the Ferris wheel, and stuff like that."

"Um, okay," I said, shaking my head. The idea of me "putting out" was so absurd that I couldn't help but laugh.

"Hey, did your parents tell you that using a tampon means you're not a virgin?" she asked.

"What?" I almost spit my mac and cheese back out onto my tray. "No!"

"Okay, just making sure," Heidi said. "Because that's what Laleh's mom said to her, but they're super-Muslim."

"We're not Muslim," I said. "We're agnostic."

"When a Persian says they're agnostic, it just means they're Muslim and ashamed of it."

"I'm not ashamed of anything," I said, my tone a little heated.

"Fine. Whatever."

"Okay, thanks for the superstrange girl talk," I said. "Are we done now?"

"Your first time should be special," she said, in a wistful way that suddenly made me wonder if she'd had sex. She stared at the sky for a beat and then whipped her highlighted hair back toward me in her inimitably dramatic fashion. "Wait, you are a virgin, right?"

"Um, yeah," I said, shocked that it needed to be asked. "Aren't you?"

"You think just 'cause I'm hot, I'm a ho?" she asked with a smirk. I was totally spooked by Heidi just then. She was being a new person, who was real and didn't take herself so seriously.

"Daria, I'm a good Persian girl. I'm not gonna have sex until, like, the last year of college. After waiting years for Mr. Right, I'll be drunk at some grad party and be like, 'I am not leaving college a virgin,' and then I'll have meaningless sex with some gross frat guy, and a few weeks later I'll meet Mr. Right."

"Wow, that's quite a narrative."

"Well, we both like to tell stories," she said. "Do you think it's a Persian thing? Like are we predisposed to love stories because it's in our blood? All those ancient poets and stuff."

"Or maybe we're predisposed to love stories because our own past is so secret and fragmented that we *need* stories. Because stories are the only way to make sense of the chaos and randomness of our world." Heidi was silent for a long time. "I'm sorry. Was that pretentious?" I asked.

"No, not at all. It's just sad, and totally true." Whatever I said must really have gotten to her, because she reached into my bowl of banana chips, grabbed a handful, and stuffed them into her mouth.

"So were you really descended from Cyrus?" I asked.

She laughed with her mouth full. Then she swallowed and said, "Please. I made it all up. My parents would rather be water-boarded than talk about their past."

"Mine too!" I said. Although I hated to admit it, there was a part of me that the Authentics could never totally get, and that Heidi always would. We were connected by a country neither of us had ever even been to.

She took another bite of chips from my tray, and then she launched into what she clearly wanted to say. "Listen, I just want to, um, thank you."

"For what?"

"For not telling anyone about seeing us buying a fake bag. I mean, you could've humiliated me. You *should've* humiliated me, given what a royal see-you-next-Tuesday I've been to you."

"So you are a royal after all!" I cracked.

She laughed, and for a moment it was like we were old friends again. "Seriously, Daria," she said. "When I realized you didn't take your chance for revenge, I felt so bad. You're like Hugh Jackman in that *Les Misérables* movie." I loved that she considered it a movie rather than a book. That was classic Heidi. "Russell Crowe is so horrible to him for so long, and then Hugh has his chance to kill him, and he just lets him go. I don't want to be like Russell Crowe."

"You are so not like Russell Crowe," I said, which seemed like a really weird compliment.

"Thanks," she said. "And also, sorry about that picture of you in the slide show at my sweet sixteen. It was a bitch move on my part, and I own it."

I didn't know what was happening, but Heidi was giving me the warm fuzzies all of a sudden. "It's okay," I said. A strange silence lingered, like neither of us knew what to say next. We just stared at each other, and then I noticed something different about Heidi.

"What are you staring at?" she asked.

And that's when it hit me. Her nose looked different . . . again. Sometimes my mouth said things before my brain had time to intercept, and this was one of those times. "Did you have *another* nose job?" I blurted out.

Heidi's face hardened. I knew immediately that I had messed up our rekindled friendship.

"I'm sorry," I said. My palms started to sweat. "I shouldn't have said anything."

I wanted to remind Heidi of all the times she had been cruel to me. I wanted to remind her that, just months earlier, she had told me how unlucky I was to be "one of those hairy Persians," sending me into weeks of experimentation with waxing, shaving, bleaching, and even a vintage Epilady machine I ordered from eBay. Of course, I couldn't tell the Authentics about my sudden obsession with hair removal, so I kept it all a secret, though I'm sure they noticed my body's disappearing mane. I wanted to remind her that she had bought me tweezers for my fifteenth birthday along with a link to a YouTube video on how to pluck a unibrow, and the fact that she'd suggested Frida Kahlo to me for doppelgänger day on Facebook, and that she reminded me countless times that I lived in Beverly Hills *adjacent* and not Beverly Hills. But I didn't say any of that because it wouldn't change the fact that I had said something totally stupid.

"You make me so sad, Daria," she said. "You act all proud,

but you're so insecure. It's painful how insecure you are."

"I should go find the Authentics," I said. I remember Baba telling me once that the key to being a gambler is knowing when to leave the table. That was also the key to a conversation with Heidi.

"You do realize it's totally absurd that you call yourselves the Authentics," she said before I could leave. "What makes you so *authentic*? The fact that you don't wash your hair?"

"I wash my hair," I protested, my hand finding its way to my scalp. Embarrassingly, I smelled my fingers, and I was pleased by their fruity scent. "Just because it's not highlighted and blow-dried, doesn't mean it's not clean and doesn't smell like citrus."

"Whatever, is Kurt *authentic* because he wears a weird hat all the time? Is Joy authentic because she dresses like she's auditioning for *Saturday Night Fever*? Is Caroline *authentic* because she's butch? Do you have to be weird, and different from everyone else, to be authentic?"

"We are not weird," I snapped. "We're just real. Being authentic is about being yourself, and having empathy for other people. And . . . that's it." I finally looked at Heidi again, defiantly, as if daring her to argue that last point.

"Well, the rest of the school calls you the Island of Misfit Toys," she snapped.

"And we call you the Nose Jobs," I snapped back.

"Fine," Heidi said, trying to calm herself down. "Fine.

Well, if being authentic is all about empathy, then I have empathy for you. I'd be insecure if I were you too."

"Oh please," I said. "I'm the one who has empathy for you."

"No, you don't," she shot back. "I have empathy for you."

For what seemed like an eternity, we both kept repeating the phrase *I have empathy for you* until it lost all of its meaning.

"Do you know why I stopped hanging out with you?" Heidi asked.

"Because you think you're better than me," I said.

"Wow, that's major projection," Heidi said, with a certainty that shook me a little. "No, Daria, it's because you were so hung up on my nose job. You just couldn't stop asking me why I did it. I did it because I didn't like how I looked. How I looked didn't reflect how I felt inside. And maybe it made me more real because it made me look more like the person I feel like I am inside."

"Why don't you just own it?" I asked. "Just say you did it 'cause you wanted to look prettier."

"See, you're doing it again. You're making me feel horrible about myself. This is why we can't be friends. You're so judgmental. Why do you want to make me feel bad about myself?"

I didn't have an answer to that. I wanted to fight back, but I couldn't help but feel that maybe she was right. Maybe there was a totally different version of history where I *had* been really judgmental about her nose job *before* she'd started being cruel to me. I mean, she had already gotten the nose job because she felt bad about herself, and maybe I had made her feel worse about herself all over again.

Heidi looked away from me for a moment, like she was formulating her next thought very carefully. When she looked at me again, she seemed calmer, more resolved. "Look," she said. "Maybe we should just stop trying to pretend we're friends or even frenemies. Maybe we just need to ignore each other from now on. We don't need to wave at each other, or smile at each other, or show up to each other's parties, or pretend to be nice. I'll just pretend you don't exist, and you do the same."

"Oh," I said.

And with that, Heidi walked away. Of course, her last words were supereloquent and my last word was *Oh*.

Standing there, all by myself, I felt every inch the misfit toy. I realized that maybe I *was* the insecure one, and Heidi was the confident one. I wanted some of that confidence, and that's when I decided to take her suggestion for a date with Iglesias. I texted him and asked if he wanted to go to the Santa Monica Pier with me Friday night.

I told my parents I was staying late at school to go to the library, but that wasn't true. Iglesias had accepted my invitation, and met me at my favorite ice cream place in Santa Monica, blocks away from the pier. When I walked in, I found him staring at the day's selection of flavors: strawberry thyme, honey rosemary, black cherry molasses, coconut curry. The first thing he said when he saw me was, "I think I need to be stoned to eat ice cream with curry in it."

"It's really delicious. I swear. My mom and I come here all the time. Of course, she always tastes one flavor and stops there, and then I order two scoops and eat them both."

"Sounds like you're a lot more fun than your mom."

I smiled. I had never looked at it that way. "I don't know," I said. "She's actually really fun. She just always knows when to stop. She's very . . ." I searched for the right word to describe Sheila, and finally came up with "appropriate."

"I prefer inappropriate," he smiled.

"You know what's inappropriate?" I asked.

"Curry in ice cream," he said.

"Wait, that's what I was gonna say."

"You know what else is inappropriate?" he asked.

"What?" I asked, unable to stop smiling.

"Having a crush on your stepmother's biological daughter," he said. "That's, like, way inappropriate. On a scale of inappropriate from one to Kanye West, it's Kanye East."

When I stopped laughing, we ordered two servings, with two flavors each, so that he could taste every flavor. We took our ice cream and went for a walk, past a row of jacaranda trees, past a Thai restaurant called Poon Thai, which he found uproariously funny, past a couple making out way too ferociously, which I found a little uncomfortable. We talked a lot, but then we got really quiet and just focused on eating the ice cream.

"Please taste this," I said, holding out a bite of my coconut curry. "It tastes like the entire country of India is in my mouth."

"That sounds kind of gross. The Ganges River is in your mouth. Isn't it real dirty?" But he took the bite anyway. And from the look on his face it was obvious he liked it.

"Now I can taste the Ganges River," I said, unable to stop smiling. "I haven't even been there."

"Well, you're in luck," he said. "The Ganges River is totally my third-date spot."

I didn't say anything. I just smiled, because I was on a *date*, and he had just said there was going to be a *third date*. I was the girl who'd thought she might never date anyone, who'd thought that her friends were enough. A jolt of excitement hit me, and a little voice in my head told me that if this was possible for me, then maybe even more incredible things were possible as well.

We stopped on a stoop, where we played each other some of our favorite music. I played him some She-Reen, and he really liked it. He said that even though he had no idea what she was saying, he could tell that whatever she was saying was angry, passionate, and totally necessary. I said it was so stupid that Americans only listened to music in English. My family listened to music in so many different languages—Farsi, French, Spanish, Arabic, Turkish, Hebrew, Greek, Portuguese—only a few of which we even spoke.

He said his parents pretty much only listened to really depressing old Mexican music. "Except once in a while my mom will play some old white dude music, like Leonard Cohen or Tom Waits. It's really strange, but I don't mind it so much. And I love the old Mexican shit. It's dope. I complain every time they play it, but secretly I love it." Then his mood changed, and he said, "So my mom comes back in two days."

"Yeah," I said. "This is it."

"You sure you're ready to do this?" he asked.

"I think so," I said. "I have to do it, right?"

He leaned back and said, "We're still gonna be *us* after you meet her, right?"

"What do you mean?" I asked.

"I mean . . ." And he sat back up now, like what he was saying was really important. "Let's say she doesn't want to see you for some reason. Then will we ever hang out again? And let's say she does want to see you. Will you just wanna see her every time you come over, and forget all about me?"

I hadn't really thought through all the permutations, so I just told the truth. "I don't know."

"It's all messed up, isn't it? I've never liked a girl the way I like you." He froze for a beat, then said, "I'm not supposed to admit that, am I?"

I should have said I had never liked a boy the way I liked him, but instead I said, "You probably just like me because you're not supposed to." I kicked myself inside for saying that.

Why couldn't I just have told him how I felt? Why did I have to doubt that everything we were feeling was real?

His face dropped a little. It was jarring to see his mood change so quickly, like when you're listening to a mix and it goes from a really happy song to a really sad song. "You're not my sister," he said. "We're not doing anything wrong."

"Still . . ." I was thinking of all the reasons why he couldn't really like me. "I mean . . . you barely know anything about me. I guess you met Caroline, but you haven't met my family, or Joy, or Kurt, and if I ever do introduce you to my family, they'll probably hate you anyway because they'll just think of you as the stepson of my birth mother, so I'm, like, never gonna introduce you to my family . . ." That's when I had an idea. "Wait, you can meet one member of my family. You can meet my grandmother!" I said, as if it were a eureka moment. My grandmother's nursing home was just blocks away from where we were.

"Really?"

"Yes," I said. And then I added, "She has Alzheimer's, okay?"

"Okay," he said.

"The thing is, she probably won't even remember meeting you. And if she does remember, and she mentions you to my parents, they'll think she imagined the whole thing."

"So it's like I'm meeting a member of your family, but also *not* meeting a member of your family?" he asked.

"Yes. I mean, no. I mean . . ." I trailed off for a moment. It had been weeks since my parents and I had last visited Maman Homa, and I was genuinely thrilled by the idea of seeing her. I missed her. And I wanted Iglesias to meet *someone* from my family.

"It's okay," he said. "I get it."

"Look, I want you to meet my whole family, eventually," I said. "But let's start with my grandmother. Come on." I stood up and grabbed his hand. Before we left, I took out my phone and opened my Twitter app.

"Are you seriously tweeting right now?" he asked.

"I'm sorry," I said. "Just give me a second. My mom reads my Twitter feed, and I told her I was at the library." I quickly composed a few thoughts of 140 characters or less that indicated I was deciding between reading Dickens and studying trigonometry. Then I put my phone away and said, "Okay, that should convince her. Hashtag, terrible daughter."

"Hashtag, covert operation," he said.

"Hashtag, training for the CIA," I replied, so happy that our conversation felt light again. If our night was a mix, we were back to an upbeat track. We made up random hashtags as we walked to the nursing home, and Iglesias said that since I spoke Farsi and lied easily, I really would make the perfect CIA agent.

Maman Homa's assisted-living facility was *darejeh yek*, as Baba would say, which literally translated into *first degree*, but what he meant was that it was top-of-the-line. The architecture was faux-Mediterranean, with terra-cotta ceilings and bougainvillea everywhere. Sheila hated the nursing home, even though it was so beautiful. She said she couldn't deal with being around old people for too long. She said she didn't want to see her future in front of her like that, and that when she was old, she would rather I euthanize her than put her in a nursing facility. "But, Sheila," I remember saying, "the nursing home is so much fun. All they do is play games and watch movies all day. And they have their own personal chef!" Sheila said I was too far away from old age to understand how horrible being stuck in one place playing games and watching movies all day really was.

Emily, the front-desk nurse, gave me a hug as soon as she saw me. That was the other thing about the nursing home. Every single staff member seemed to know every single patient's family members by name.

Emily led us to Maman Homa's room, past four old men playing poker, past a man and two women playing Monopoly. Maman Homa was alone inside, watching the Persian news on television. "Hey, Maman Homa," I said as I walked in.

Visiting Maman Homa was kind of like a box of chocolates—you never knew what you were gonna get. Except that with a box of chocolates, you got a guide, so if you were smart and planned ahead, you actually did know exactly what you were gonna get. But with Maman Homa, there was no way to prepare, and no guide. Some days she remembered you. Some days she didn't. The smile on her face when we entered made me hopeful that this was one of those good days when she was happy and recognized me, but then she said, "Sheila *djoon*, how are you?" in Farsi, and I knew that it was not one of those good days. In fact, this was a new kind of day altogether— a day in which she mistook me for my mother.

"No, Maman, it's me, Daria. Your granddaughter," I said in Farsi.

"Sheila *djoon*," she said. "I've spoken with your mother. She refuses to leave."

"Maman, I'm not Sheila," I said.

"And I want you to know that family is very important to me. And that if I were you, I would stay here with my family. Even though it's dangerous. At least you will all still be together." It suddenly hit me that Maman Homa didn't just think I was my mother, she also thought we were in 1979. "But I also want you to know," she continued, "that if you do decide to accept my son's proposal and leave Iran with us, then we will be your new family. You won't be without a mother, because I will be your mother."

"Yes, Maman," I said. "I understand."

"I know it won't be the same as having your real mother by your side. But I hope I can be a decent substitute. Did you know I was raised by my aunt?" she asked.

"I didn't know that," I said.

"My mother died giving birth to my younger brother,"

she said. "I was five. My aunt took us in. And I called her Mommy. And she was my mommy as far as I was concerned. Do you know that if you keep repeating something, eventually you will believe it?"

"I do know that," I said.

"Well," she said, "I can't believe your family is staying here. The country is clearly going down the toilet. But everyone makes their own decisions."

Emily turned to leave, but before she left, I said, "Emily, she thinks I'm my mom. And that we're in the 1970s."

Emily smiled reassuringly, clearly used to this. "Never a dull day," she said, and then she left.

As Iglesias and I sat by her bed, Maman Homa kept talking about her childhood. She told us all about the aunt who raised her, and how she made a skin mask out of kitty litter because she believed it firmed your skin. And she told us all about her grandfather and how he could've been an Olympic ski champion if he hadn't stepped on glass and gotten an infection in his foot, which then had to be amputated. And she told us all about her cousin who tried to steal her husband away from her, at the wedding.

I translated everything for Iglesias, who seemed very entertained by the stories, and I made mental notes of everything, in case it could inspire my genealogy assignment. Unlike Heidi, my plan was not to make it all up and pretend to be descended from royalty. But then Maman Homa said something really interesting. She told us about her great-great-grandmother who was descended from the Qajars. I couldn't stop laughing.

"What's so funny?" Iglesias asked.

"Heidi pretended to be descended from royalty," I said. "And my grandmother says I really am descended from royalty."

"Whoa. You're a real Persian princess," he said.

"I mean, my grandmother isn't the most reliable source," I said.

"Just own it." Iglesias suddenly stood in front of me and then bowed down. "Your Highness, may I have your hand?"

I lifted up my hand, very demurely, and then he kissed it.

And I blushed.

Maman Homa said, "Sheila *djoon*, who is this man? If you're going to be spending time with other men, then I'm going to tell my son to rescind his proposal."

Before heading back home, we walked along the shore, and Iglesias said the ocean was beautiful, and he said it was no wonder I was named after the ocean because I was beautiful too. I let him say it. And for the first time, I let myself believe it.

When we finally made it to the Santa Monica Pier, we ordered cotton candy and ate it with our hands, licking the stickiness off our fingers. I said there was nothing better than the feel of cotton candy on your lips.

"Nothing better?" he asked. "Not even curry ice cream?"

"Nothing!" I exclaimed.

Then we rode the Ferris wheel, staring at the sunset, and the city became a sea of lights all around us. "Thanks for introducing me to your grandma," Iglesias said. "I couldn't understand a word she said, but she seemed really cool."

"Yeah," I said. "I wish you could've met her before she got sick."

"I'm sorry about that," he said.

"Forgetting things must be awful," I said.

"I wish I could remember what I wanna remember, and forget what I wanna forget," he said as the Ferris wheel descended back down.

"What would you wanna forget?"

"My mom's death. Every time my dad mentioned my mom's death." I gulped down hard, and my stomach sank. Iglesias, perhaps sensing the mood change, added, "Oh, and my first girlfriend. I really wanna forget her!"

"Wait, what? How come she's never come up?" I didn't want to admit it, but I was a little jealous.

"I don't know. It was a long time ago."

"A long time ago? You're only eighteen."

"Two years ago," he said. "Let's talk about something else, like the things I wanna remember."

"Okay," I said. "So what do you wanna remember?"

Without missing a beat, he said, "I wanna remember this."

"This?"

"Yeah, riding the Ferris wheel with you. I mean, I wanna remember you in general. I've never met anyone like you, before you."

My face got all red, and I didn't know what to say. All I could think of was, "What am I like?"

"Smart," he said. "And funny. And real." I held on to the rails of the Ferris wheel as it slowly crept back up to the top of its circular path. "So is this a moment worthy of your first kiss?" he asked.

"I don't know," I said, scared. I looked around and took a mental picture: the dark ocean out of focus in the background, the lights of the city glowing all around us, Friday-night lovers hand in hand below us, families eating ice cream, and Iglesias sitting so close to me I could feel the warmth of his leg against mine. Finally, I said, "Yeah, it's a worthy moment."

He leaned into me, but I wasn't ready. I held him back and said, "Wait until it gets to the very top. Then it'll be perfect."

He waited.

I waited.

And then the Ferris wheel got to the very top, and I closed my eyes and felt his lips against mine.

It was better than cotton candy.

Chapter Twelve

I'D THOUGHT THAT HAVING A new granddaughter would have distracted Sheila from throwing my sweet sixteen party, but I'd thought wrong. If anything, it had galvanized her even more. After all, this gave her an opportunity to dress up not only her daughter, but also her granddaughter, and flaunt us both in front of all her friends. Which is why Sheila, Lida, and I were in the baby section of Barneys in Beverly Hills on Saturday morning, searching for an outfit for Rose. I was lost in a daydream, playing that kiss on the Ferris wheel again and again in my head. It felt like a dream, a very nice dream, which I was abruptly taken out of when Sheila hoisted a pink cashmere baby dress in my face. "Daria, for the last time, what do you think?" She demanded to know. "Isn't it adorable?"

Still in my reverie, all I could manage was a feeble "Yeah, supercute."

"Are you even paying attention, Daria?" Sheila asked. "This is *your* birthday we're planning."

"Oh, come on, Sheila," I said. "We're not planning it. *You're* planning it. I hate my birthday."

"Why would you say that?" my mother asked.

I thought for a beat. Why did I hate my birthday so much? I guess I hated how I had to pretend it was the best day of the year to make other people feel good. I hated all the obligatory Facebook birthday posts I had to "like." Or maybe my birthday reminded me that I was born on the cusp of Aquarius and Pisces, so it was basically like the universe couldn't make a decision about who I was supposed to be, and where I really belonged. But I didn't say any of that. "I don't know. I just do," I said instead.

Sheila took a long breath, composing herself. "Look, I know you're upset now, but in ten years, when you're looking at the beautiful photos from the event, you'll thank me."

"Ten years," I repeated, laughing. "Wow. Okay. So way over half my life from now, I'll thank you."

"Yes," she said. "And when you look at those photos in ten years, you'll love me even more if all our clothes don't clash, so please help me pick the right outfit for Rose."

I just shrugged, unable to hide my annoyance. Lida put a supportive hand on my arm, and then, probably afraid of being accused of taking sides, put one on Sheila's arm as well.

Sheila gently pushed Lida's hand aside, and announced, "I've already decided that I'm going to wear my new red Valentino with the black-and-white flowers. You, well, I was thinking you should be in white, and Rose can be in this—"

"She's a baby," Lida interrupted, taking in the dress Sheila was holding up. "Why would you buy cashmere for a baby? She's just going to spit up all over it."

"She's only going to wear the outfit once," Sheila replied, as if this were obvious. Then she shifted her attention to a pink infant headband, bedazzled with rhinestones.

Before Sheila could say a word, Lida said, "She has no hair, Sheila. That will look ridiculous on her."

"Lida *djoon*, you're my sister and I love you, but aren't you going to miss your flight?"

Lida was going back to Iran that day, and she seemed very excited about it. She had told me that morning that as much as she loved seeing us, she didn't like feeling like a tourist all the time, which made me wonder if Sheila and Baba still felt like tourists in America. Which made me wonder if that's how Encarnación Vargas felt. Which made me think of Iglesias and that kiss on the Ferris wheel. Okay, let's face it, everything in that moment made me think of the kiss on the Ferris wheel. I must have missed the next round of back-and-forth between Sheila and Auntie Lida, because the next thing I felt was Sheila's hand on my shoulder, and her voice bellowing in my ear,

"Daria, say good-bye to your auntie."

"Oh, you're leaving now?" I asked.

"Have you not been listening to a word we've been saying?" Sheila asked. "I don't know what's going on with you these days, Daria. You're either angry or checked out. Is everything okay?"

I could have said, *Well, let's see. I found out you adopted me, lied to me my whole life about it, and now I'm in love with my birth mother's stepson. So excuse me for not caring about picking out an outfit for my one-week-old niece right now.* But instead I just said, "I'll miss you, Auntie Lida." Which was true.

Lida gave me a big hug and said we should try to see each other again next year. "And don't let her take over your birthday," she whispered in my ear. "Remember it's *your* day." That made me laugh, because it was so blatantly untrue.

After Auntie Lida left, Sheila decided we would continue our mother-daughter bonding day by finding me the perfect white dress for my sweet sixteen. I don't know why she was so fixated on my wearing white. It was like she thought I was a debutante, or a bride, or something associated with purity. I was too tired and distracted to fight with her. All I could think about was the fact that in just a few hours, I would be meeting Encarnación Vargas. Iglesias said she and his dad had returned from Mexico, and that they would be having a quiet family dinner. I was rehearsing what I would tell Encarnación when Sheila got my attention once again, this time holding a white dress. "This is the one," she said. "This one is so you."

I wanted to tell her that she had no idea what was "so me" anymore, but all I said was, "Sure, I'll try it on."

Later, as we walked through Beverly Hills, we passed the Chanel store and peeked in at the new bags. "You'll have one of those when you graduate from college," Sheila said.

"I know," I said. "When I'm officially a woman. Let's just hope they're still in style then."

"A Chanel bag never goes out of style," Sheila said.

Speaking of style, I spent a fair amount of time deciding what to wear to the Vargas family dinner that evening. I wasn't one of those girls who tried on outfit after outfit every time she left the house, but I'd turned into one of those girls before this dinner. Luckily, Joy had agreed to come over and be my style consultant.

At first, I put on a fancy floral cocktail dress that Sheila had bought me for my previous birthday.

"I mean, it's a pretty dress. I love the fabric," Joy said.

"But?" I asked.

"But it makes you look like you just left the country club."

Trying to move as far away from that as possible, I tried on a pair of jeans and my favorite gray hoodie.

"Now you look like you put no effort into your appearance," she said.

"I'm gonna see Iglesias," I said. "So I want to look cute."

As Joy searched my closet for the perfect outfit, she said, "I love that you have a crush."

"What about you?" I asked. "No butterflies in your stomach when Lance Summers talks to you?"

"Um, not at all," Joy said. "Although I did get my parents to reconsider the internship if I get straight As this semester."

"Wow, you negotiated," I said. "How Persian of you."

Joy pulled out my new bag of clothes from Local. She looked at the new jeans that were inside, and the green V-neck sweater. "Ooh, I love this green."

I threw on the jeans, one of the supersoft Local T-shirts, and the sweater. They all fit perfectly.

"I think that's the outfit," Joy declared. "You look nice but not *too* nice." It felt right. After all, that's how I had found Encarnación. She used to work at Local. This would show her that I'd put real thought into this encounter.

When we opened the door to leave, Sheila peeked in and saw all the outfits I'd rejected strewn about my room. "I'll clean up later," I said.

"You girls are going to a movie with Caroline and Kurt, right?" she asked.

"Mmm-hmmm," I mumbled.

"What movie are you seeing?"

"I don't know," I said. "What are we seeing again, Joy?"

Joy's face flushed a little. "Whatever starts when we get there."

I groaned internally. Clearly, I'd chosen the wrong person to cover for me.

"You put an awful lot of thought into your outfit choice for a night at the movies," Sheila said with a knowing glare.

I could feel my face warm up, so I rushed out of the house before I could incriminate myself further. "We're gonna be late!" I said, and gave her a quick peck on the cheek before running out. Sheila definitely knew something was up. Persians always kiss each other on *both cheeks*.

My friends were so awesome that all three of them agreed to accompany me to Encarnación's house. But our first stop, since my mother is a stealth web stalker, was at the movie theater. I took a picture of the movie options and tweeted, "What should we see tonight, people? #moviechoices." Then we took an Authentics selfie in front of the theater, and I posted it to Instagram with the caption "Movie Night with My BFFs." And finally, I "checked in" on Facebook.

Having covered the required digital bases, we took a car toward Encarnación Vargas's home. Kurt sat in the front passenger seat, and I was in the back, between Joy and Caroline. My hands were shaking. I was on the verge of full-blown panic.

"You guys, I'm really scared," I said. They all eyed each other, like they were trying to decide who would do the best job of giving me a pep talk. When none of them said anything,

I kept going. "I'm kind of freaking out here. Like, maybe we should just turn back, guys."

"No way," Caroline said. "I'm not letting you chicken out."

"We can go out to dinner instead, or play Apples to Apples, or—"

"This is your moment, Daria," Caroline said. "If you don't do this, you'll be so disappointed in yourself. And you won't have any of the answers you need."

"I mean, what if she rejects me? What if she doesn't want to see me? What if she tells me to leave her alone?"

"Then I'll kick her ass," Caroline said.

Our driver turned the music down. I think she could tell how intense this was for all of us. "Thanks, guys," I said. "I don't know how I'd do this without you."

Trying to lighten the mood, Kurt said, "I'd be happy to quickly do your birth mother's chart for you." We all groaned.

"Seriously, Kurt," Caroline said. "She's never met the woman. How would she know her astrological sign?"

"You can ask Iglesias," Joy suggested.

"Who?" Kurt asked. There was silence, which was probably the worst possible reaction. "You guys, who is Iglesias?" he asked again.

More horrible silence. Finally, I said, "Iglesias is her stepson."

"Oh," Kurt said. "Is there some reason everyone's acting like they killed a puppy every time someone says his name?"

"It's just that . . ." I trailed off and then finally said, "It's just that we went on a date. I wanted to find the right time to tell you, Kurt. I didn't know how you'd react, and I wanted to be . . ."

"Oh, that's great," Kurt said. "That's better than great, actually. That's fantastic."

"It is?" I asked.

"Why wouldn't it be?" he asked.

"It's just that moment on the ice rink . . ." I said.

"What moment on the ice rink?" Caroline asked. "There was a *moment* on the ice rink?"

Joy elbowed Caroline.

"There was no moment on the ice rink," Kurt said. "And even if I might like Daria, we can't date because the Authentics come first, so I'm very happy for her. Can we move on, please?"

We rode in silence the rest of the way. When the driver finally pulled up to the house, we all got out of the car, and I hugged all three of them. But Kurt's hug felt limp. He got in the passenger seat of the car, and then Joy got in the back. Caroline gave me one last hug, and whispered in my ear, "Don't worry about Kurt's feelings, okay? You are going to meet your birth mother right now. You just stay strong and carry on, or whatever. And seriously, if she's mean to you in any way, then you text me, and I will come take her down."

✳ ✳ ✳

As I approached the house, the first thing I noticed was that the Christmas decorations were gone. I kind of missed the wreath on the door. It reminded me of the first time I met Iglesias. I stood outside the door for a brief moment, breathing in and out as calmly as I could, and then when I felt ready, I knocked on the door. I sighed with relief when Iglesias answered. "Hey," he said. "I'm so sorry."

"About what?" I asked.

And then I noticed that he was wearing a tuxedo.

"I totally forgot," he said. "I'm not the best planner."

A woman in a peach dress came bolting through the house, her dark hair swept into a bun atop her head. I immediately recognized her as an older version of Encarnación Vargas. I also immediately recognized her as my biological mother. "Where are my keys, Enrique?" she asked in Spanish. "We're going to be late."

"I didn't touch your keys," Iglesias bellowed.

"I've got them," a man said as he entered the room, also wearing a tuxedo. He was an uncanny older replica of Iglesias. Same face, just more wrinkles and thinning hair.

"Okay, then let's go," Encarnación said. "I am not going to have your aunt blaming me for starting late."

"Um, Mom," Iglesias said. "This is my friend Daria."

Encarnación looked up and finally noticed me. "Nice to meet you, Daria," she said. I was hoping she would take one look at me and immediately recognize me as her child, but that didn't happen. "We're late for my niece's quinceañera, so if you don't mind . . ."

"I had told Daria she could have dinner with us tonight," Iglesias mumbled under his breath.

Encarnación's eyes opened wide, and she looked to her husband knowingly. "Oh, I see. You wanted her to meet your folks, huh?"

"Well, yeah," Iglesias said.

"I'm Enrique's dad," the man said as he approached me. "Are you in school?"

"Yes," I said.

"Are you going to go to college?"

"Um, definitely," I said.

"You can call me Fabio," he said, and then he gave me a big hug.

"Hi, Fabio," I said. "It's nice to meet you, and Mrs. Vargas, I . . ."

"I'm Mrs. Lunes now," she said. And then, "You knew my maiden name. Wow, you and Enrique must be very close."

"Enrique has never brought a girl to dinner before. There was, of course, the girl we found him in his room with . . ."

"Dad!" Iglesias's eyes begged his father to stop.

The situation was spinning way out of my control. Encarnación and Fabio thought I was Iglesias's new girlfriend, which wasn't entirely wrong. But, of course, it also wasn't why I was here. Before I could attempt to get back on track, Encarnación took my hand and said, "I have a great idea. Come with us."

"Oh, I can't," I said. "I just really wanted to meet you over dinner and . . ."

"You look like you're exactly the same size as me," she said. And then she took my hand in hers and led me into the house, yelling back, "Fabio, call my sister and tell her we're going to be late."

Encarnación took me to her bedroom. It was so different from Sheila and Baba's bedroom. The bed was smaller, and there was no flat-screen television. Encarnación found a lilac dress and tossed it my way. "Try this on. I wore it when I was a bridesmaid for my sister's wedding."

"Mrs. Vargas," I said.

"Mrs. *Lunes*," she corrected me. "And you can call me Encarnación."

"Encarnación," I said. "I really wanted to meet you."

"Aren't you sweet? I'm glad to meet you as well. You seem so much nicer than Enrique's last girlfriend."

"What was she like?" I asked.

"There's plenty of time for girl talk another night," she said. "But we're going to be late, so see if this dress fits."

I took off my sweater and laid it on the bed. I could see Encarnación stare at the Local label as I tried on the dress. "Local?" she asked. "You like that store?"

"I love it," I said. "They make great clothes."

She stared at the sweater for a long time, then touched it tenderly, like it was taking her back in time. "I used to work there," she said. And then, composing herself, she added, "I'm happy they're still using quality fabrics."

I pulled the dress down over my knees, and before I could answer, she said, "It fits! I knew it would. Let's go."

"I don't know how late I can stay at the party," I said, grabbing my sweater and jeans. "I should take my clothes with me."

"Go home whenever you need to. You can keep the dress. It doesn't fit me anymore, anyway."

As she pulled me down, she whispered in my ear, "His last girlfriend had a fake tan, a septum piercing, and a misspelled tattoo on her shoulder. That's all I'll say."

"Can't use spell-checker on a tattoo," I said.

And she laughed. "I like you already," she said.

I smiled big. She liked me.

Iglesias and I sat in the backseat on our way to the quinceañera, him in his tux, and me in my lilac dress. We looked like we were on our way to the prom, or to a wedding, and it felt kind of nice. He took out his phone and started typing into it, and it wasn't until I felt my own phone vibrate that I realized he was texting me.

Iglesias: This is disaster. I sorry.
Me: I'm kind of excited. I never been 2 quince.

Iglesias: They R boring and my aunt sucks.

Me: But your parents seem so cool.

Iglesias: I guess. But they think we're dating!

I stopped cold. "They think we're dating" meant, of course, that we were *not* dating. My face must have given away my emotion, because he typed feverishly and sent me one more text.

Iglesias: Sorry. Didn't wanna assume. Makes an ass outta U + me. Or just me.

There was new and palpable tension between me and Iglesias as we entered an old church in La Mirada, which was one of those towns I had only ever heard about on the local news. Iglesias whispered to me, "I'm sorry. Are you still pissed?" I didn't know what to say, so I just shook my head. But I was kind of pissed. How could he not assume we were dating after he'd kissed me on top of a Ferris wheel?

A Mass was already under way when we entered the church. A woman in a tight sky-blue dress and with too much makeup on strode directly toward us and accosted Encarnación. It was obvious from their rapport that they were sisters. "We did not delay the Mass for you, Encarnación," the woman whispered.

"She looks beautiful, Magnolia," Encarnación said, indicating the fifteen-year-old girl in the white Cinderella dress with rhinestone overlays who was in the process of being blessed by a priest.

"You just had to show up late, didn't you?" Magnolia asked. "You would just love to ruin the most important day of my daughter's life."

"Ruin her day?" Encarnación whispered. "I sewed her dress!"

"You don't understand," Magnolia said. "Nothing can go wrong today. Nothing." With that, Magnolia sat back down. Encarnación, clearly perturbed after her tiff with her sister, found an open pew and took a seat. We all followed her.

I watched silently as a priest blessed a teenage girl. I had never been to church before. Lala had always wanted to take me, but Sheila and Baba had strictly forbidden her. Sheila once said that she would rather I become a drug addict than a religious fanatic. But the thing was that Lala was nothing like a religious fanatic. She was just a woman who went to church on Sundays and read her Bible quietly to herself at night. But in my parents' eyes, that was one step away from joining some kind of dangerous Jesus cult. I guess because of the Iranian Revolution, my parents thought any form of worship was a gateway drug that inevitably led to killing your people, hiding your women under heavy fabrics, and overthrowing your government, or something like that.

My wandering thoughts were cut short when Iglesias took my hand in his and squeezed it. I squeezed back. Then he whispered, "That's my cousin Virginia. She's dedicating her life to God right now. She's vowing to maintain spiritual devotion and remain a virgin until she gets married." He paused and then added, "Which would all be really moving if she hadn't lost her virginity five times already."

After the Mass, everyone moved to a nearby salon where a party was already under way. The place was decorated with balloons, and a band was playing Latin music for the crowds. And when I say crowds, I mean it. Not only was everyone from the church there, but hordes of other people were arriving as well. Magnolia was the center of attention, trotting her daughter Virginia around from person to person, proudly greeting them. Finally, they reached us. "Enrique," Magnolia said with a snarky smile. "Do introduce us to your new friend."

"This is Daria," he said. "She's, um . . . We're, um . . . dating."

"Are you wearing the dress my sister wore at my wedding?" Magnolia asked.

"Yeah, I guess I am," I said.

"It looks good on you," she said. Virginia was barely listening to the conversation. She had slipped a phone out of her purse and was texting. "Virginia, put the phone away. This is the greatest day of your life. Be present for it!"

"I'm sorry," Virginia said, under her breath. For being the

star of the night, she seemed pretty over it all. I wondered if that's how I would feel the night of my sweet sixteen.

"Okay, come on, Virginia, we have more people to greet," Magnolia said. "Did you thank your cousin for coming?"

Virginia smiled a fake smile at Iglesias and said, "Thanks for coming, cousin dearest."

"I never miss an opportunity to come," Iglesias said with a crooked smile.

"If you think we're too dumb to get your dirty jokes, you're wrong," Magnolia said.

After Magnolia pulled Virginia away, I turned to Iglesias. "Were you flirting with your cousin?"

"Ew, no," he said. "That would be gross."

"Not really," I said. "She's not your blood relative, right? She's no more related to you than I am."

"Yeah, except I've known her since she was in pigtails, so it's a little different."

I stewed silently and finally said, "What are we going to do?"

"I don't know," he said. "We could dance."

"I mean, about your mom?"

"I think what you mean," he said with a smile, "is *your* mom."

"This is not funny," I said. "This is terrible. We have to tell her."

"Go ahead," he said. "She's right there." Iglesias pointed to a large table where Encarnación and Fabio were engaged in discussion with three other couples, all of them drinking, telling stories, and laughing. "Maybe you should tell her in front of all her friends. That would go over well."

"This is all wrong," I said. "I was supposed to tell her I'm her daughter first, and then broach the bizarre nature of our relationship."

"So we're in a relationship?" he asked.

"I don't know," I said, increasingly tense. "Maybe not. You're the one who asked me if we were dating after you kissed me." He tried to speak, but I didn't let him. "I don't kiss guys I'm not dating, Iglesias. But maybe that's the kind of girl you want. Maybe you were hoping I was like your last girlfriend, with her misspelled tattoo."

"Why are you so pissed off at me?" he asked.

I could have said I was pissed off because he'd completely messed up my plan. Tonight was supposed to be about me connecting with my birth mother, and now it had become about something completely different. Now I was thrust into his entire social universe as his new girlfriend, who he wasn't even sure he was dating. I could've said all of that, but instead I just said, "I don't know. I just am."

I walked outside alone. I took a deep breath, hoping for some fresh air, and inhaled some cigarette smoke instead. I looked up and saw Virginia's flat shoes poking out from behind a Dumpster. "Hey," I said, approaching her.

"Oh, hey," she said. "I needed to get out of there."

"Yeah, I get it," I said.

"Have you had yours yet?" she asked.

"My what?" I asked.

"Um, your quinceañera," she said, as if stating the obvious.

It took me a moment to process the fact that she assumed I was Mexican. I could've corrected her, but I really wasn't in the mood. And besides, I *was* Mexican. Kind of. So I just said, "Not yet."

"Well, I hope your mother is more chill than mine."

"Hardly," I said.

She smiled and held out her pack of cigarettes for me. I shook my head, and then she used her last cigarette to light a new one. "Don't smoke. It causes bad skin," she said with a laugh. "That's what my mom cares about. Forget cancer!"

"Why do moms use their daughters as excuses to throw parties for themselves?" I asked.

"Now, that is the million-dollar question," she said. "My mom even invited Sharon Alvarez, who wrote the word *slut* on my locker last year."

"That's awful," I said. Heidi may have made my life difficult, but she'd never done anything that bad. "Does your mom know she did that?"

"She knows I hate her. That should be enough."

"Yeah," I said, thinking of my mother inviting Heidi to my

birthday. "My mom's already invited my former best friend to my . . ." I was about to say *sweet sixteen* when for some reason, I said, "quinceañera."

"What is that about? If it's supposed to be our day, then it should be *our* day. Is she gonna make fourteen of your friends dress up as past versions of you?"

"What?" I asked.

Through the glass, Virginia cocked her head toward a row of fourteen girls dressed in matching shades of baby pink. "They each represent one year of my life *before I became a woman*. It's all such a show. And my mom is spending all her money on this party. I was like, 'Mom, give me the money. I'll take myself on a vacation to Brazil. Jesus.' I don't get her priorities."

"I totally understand," I said.

"I thought you looked kind of square when you walked in, but you're actually cool," she said.

"I borrowed this dress from Iglesias's mom," I said. "It's not how I usually dress."

"Iglesias!" she squealed. "As in Enrique Iglesias. Genius. How have I not been calling him that?"

"No, please don't. He hates it. I mean, he lets me call him that, because I'm kind of flirting when I do it, but you're his cousin, so that would be weird."

"First of all," she said, "I am only his cousin by marriage, so I could totally flirt with him without it being weird. Second of all, we practically grew up together, and I have no interest in him. And third of all, the nickname is hilarious, and it's so much less embarrassing than being called Rico."

I suddenly felt really guilty about lying to her about having a quinceañera. She seemed really awesome, and I realized that in a way, she was my cousin too. And I didn't want her to think I was a liar. "Listen," I said. "I said something kind of stupid. I'm not actually . . ."

Before I could finish, she held her hand up. "Hold that thought. It's time for my Cinderella moment." Virginia ran back inside. Through the glass, I could see an older man, presumably her father, slip off her flats and replace them with a pair of high heels. The whole crowd clapped. And then the dancing resumed.

I watched from outside as Encarnación took Iglesias's hand and danced with him while Virginia danced with her father and Magnolia took photos of the scene. I wondered how different my life would have been had I been raised in this community. After all, Virginia's quinceañera was just another version of my sweet sixteen. Magnolia and Encarnación, with their constant bickering, were another version of Sheila and Auntie Lida. The father dancing with Virginia, he was basically Baba with fuller hair.

I walked back inside to say good-bye to Iglesias, and to Encarnación, but I couldn't bring myself to interrupt their celebration. They looked like they were having so much fun.

Iglesias was teaching his mom how to krump, and Encarnación was laughing at her son. Fabio was taking pictures of both of them with his phone. Even Virginia, who had complained about her quinceañera, was happily twirling in the arms of her father, a carefree smile on her face. The crowd of revelers was singing along to the song blaring through the speakers, articulating every Spanish word with delight. I had never heard the song before. I felt completely out of place, the only apple in a bowl of oranges, a blue M&M in a bag full of reds. I was just a visitor here, a tourist, and it was time for me to go home.

Chapter Thirteen

I COULD BARELY SLEEP THAT night. My heart raced, my hands trembled, and was having night sweats. I laid a towel down under me and stared up at my ceiling, wondering what I should do next. I couldn't even figure out what was making me anxious. Was it the fact that I had fought with Iglesias, or was it the fact that I hadn't told Encarnación who I was, or was it both? I played out different fantasies in my mind. In one, Iglesias and I moved to Mexico City together, where he became a hip artist, and I became his agent, selling the world on his brilliance. We never told Encarnación that I was her daughter, but because I was married to Iglesias, she became my mother-in-law, and so I started calling her Mama. Our wedding was on a Mexican beach—I don't know which one since I've never been to a Mexican beach (hey, it was a lucid dream)—and the day of the wedding, Sheila and Encarnación fussed over me together. And then Baba gave me away. When we grew old together, I asked Iglesias if we had done the right thing by never telling our parents the truth, and he said, "Of course. Because all that matters is that we know the truth. And the truth is that I love you."

In another daydream, I stormed out of bed on that very night and banged on Encarnación's door. She opened it in her nightgown and asked what was going on. I told her that I was her daughter, and she shook her head with tears in her eyes. She told me I had lied to her. She told me I was forbidden from dating her son. I told her he was her stepson, but she didn't care. She slammed the door in my face. Iglesias and I tried to see each other again, but the weight of it eventually crushed us, and we went our separate ways. I ended up marrying Kurt, who forced me to give birth to all three of our children by C-section so that they could be born at a time of astrological compatibility with us. But eventually we got divorced. Then I married a Persian doctor who Sheila set me up with, but he cheated on me. Finally, in my old age, I saw Iglesias at a gas station, and realized he was the one I loved, and that we were now too old to do anything about it. So I just drove away without saying a word.

The fact that both of these fantasies saw me through to old age probably gives you some idea of the hours of sleep I was losing that night. And there were others as well, each with a running theme, which was that if I told Encarnación who I was, there was no way Iglesias and I would be allowed to continue our relationship. I had to make a choice—at least that's what my subconscious was telling me.

At some point, I must have fallen asleep because I woke up at noon to the sound of yelling downstairs. I could make out Sheila and Baba yelling in Farsi, but there were two other voices, yelling in another language. Groggy, I opened the door and shuffled to the living room, where I found Sheila and Baba huddled on one side, and a middle-aged Chinese couple huddled on the other. My parents and Andrew's parents glared at each other like they were planning nuclear attack. In between the two couples stood Amir and Andrew, one looking more exhausted than the other.

"Good morning," I said, in English, hoping the neutral language would settle the mood.

"Daria," Sheila said, forcing a smile. "You remember Andrew's parents, Meili and Fang. You met them at the wedding."

Meili and Fang each took my hand and smiled. I looked down at my bare feet and my worn pajamas, and then ran my hands through my frizzy hair. "I'm sorry, I just woke up."

Meili looked at her watch. "It's past noon," she said. "You usually sleep past noon?"

I was taken aback by her hostile energy. "Um . . . sometimes . . . I mean . . . It's Sunday."

Meili shot a knowing look to Fang, which was not lost on Sheila, who said, "If you have something to say, just say it out loud."

"She sleeps a lot," Meili said. "That's all."

"Mom, please," Andrew whispered. "Is that necessary?"

"Perhaps she was studying all night," my mother countered, which of course wasn't true, but I appreciated her desire to defend me. What I wished my parents had noticed was that something was different about me. I wasn't a girl who usually stayed in bed until noon, and I wanted my parents to intuitively know that something was wrong.

Meili shrugged. "It is not for me to judge. You let your child sleep all day. You don't pick us up at the airport. You send us to a hotel. It is not for me to judge."

"For the last time," Sheila said with a sigh, "I booked you a room at the Beverly Wilshire because I thought you would be more comfortable there. It's a beautiful hotel."

"Comfortable? The stranger you sent to pick us up left us there, and they said our room won't even be ready until three p.m.!"

"We apologize," Baba said.

"I was only trying to treat you as I would want to be treated," Sheila explained. "If I came to Beijing, I would want to stay in a beautiful hotel . . ."

"You wouldn't want to stay in our home?" Meili asked. "Why? It's too dirty for you? You're afraid there will be chickens walking on the floor? You're afraid I'll skin a dog, boil it, and serve it to you for dinner?" Fang put his hand gently on his wife's arm, but she shoved it away. "We are family," Meili said. "And family picks family up at the airport. And family stays with family when they visit. That's not too much to ask."

Amir and Andrew looked at each other like they were trying to devise a way to defuse this situation.

"We live in a small apartment," Sheila explained as Meili and Fang gazed at our palatial living room, probably calculating its square footage in their heads. "The only room we could put you in is Lala's old room, and it only has a single bed in it anyway. As does Daria's room. There's just no room for you, unless you want to sleep on the floor of the living room." This was all true. We had lived in a bigger house before Amir went to college, but then Baba had downsized, much to Sheila's chagrin.

"Well," Meili said, "you could have purchased an air mattress. It's bad enough our son doesn't want us staying with him."

"Oh, come on, Mom," Andrew said. "You know we don't have the space, but I told you that you can hang out at our place from the moment you wake up until the moment you go to sleep."

I had a deep desire to crawl back into bed, to escape this hellish battle. And that's when I verbalized the insane idea that popped into my head. "How about this?" I proposed. "One of you can stay in my room, the other can stay in Lala's old room, and I'll stay in the hotel." I had a quick flash of Iglesias and me ordering room service in a crisp white bed at the Beverly Wilshire, pretending we were grown-ups on a glamorous vacation, or newlyweds on our honeymoon.

"I think you're joking," Sheila said.

"Of course she's joking," Baba said. "We're not letting her stay in a hotel by herself."

The truth was that I had been joking, but now I wanted to turn the joke into reality. "Why not?" I said. "It's right down the street."

"*Abada*," Sheila said, which is Farsi for *no effin' way*.

"If you say yes," I said to my mother, "I won't complain anymore about the awful sweet sixteen you want to throw me. I'll wear whatever you want me to, and even let you pick the music."

I could see my mother considering this offer very seriously, but finally, she shook her head.

"Come on," I said, trying another tactic. "You let me sleep over at Joy's and Caroline's all the time," I pleaded.

"Because there are adult chaperones present, *aziz*," Baba said.

"Um . . . Concierge. Receptionist. They sound like adult chaperones to me." From the half smile on Baba's face, I could tell I was winning him over. "And at least they'll be awake at night, unlike Joy's parents, who sleep like logs. For all you know, we sneak out and rage all night when I stay at Joy's."

"Do you?" Sheila asked, worried. Then she turned to Amir and asked, "Does she?"

"Of course not!" I pleaded. "And I won't if you let me stay in the hotel either. I'll just order room service, and watch movies, and do my homework by the pool. And tomorrow I'll go to school."

"This is what you get for reading Eloise to her too many times," Amir smirked.

"Don't you trust me?" I asked, knowing that was the clincher.

"Of course we trust you," Sheila said, softening. "But . . ." Sheila was still unsure, and then Meili came in to save the day.

"You even consider letting a fifteen-year-old girl stay in a hotel alone?" she asked. "Ridiculous!"

"What's ridiculous about it?" Sheila asked. "I trust my daughter, and I don't believe that keeping her in some kind of prison is the right way to raise her."

"Ha," Meili said. "Maybe in the hotel, she'll sleep until *six* in the afternoon!"

"It's decided," Sheila said. "Daria, you will move to the hotel."

"Wait, seriously?" I asked.

"Wow, unbelievable," Amir said, shaking his head. He pulled me in close. "Nice work, Daria. You clearly have the

Esfandyar negotiation gene."

I smiled. I had never expected this plan to work, and had Meili not butted in, it probably never would have. Sheila was so desperate to be *unlike* Meili that she was letting me go to make a point.

"Then it's decided," Meili said with a nod. "Your daughter will go to a hotel, where she will sleep all day if you're lucky, and binge-drink if you're unlucky. Can I move into my room now? I'm exhausted from the flight."

Amir and Andrew helped Meili settle into my room, and Fang settle into Lala's old room. At three o'clock, my parents drove me to the Beverly Wilshire and checked me in. They explained to the concierge that I was a fifteen-year-old girl staying alone and would need supervision. "Can we nanny-cam her room?" Sheila asked. Luckily, they did not offer surveillance services.

In the room, my mother lay down on the bed, her hair flowing onto the fresh white pillow. "I love hotels," she said. "I wish I could stay here with you instead of going home to that woman and her husband."

"She'll soften up when they meet Rose," I said. "Maybe."

"Let's choose to be kind to them," Baba said. "They're our family now, and they raised a wonderful child, so how bad can they be?"

Sheila laughed. "Your father has too much compassion," she said. "That's why half of his friends owe us money."

"Two friends," Baba said. "And they'll pay it back."

"Maybe if they had paid it back already, we'd live in a home with a guesthouse that we could quarantine those two inside. Instead, they'll be right next door to us."

Baba didn't say anything. I could tell her words stung him a little. Sheila always wanted more of everything, and it was up to Baba to give it to her. Instead of responding to her, he turned to me and said, "You'll call us if you need anything?"

"Of course," I said. "Who else would I call?"

"Maybe we'll take them to a movie later so we don't have to talk to them," Sheila said. "What did you see last night?"

It took me a moment to realize that she was talking to me. "Oh, um, we saw . . ." I had to think hard, but finally I remembered what our lie was. "*Free Charity.*"

"Was it any good?" Sheila said.

"Terrible," I said. The last thing I needed was Sheila seeing the movie and asking me to compare notes. "See something else."

After many more questions and requests, most of which were versions of "You'll call us every half hour, right?" or "Order room service, but no caviar, please. We're on a budget," Sheila and Baba finally left.

I looked nervously around the room. I had stayed in hotel rooms before, but usually there was a door leading to my parents' adjoining room. Now the umbilical cord was cut, and

I was on my own. I opened the minibar, full of tiny alcohol bottles. I took in the bathroom, with its carefully wrapped mini toiletries. So many of the items in the hotel room—the toiletries, the alcohol bottles—were miniature. These items were manufactured for a temporary life. *My* temporary life, where every day housekeeping would wash the sheets and towels clean of yesterday's mistakes and memories.

I rushed out to the balcony and took in my view of downtown LA, its skyscrapers breaking through the dense blanket of smog, reaching toward the eternally blue Southern California sky. Just a few hours ago, I'd been sleepless in bed, riddled with anxiety, unstrung by the unknown variables of my life. But now, in this nondescript room that bore no sign of me, or of anyone else, I felt great. My nervousness quickly turned to excitement. Here, I could be anybody I wanted. If I didn't like who I was, I could pick someone else. Here, everything was temporary.

I thought of Iglesias. I could call him right now, and see if he would come over. He might be upset about the night before, and how I'd left without saying good-bye, but he'd probably come over, right? I mean, when a girl invites a guy to a five-star hotel room, he shows up, right? I took out my phone and scrolled to Iglesias's name. I was about to call him when I decided that what I needed even more than Iglesias in my bed was someone to talk to *about* Iglesias. I needed the Authentics.

✳ ✳ ✳

Unfortunately, Kurt didn't answer my call or respond to any of my texts, which meant he was definitely still pissed at me. But Joy and Caroline arrived forty-five minutes later, so excited that they were clutching each other's hands. Caroline was wearing blue jeans and a T-shirt that read "Deport Bieber," and Joy was in a typically mismatched but perfect ensemble that consisted of layer upon layer of striped cutoff shirts. "This is fabulous!" Joy squealed. "Your very own hotel room. You're like Scarlett Johansson in *Lost in Translation*."

"Except we're not in Japan," Caroline pointed out.

"You know what I mean," Joy said. "You should put on a lot of makeup, pretend to be in your twenties, go to the hotel bar, and meet an old man who changes your life."

"Totally," Caroline said. "And then bring him back to your room, raid the minibar, and wake up naked surrounded by empty little bottles of booze."

"Um, okay, guys," I said. "Have you forgotten who I am?"

"Of course not," Caroline said. "But you're changing, Daria. Right before our very eyes. Our little girl is changing." Caroline ran her hands through my hair playfully, and I laughed. She was right. I was changing but not that quickly, which was why I dutifully called my parents.

My mother answered, and I told her she was on speaker with Joy and Caroline. Sheila said she wished she were with us. She said they had all visited Amir, Andrew, and Rose, but

184

left when it was Rose's nap time. Now they were at a Chinese restaurant in Alhambra owned by Meili and Fang's second cousin's brother-in-law. Sheila did not sound happy.

I convinced Joy and Caroline to stay long enough to order room service. I ordered a club sandwich with fries. They decided to split three appetizers. Once the food arrived, we sprawled out on the giant hotel bed, with four dishes laid out in front of us, and went to town. "So, have you guys spoken to Kurt?" I asked.

They both shook their heads.

"I think he's as upset with us as he is with you," Joy said. "He feels like we should've told him."

"I should've told him," I said. "I screwed up."

"He's hurt," Caroline said. "And possibly heartbroken."

"Is he, though?" I asked. "I mean, do you think he really likes me?"

"Who knows?" Caroline shrugged. "Kurt is a bit of a mystery. Maybe he's gay. Maybe he's in love with you. But even if he is, we all have to have our hearts broken at some point or another, right?"

"Well, not all of us," Joy said. "Some of us marry our high school sweethearts."

Caroline laughed. "You're right. Some of us do." Then she added, "Sweetheart."

Joy rolled her eyes. "Okay, Daria, it's time for you to fill us in on everything that did or did not go down."

I told them about Encarnación lending me her dress, the quinceañera, my fight with Iglesias, and my doubts about telling Encarnación who I was.

"Okay, stop," Caroline said. "You *have* to tell her who you are. That's the whole point of all this."

"But why, if it's going to ruin everything with Iglesias?" Joy asked.

"You guys, we're the Authentics." Caroline sat up straight and spoke forcefully. "You have to tell her because it's the authentic thing to do. Because it's honest."

"Yeah," Joy said. "But she's met her. She knows who she is now. She can be authentic within herself without rocking the boat."

I tried to get a word in, but Caroline beat me to it. "That's not how it works," she said. "Being one thing inside and another thing outside is the definition of inauthentic. That's, like, textbook inauthentic."

"Well, that's easy for you to say," Joy said. "Your parents didn't even bat an eyelash when you told them you're gay."

"Don't diminish my bravery," Caroline said. "Maybe my parents are more open-minded than yours, but coming out at thirteen wasn't easy."

"Whatever." Joy suddenly stood up. "I've gotta go," she said. "My parents are gonna start wondering where I am."

"Go be the good girl," Caroline taunted her.

"How am I a good girl?" Joy asked. "I'm the one who fought

my parents about that internship, and they're letting me do it."

"Whatever," Caroline said. "Do they know you only got the internship because the producer's son thinks you're hot?"

"Will you relax about Lance Summers?" Joy pleaded. "I don't even find him remotely cute."

I wasn't sure what was happening, but it was clear that Caroline and Joy were not talking about me and Encarnación anymore.

Images and memories popped into my head: Caroline trying to kiss Joy at midnight on New Year's Eve. Caroline asking Joy for permission to go meet Iglesias with me. Caroline telling Stuey she didn't need to be set up. Caroline and Joy walking into the hotel room clutching hands. Caroline sarcastically calling Joy "sweetheart." It hit me like an MMA fighter: hard, fast, and from all angles.

"Um, wait, are you guys . . . together?" I asked.

They were silent, which was all the confirmation I needed.

"How long has it been?"

They eyed each other, probably trying to secretly communicate an appropriate length of time that would be close to the truth, but not so long that it would hurt me too much.

"Seriously, guys, just tell me the truth. We're the Authentics, right, Caroline?"

"It started last summer!" Caroline blurted out.

"Last summer?" I asked. And then louder and without a question mark. "Last summer!"

"It was the end of August," Joy said desperately. "Practically fall."

"Um, no, that's summer!" I countered. "That's *definitely* summer."

Caroline looked at Joy sheepishly, but Joy wouldn't even look at her. "We had to tell her the truth eventually," Caroline pleaded. "She's our best friend."

"Sometimes the truth hurts people," Joy said, her gaze fixed on the floor. "Like my parents would be hurt if I came out to them. No, not hurt. Devastated. Livid. Apoplectic. They'd probably send me back to Nigeria to live with my grandparents. Daria, you're from an immigrant family. You know how hard it would be to come out, right?"

"You've gotta be kidding me," Caroline said. "Her *brother* is gay and has a husband and child. And the world keeps turning!"

I waved my hands manically in the air, one in front of each of their faces. "Hey, guys, this is about me right now. This is about how you hid this from your BEST FRIEND for months!"

"Yeah, well, you hid that *moment on the ice rink* you had with Kurt," Caroline said, in an attempt to even the playing field.

"Yeah, that's different," I said. "Because nothing happened. And nothing would've happened because I wouldn't jeopardize our group of friends over something stupid."

"This isn't stupid," Caroline said. "I love Joy."

Now Joy finally looked at Caroline, with a look that let me know she loved Caroline too. How could this be happening? How could my two best friends *fall in love* without me even noticing? I felt pissed at them for hiding it from me, and even more pissed at myself for being so self-involved that I could miss something so big.

"I'm sorry," Joy said. "I just . . . I didn't want to talk about it. And then we made it our New Year's resolution to tell you and Kurt, but you had all this stuff going on, and we didn't want to add this to your pile of stuff to process."

"Yeah, well, now I have to process the fact that you both lied to me." They had no response. "It's like I'm replaying every time we've hung out since August, and the fact that you basically lied to me every single one of those times."

"When you put it that way . . . ," Caroline said, and then trailed off. Caroline always finished her thoughts. This was a first.

"I need to be alone right now," I said, and turned away from them.

"We'll see you at school tomorrow?" Joy asked, her voice tentative.

"Yeah, sure," I mumbled, unable to conceal my hurt.

"See you tomorrow, then," Caroline said, reluctantly walking toward the door. "I better not get called on in Farrell's class. I still haven't finished my essay."

I knew Caroline was trying to ease the tension by bringing up a neutral subject, but I didn't take the bait. I just shrugged and then watched them leave.

I barely had a moment alone when there was a knock on the door. "Go away," I said.

From the other side of the door came Joy's voice. "Please open the door, Daria." I didn't want to, but I did. Joy was alone in the doorway. "Don't be mad at Caroline," Joy said. "She always wanted to be honest. I was just so scared of my parents finding out that I didn't want to tell *anybody*. So if you have to hate someone, hate me, please."

The thing is, Joy was *impossible* to hate, but in that moment, I just felt too hurt to tell her that, so I only said, "Okay," and closed the door again.

I felt gutted. What I hadn't told Caroline and Joy, what I was only beginning to understand, was how rootless I felt. I had *believed* in their authenticity. I had aspired to be as real as they were. Now that I knew they were hiding something so major, what was I left to believe in? I'd already been raised agnostic, and had just lost faith in my parents. With this latest revelation, I had officially lost faith in *everything*, and I felt so alone, like a single star all alone in the smoggy Los Angeles sky.

I opened the minibar, those tiny bottles daring me to open them, and I pulled one out. It was tequila. I twisted the little bottle open, and quickly swallowed the entire thing, feeling it burn my throat as it entered the desolate void that was my body. My little world had changed so much. I felt like the entire planet had shifted off its axis, and was spinning rapidly around a burning-hot new sun. In this new universe, who would care if I got drunk? And who would care if I texted Iglesias the address and room number of my five-star hotel room? What was left to lose?

By the time Iglesias arrived, that little bottle of tequila had changed everything. I felt tipsy, literally tipsy, like the ground beneath my feet was being subjected to a mild, prolonged earthquake. "Welcome to my new home!" I slurred as Iglesias took in the room.

"Whoa," he said. "How in the world did you get your parents to let you stay here alone?"

"It was easy," I said. "My brother's in-laws said that letting me stay here would be insane, and my mother thinks they're too rigid, so she let me stay here to prove that she was nothing like them." I opened the minibar and pulled out a bottle of tequila for him. "Here," I said. "You need to catch up with me."

"I thought you didn't drink," he said.

"Well, there are a lot of things I didn't used to do. That was the old me."

"I liked the old you," he said.

"You don't like the new me?" I asked.

"Well, I don't know the new you yet. Give it time."

"I think I need a drink to deal with that statement," I said, twisting open the tequila in my hand.

Iglesias put his hand on mine, taking the bottle from me. He set it next to the television. "Hey," he said. "You're already tipsy."

"So?" I asked.

"So," he said. "If you get any drunker, I'm gonna feel like I'm taking advantage of you when I make out with you. And I don't wanna take advantage of you." He smiled big, and came close to me, interlocking my hands in his and squeezing them gently. He pulled me in, swayed me back and forth, and spun me around, like we were slow dancing to an imaginary song in his head. I felt dizzy, so I stopped him. "What?" he said.

"Nothing," I said. Then I added, boldly, "I thought we were gonna make out."

"We are. I'm just enjoying the anticipation."

"Oh, okay," I said. "So let's anticipate some more."

"Cool," he said, and tried to spin me again.

"It's just . . . Can we anticipate lying down? 'Cause I feel like I'm gonna puke."

"Vomit is such a turn-on."

"I aim to please," I said.

And we both laughed as he laid me down on the hotel bed. "I have to be home in three hours," he said. "And I took the bus."

"Okay," I said. "So let's not anticipate too long."

"We won't," he said.

I placed my head on his chest and stared up at the ceiling. The room finally stopped swaying. "Do you think anyone is really, truly authentic?" I asked.

"I don't know," he said.

"I mean, my parents lied to me, my best friends lied to me, and now I'm lying to my parents."

"Not all lies are bad, right?"

"Is that a question or a statement?" I asked.

"I guess it's a statement. Sometimes you lie to protect people. Or to give them a fantasy that makes their lives better. Like telling a kid that Santa Claus is real."

"No one ever told me Santa Claus was real," I said.

"Well, that explains everything," he said.

"Like what?" I asked.

"Like why you're so cool." He smiled and shifted me so I was on top of him, then he kissed me. I felt so warm, like I was literally melting into him. "I really like you, Daria," he said.

We were alone, in a hotel room, and it suddenly hit me what was supposed to happen next. "Do you . . . do you want to . . ." I couldn't get the words out.

"Not tonight," he said. "Not when you're drunk. Your first time has to be perfect, just like your first kiss."

I smiled, relieved. Then I lay back down on his chest, and I closed my eyes. "Good," I said. "Because I'm really tired. Sing to me in Spanish."

He laughed. "Seriously?"

"Seriously."

The last thing I remember was Iglesias singing me one of his mother's favorite Chavela Vargas songs as he stroked my hair. I must have drifted off to sleep, because the next thing I remembered was the slam of a door and the sound of Meili's voice. "This is what you get for letting your daughter stay in a hotel room alone."

I looked up, groggy. Iglesias was lying next to me in bed. There were two open tequila bottles on the counter. And hovering over me were my horrified parents, bookended by Meili and Fang. My mom had no doubt brought them to show what a good, studious girl I was being.

I pulled the sheets above my head, willing myself to disappear.

"Show your face, Daria," Sheila demanded.

"I'm so disappointed in you, *aziz*," Baba said in a whisper, which made this feel like the worst moment of my life.

And then Iglesias uttered that old cliché, "It's not what it looks like." From under the covers, I eyed Iglesias's thick calves, exposed by the shorts he was wearing, and I pinched his skin. Hard. That was meant to indicate he should just shut up, but I'm not sure he got the message, because he then said, "Nothing happened, if that's what you're worried about."

At this, my mother seethed. "Nothing happened? It looks to me like quite a lot happened. My daughter lied to me. My daughter drank tequila. My daughter has a tattooed boy-friend!"

"He's not my boyfriend!" I said as I threw the sheets off me. Iglesias turned to me, hurt in his eyes.

"If he's not your boyfriend," Sheila said, "then I am even more concerned."

I froze for a moment, because she was so right. How had I gone from the girl who never dated to the one who got trashed in a hotel room with a guy she'd just met? "It's complicated," I said. That was seriously the best response I could think of.

Meili laughed. She was about to jump in, but Fang placed a hand on her arm.

"What is it?" Sheila asked Meili, almost daring her. "Is there something you need to say?"

"No, of course not," Meili said with a satisfied smile. "It's not my business."

I closed my eyes and silently prayed that Meili stayed very much in my business. The more Meili attacked me, after all, the more Sheila defended me. There was nothing like a common enemy to shift my mother to my side.

"Perhaps we should go to the coffee shop downstairs," Fang said.

Before he could finish, Meili said, "Thank you. I'll have one of those blended green tea things."

Fang eyed Meili, clearly urging her to vacate the room with him. But Meili stayed put as her husband reluctantly left alone, afraid of what his wife might say or do in his absence.

"So, let's discuss what's happened here," Sheila said. "I just caught my daughter in bed with a . . ." She trailed off, then turned to me and asked, "Is he a Mexican?"

"Sheila!" I said. "Seriously?"

"What?" she responded. "I'm just asking a question. I'm not upset if he's a Mexican!"

"First of all," Iglesias said, "I'm not *a* Mexican, I'm just Mexican. And you do sound kind of upset about that, which is kind of upsetting to me."

"Iglesias, don't bother," I said. "She always wins arguments like this. She's a master debater."

"I'm upset my daughter lied to me," Sheila said, ignoring me. "And I'm upset you have tattoos."

Iglesias turned to me, probably waiting for me to come to his defense. And I wanted to defend him. I wanted to tell Sheila that his tattoos were works of art, and that he didn't deserve to be attacked, and that if anyone should be judged, it was her for withholding my entire identity from me, but instead I said, "There's a difference between flat-out lying and what I did." I was such a terrible debater.

"I don't trust people with tattoos. And neither does my husband." Sheila glared at Baba, who just looked down, unable to verbalize his emotions. "People with tattoos don't understand the difference between what should be temporary and what should be permanent, and this"—Sheila waved her arms across the hotel room—"will be temporary."

Meili stifled a laugh, and then opened the minibar and found a bag of mixed nuts. She sat down on the desk chair, happily snacking as she watched the show.

"I bet you'd trust Angelina Jolie," Iglesias said. "But then, she's a white girl with tattoos. And I'm a scary Mexican man with tattoos."

I kicked Iglesias, and he glared at me, as if to say, *You can't possibly be on her side in all this.*

"I didn't even *know* you were Mexican," Sheila said, digging herself in further. "For all I knew when I walked in, you were Italian or Iranian or Colombian or Israeli. No one ever knows what I am either."

"Wow," Iglesias said. "I'm gonna go home now, but this was a nice chat."

Baba put his hand on Iglesias's chest and pushed him back down. It was the most aggressive I had ever seen Baba be. "Not so fast. We're not done with you yet. And please speak to me and my wife with respect."

"Oh yeah," Iglesias said. "Because racism should always be met with respect."

"Iglesias, please don't," I whispered, desperate for this argument not to get any worse than it already was. But he ignored me, and so did my parents. It was like I was invisible.

"We are not racist," Sheila said. "We are just realistic."

Meili, her mouth full of nuts, finally spoke. "I don't mean

to interrupt, but you *are* racist," she said. "Our son told us everything when he met Amir. He told us how this woman right here"—finger pointed at Sheila—"felt she could hardly handle a gay son, let alone a gay Chinese son-in-law."

Sheila scoffed. "I was just worried about the cultural differences."

"Is that why you were so rude to us at their wedding?" Meili said. "Because of *cultural differences*?"

Meili stood up and took a step toward Sheila. Sheila took a step toward her. Baba often talked about how World War III was inevitable in the Middle East, but now I thought World War III might start right here, in a Beverly Hills hotel room.

But just as the two women came perilously close to starting another global conflict, Fang arrived, holding iced blended green teas for everyone in the room. "What's happening?" he asked Meili as he handed each of us a frothy drink. "What have you done?"

"Nothing," Meili said, grabbing her drink and taking a big sip. "I have been perfectly well behaved."

But Fang clearly didn't believe her, because he took her arm and announced, "We'll wait for you outside. This is a family matter."

"But we *are* their family," Meili protested.

And to everyone's surprise, Fang took her hand and just led her out of the room.

For some reason, the tension in the room got even worse

when Meili left. I felt awful. My night in the hotel room was supposed to be like Eloise, but there was no part of that book where Eloise disappointed everyone around her. That's what I felt like in that moment, like I was ground zero of disappointment. I sucked up my entire iced blended, grateful for the brain freeze that made me momentarily forget where I was.

"Okay," Baba said. "Now we are alone with Daria and her boy—" He stopped himself. I knew he was going to say *boyfriend*, but instead he asked, "Who are you, anyway?"

Iglesias was sweating, a few beads resting above his upper lip. "My name's Enrique Iglesias, sir." I pinched him again. "I mean, sorry, sir, she just calls me Iglesias."

"Do you go to school together?" Baba asked.

"No, sir," Enrique said.

"You don't have to call me *sir*," Baba said.

"Oh," Iglesias responded. "I was just trying to address you with the *proper respect*."

I kicked Iglesias again. "Please," I whispered. "Don't make it worse than it already is." Iglesias glared at me.

"If you don't go to school together, then how did you meet?" Baba asked.

Iglesias looked at me, silently begging me to take over. This was my moment to finally tell my parents the truth, to confess that my lie was so much bigger than hiding a boy. But I wasn't ready to tell the truth. So I let Iglesias struggle through it. "We just met recently," he said.

"It can't be that recent if she has a nickname for you," Baba responded.

"Well, she gave me the nickname the day we met." Iglesias and I both smiled at that, perhaps transported back to that first day I knocked on his door, a day that seemed so much better than this one. I wished I could go back in time to that moment, restart everything, and make different decisions, starting with never swabbing my cheek and sending it in for DNA testing. I craved ignorance. I wanted a return to the innocent person I had been only a few weeks ago, a person who would never have raided a minibar or lied to her parents.

I remembered telling Baba once that it seemed like nothing ever really changes. Baba said life was like a spiral. You don't think you ever move forward because you're going in circles, but if you look back, you see that each spin around the circle has led you one small notch forward. I always thought of that when I held one of my spiral notebooks. Baba was right. We do move forward slowly, almost imperceptibly, but what if we want to move backward? What if we want to spin slowly back down the spiral of our lives and get a second chance at our last loop? That was what I wanted.

Then Baba said something to Iglesias that stopped me cold. "I assume it was you who visited my mother with Daria."

So he knew?

"Yeah," Iglesias said. "She's a cool lady."

"You're a smart girl, Daria," Baba said. "You must have

known the staff would call me and let me know you'd visited with a boy. I'm just shocked they didn't call me immediately. You would never have been in this hotel room had we known."

"I'm sorry," I said. The truth was, I'd never thought the staff would say anything. I'd figured they would assume he was a friend. But maybe, on some subconscious level, I'd wanted them to tell my parents. Maybe I'd wanted my parents to find out, to know everything. If I had, why couldn't I just tell them?

"I'm sorry is not enough, Daria." This was my mother. "We need answers. Who is this boy? How did you meet him? How long have you known him?"

I was about to launch into the truth, but I stopped myself. I knew Sheila wouldn't want to play that scene in front of a stranger.

"I really think I should go," Iglesias said, disappointed in me. I suddenly imagined myself through his eyes: weak and pathetic.

Once again, Baba said, "Not yet. And not until we call your mother. She has a right to know what you're up to."

Iglesias laughed nervously. "Sure, let's call my mother. Good idea, Daria?" He was practically daring me now, probably exhausted by my cowardice.

"Let's just go home," I said. "Trust me, you don't want to have this conversation here. And I'm not ready to have it. Not here. Not—"

Before I could finish, Sheila snapped. "Enough, Daria," she shouted. "I demand to know who this person is. I demand for you to stop acting like a child, and begin acting like *my* child."

"What does that even mean?" I spat back.

"*My* child," she said, "does not get drunk in hotel rooms with strange boys. *My* child does not sneak around behind her parents' backs."

"Well," I said, my throat tightening up so much that it was hard to speak, "maybe I'm not your child."

It was a vague statement, and I could tell Baba didn't read much into it. But my mom froze like a deer in headlights when I said it. "What are you saying, Daria?" she whispered.

I could tell she knew exactly what I was saying. I took a deep breath. I looked to Iglesias for strength. He gave my hand a squeeze. That was all I needed to go on. "I'm saying that Iglesias is the stepson of my . . ." I stopped for a moment before I whispered the words. ". . . biological mother."

Now my mother's eyes welled with tears. Baba's too. "You're right," Sheila said. "We'll discuss this later. Privately."

"Oh, come on," I said. "It's too late for that, Sheila. I found out, okay? And I went searching for my biological mother, and I met Iglesias. And she was out of town, so I spent some time with him because I wanted to get to know her, which is what anyone else would have done—"

"Wait, so you just hung out with me to get closer to my mother?" Iglesias asked, pulling his hand away from mine.

202

"No," I said. "Of course not. But it's just . . . I mean . . . I wouldn't have hung out with you if you weren't her son—"

"Why? 'Cause I'm below you? 'Cause I have too many tattoos?"

"No!" I protested. "I'm not my mother."

"I thought you were being real," he said.

"I was being real. I *am* being real," I said. And then, I added desperately, "I'm trying to be real, okay? Isn't that enough?"

Iglesias stood up. Upright, he was so much taller than my parents. He suddenly seemed like the most powerful, imposing person in the room. "I get it now. It all makes sense. I was such a dumbass to think someone like you would ever like someone like me."

I stood up to face Iglesias, trying to take his hand in mine, but he kept pulling away. I wanted to hold his hand so badly. I wanted to feel like I did the first time he gripped my hand in his. "What does that even mean, Iglesias? *Someone like you?*"

"Oh, come on, Daria," he spat back. "Admit that you were using me. This whole thing was always about you. I was just a stepping-stone."

"No," I said. "You were just a surprise." That was the truth. He was a beautiful surprise, and now he was slipping away from me.

"You know what you are, Daria?" he said, his face flushed. "A cultural tourist. Well, you've had your little vacation, okay?"

"Iglesias, please don't be mad," I whispered. "I don't think

I can handle one more person being mad at me."

"There you go. Once again, it's all about you," he said. I hated myself a little just then, because he was right.

Baba stepped forward, gently, and said, "Please don't talk to my daughter that way."

"How about I don't talk to her at all?" Iglesias asked, and headed to the door. "I'm done being caught in this cross fire. Good-bye to you and your whole fucked-up family. This Mexican is off to get more tattoos."

"Wait!" I yelled as I ran toward the door.

"Daria, let him go," Baba demanded.

"Iglesias! Wait! Please!" I begged, clutching onto Iglesias's arm.

Baba approached me from behind and placed a hand gently on my shoulder. "Let him go," Baba said.

"I don't want to let him go," I said, still clutching his arm. Then, looking into Iglesias's eyes, I said, "I don't want to let you go."

Iglesias didn't say a word. He didn't need to. He was angry and disappointed and had every right to be. I knew there was nothing else I could say. I let go of his arm and watched him leave, the door slowly closing behind him.

I felt so alone when he was gone, but of course I wasn't. I had four eyes glued to me. I couldn't look at my parents. I could only look at the floor, trying to lose myself in the geometric design of the hotel carpet, holding back tears.

"Aren't you going to say anything else?" Sheila asked.

I shook my head, unable to face her.

"I'm so disappointed in you, Daria," she said.

Without thinking, I said, "Well, I'm disappointed in you, Sheila." And then I finally looked up.

We faced each other for what seemed an interminable amount of time, each daring the other to speak first, blink first, or, most important, apologize first.

Finally, Sheila said, "I had my reasons." Her voice shook a little.

"*We* had our reasons," Baba corrected, taking Sheila's hand in his.

"You had your reasons? Seriously, that's your answer?" My rage surprised even me.

"I don't have to explain myself to you," Sheila said, hardening. "I made the decision I thought was best for you. I have always made the decisions I thought would be best for you."

"*We* made the decisions," Baba said sharply, clearly feeling left out.

"Oh, that's bullshit!" I yelled at Sheila.

"Daria, watch your mouth," Baba said.

"You did what was best for *you*. You did what was most *comfortable* for you. That's all you care about. Your own comfort!"

"Comfort?" Sheila echoed, with a sharp laugh that hit me like a dagger. "You, my beautiful, complicated daughter, know nothing about the discomfort I have experienced in my life.

You know nothing of losing a brother, losing a father, losing a country. You know nothing of losing one child after another, asking a God you don't even believe in why you are defective."

I swallowed hard. It was easy to judge Sheila when she was hiding behind her shell of perfection. But when she was unleashing honesty, it was much more difficult.

"I know how horrible discomfort is," she continued. "I know how terrible pain can feel. And so I have tried to give *you* a comfortable life. I have tried to give you not just nice things, but also the stability I never had."

"I know," I whispered. "But it was all a lie."

"It wasn't a lie," she said. "Because even I believed it. I always believed you were my daughter. And I didn't see anything wrong with letting you believe it too. You looked like us!"

"I don't look anything like you," I said. "We're just both dark."

"Well," Sheila huffed. "I don't know what to say. I just wish you had never betrayed our trust."

"Don't blame me for how I handled your lie," I said. "It was *your* lie, not mine."

And then I burst into tears. And Baba took me in his arms and shushed me like I was an infant. "Don't cry, *aziz*," he said.

"You named me after the ocean," I sobbed. "Well, I'm an ocean."

"We named you after the ocean because oceans are beautiful and inspiring," he said. "And because no matter how bad the waves can be, the ocean always comes back to its natural, peaceful state."

Baba led me out of the hotel room and into the dimly lit hallway, where Meili and Fang, their iced blended green teas almost empty, awaited us. My mother followed behind us, and she briefly faced off with Meili. "Don't worry," Meili said. "I couldn't hear everything." After a beat, she added, "Just enough."

But Sheila had no fight left in her. She simply hung her head low and led the way to the elevator. With a manicured nail, she pressed the down button. We all entered the elevator together and before we reached the lobby, a French couple entered. They were clearly discomfited by the scene they were caught in, if only for a brief instant. Sheila realized we were the source of their discomfort, and so she forced a smile their way, and in her perfect French, she said, "Welcome to Los Angeles." I was crying too hard to roll my eyes, but I wanted to. Somehow, despite the level of emotion contained in this small elevator, she had found it in her to save face for two European strangers. When we reached the lobby, my mother let the French couple out first, and said, "Enjoy your stay."

And then our broken family shuffled out into the lobby.

Chapter Fourteen

WHEN I OPENED MY EYES, I was back in my bedroom at home. I had a vague memory of coming back home, of Sheila telling Meili and Fang they were moving to a hotel whether they liked it or not, and of Meili saying she would rather stay in a hotel than spend another second in this lunatic asylum. All things considered, I couldn't argue with Meili. And I didn't. In fact, I hadn't said another word since we left the hotel. Perhaps I was in shock. Or perhaps I was afraid of the words that might come out of me if I spoke, afraid of my anger, and of my sadness.

When I woke up, the sun had risen, and the pain in my head was like no pain I'd ever known before. It was like Baba had decided to build his latest condo development inside me, and a team of his construction workers was working inside my head, hammering away at the outer edges of my skull. *I guess this is what a hangover feels like*, I thought to myself as I willed my eyes shut. My eyes. My poor eyes.

But before I could attempt more sleep, there was a light knock on the door and then a grand entrance from Sheila, who, let's be honest, only made grand entrances. She placed a plate of fried eggs on my bed, and a cup of coffee on my bedside table.

"I figured you would be hurting after that bender," she said. "Eggs have some kind of enzyme in them that helps with hangovers. And coffee will wake you up."

I wanted to tell her that I had no interest in waking up. That my deepest desire in that moment was to go back to bed for a very long time, and maybe to wake up in a different body. But I just nodded. It struck me that this was the first time Sheila had cooked for me. For all my life, it was Lala who had cooked for me. My days and nights were full of the love of her rice, the warmth of her stews, the sweetness of her *tres leches* cake. Now that she was gone, Sheila had finally flared up the stove for me. But this meal, the first she'd cooked for me, was not made from love. No, these were eggs of disappointment.

"I called your school," Sheila said. "I said you got food poisoning from raw tuna. One should always be specific when one lies."

I didn't say a word to my mom. I simply nodded, and then she left. And, ever the dutiful daughter, I took a bite of the eggs, and a sip of the coffee. Within minutes, my head and my eyes and my stomach responded positively, and so I took another bite, and another sip, until I started to feel human again.

When I was almost done, there was a light knock on the door again. I sighed, expecting Sheila's grand reentrance. But nobody came in, which meant it must be Baba on the other side of the door. Unlike Sheila, Baba always waited for my okay to enter my room.

"I'm awake, Baba," I said.

He entered the room with a half smile, his face betraying the trials of the day. "I'm just checking on you," he said. "Are you sure you're okay?" I shrugged. "Do you need anything?" he asked. Again, I shrugged. "Do you want to talk?" I shook my head from side to side. "I understand," he said gently. And instead of leaving, he sat down on the edge of my bed. "I'll just sit here a little while. In case you decide you do want to talk. But you don't have to. I don't mind the quiet." He gave me a supportive smile, and then, as if he couldn't stand the seriousness of the moment, he added, "Truthfully, after having Meili and Fang in the house, I welcome a little silence." I guess he wanted a smile from me, or maybe even a laugh, but he didn't get it. I couldn't even look at him. I was too ashamed and hurt.

We sat in silence for almost an hour. Baba and I had sat in silence before. Sometimes we would sit in the living room for hours, Baba reading the newspaper, me reading a schoolbook, not saying a word. We would look up at each other and smile, acknowledging how nice it was to sit side by side without needing to speak. Those silences were weightless. They felt free. This silence was different. It felt heavy. It was full of every tender moment between us, now being reassessed in light of new revelations.

Finally, I broke the silence with a question I already knew the answer to. "Baba," I said. "Are you my biological father? My DNA test said I was half–Middle Eastern. Did you, I don't know, have an affair with her . . ."

Baba put a hand on my leg and squeezed it, and then placed his hands on my cheeks. He looked me sadly in the eyes and shook his head no. I closed my eyes and tried hard to feel safe, the way I used to when my face was cradled in his steady hands. But his little trick didn't work anymore.

When he left, I let out a quick sob. Tears filled my eyes, and I grabbed my pillow and held it tight in front of me, pushing my face into it as I screamed. I knew it wouldn't work, but it felt good nevertheless. As I unleashed my ire into my poor pillow, I thought of how I had alienated just about everyone in my life, from my parents to Iglesias to Kurt, Caroline, and Joy. I knew where I needed to go.

Sheila had said I was grounded, so I tiptoed out of my room. Luckily, Sheila and Baba had the TV on superloud, so I managed to sneak past them without being overheard.

I took the bus toward Amir's house, and sat next to a group of friends on their way to a hike. I had a sudden regret that I wasn't raised near nature. My parents' idea of nature was spending time in the communal yard of our apartment complex, picking a lemon from its potted lemon trees, and posing for selfies with the hot-pink bougainvillea when it bloomed. These bright flowers were Sheila's favorite, and Baba, in his role as president of our homeowner's association, had them planted in her honor. She said they reminded her of the South of France, and Baba did his best to give her the illusion of living in France.

When the bus stopped at Griffith Park, I decided to get out with the hikers. I wanted to disappear, to be surrounded by trees. I walked toward the observatory, past the bust of James Dean, the patron saint of alienated teenagers. I remembered seeing *Rebel Without a Cause* when I was thirteen and thinking, *Why is every teenager in this movie so angry?* Now I got it. I gave James a silent nod and then began to hike.

There were a few hikers around me—some hipsters, some couples, and two nuns—and they all followed the trail. But I was done following the path that had been laid out for me. I was my own woman now, and I wanted to forge my own path. So I veered away from the trail, the ground crackling beneath my feet. I walked until I couldn't hear any more footsteps that weren't my own. When I was confident that I was far enough away from any other human, I lay down on the scorched earth and stared up at the sky peeking through the trees and smog.

I imagined a world in which there was only me. No one could betray me. No one could hurt me. No one could make me feel anything. I reveled in the silence. I breathed in the quiet. I let the stillness fortify me. And I asked the calm to give me strength for what came next, because the truth was that I didn't want to live in a world without other people.

By the time I made it to Amir's house, I was starving. The fried eggs had apparently been digested, and my rumbling stomach demanded more food. Lala opened the door for me, and immediately took me in her arms. "You worried us all sick," she said in Spanish.

"I'm sorry," I said.

"Where have you been?" she asked.

"Hiking."

Lala walked back into the home and went straight to the phone. I knew she was going to call my parents.

"Wait," I pleaded. "Tell them I'll be home in an hour. I want to talk to someone who isn't mad at me, someone who's on my side, someone I can trust. I want to talk to you."

She held the phone in her hand, weighing her decision. And then she called my parents, and she told them I was safe, and that I would be home in an hour.

"Thank you," I said as Lala put the phone back down. And then, struck by the lack of chaos, I asked, "Are you alone?"

"Rose is sleeping," she said. "Amir, Andrew, and his parents went out to lunch."

"They're staying here?" I asked.

Lala nodded. "They're sleeping on an air mattress Andrew bought for them. I don't know what they have against hotels. I would love it if someone would pay for me to stay in a hotel."

"Don't talk to me about hotels right now," I said.

"Right," she said. "Or perhaps we *should* talk about hotels."

"I'm hungry," I said. Without missing a beat, Lala opened the fridge, which was full of food, just like ours once was. She took out two Tupperware containers and prepared me a plate of rice and *ghormeh sabzi*, then placed it in the microwave. "So, how much do you know?" I asked.

"Your parents called when they realized you weren't in your room," she said. "They told me everything. Well, everything they knew. I'm sure there's a lot they still don't know." The microwave *ding*ed. She placed a spoonful of yogurt on the side of my plate, just how I liked it. "Eat," she said.

I took a bite of the delicious stew, and then another. "I knew," she said as I reveled in the flavors.

"Knew what?" I asked, my mouth full.

"Daria, I knew everything. I've always known everything." I looked up at her, seeing her as if for the first time. "I know you're angry with your parents for lying to you, and maybe you came here because you think I'm the one person who *didn't* lie to you, but I did. I knew all along." I realized that in my shock, I had held a lump of rice in my mouth, and I swallowed it deliberately. "I'm sorry for it. And I'm not sorry for it too. At the time, it seemed like the right decision. We all thought you never had to know. Maybe it was stupid. Maybe it was naive. But it's what we thought. Me. Your father. Your mother. All of us."

"But it was *her* idea, wasn't it?" I asked.

"Why do you want your mother to be the enemy?" she asked.

"I don't," I said unconvincingly. "I just . . ." I didn't know what to say. I guess I wanted someone to be the enemy. Having someone to blame would've been easier than this horrible feeling of emptiness, and my mother had always been my easy target.

Lala sat down next to me. Placed a hand on my knee. "Remember how you always used to ask how come Amir was so much older than you? You would say how all your friends had brothers and sisters they could play with."

"Yeah," I said.

"Well, your parents tried to have another baby after Amir. But it never worked." I looked at Lala, waiting for more. "Do you understand what a miscarriage is?" Lala asked.

"I'm fifteen, Lala," I said. "Not six."

"I know," Lala said. "You might understand what a miscarriage is technically, or scientifically, but I don't know if you understand what it is emotionally. When a woman carries life inside her, she begins a relationship with that life, with that child. She talks to that child. She sings to that child. She builds hopes, dreams, and expectations. When a woman miscarries, she doesn't just lose a pregnancy, she loses all of those hopes, all of those dreams, and all of those expectations. And, perhaps worst of all, she blames herself."

We were talking about Sheila, but the way Lala was talking, I knew she had gone through this heartbreak as well, so all I could think of to say was, "I'm sorry."

"For what?" Lala asked.

"I don't know," I said. "I just thought . . ."

"*Mi amor,*" Lala said. "Miscarriages are very common, especially in the first trimester. Most women who miscarry never even know they were pregnant. I miscarried once. Two months into the pregnancy. And I mourned that child."

"I understand," I said. "I think I do."

"Then understand this," she said. "Your mother had nine miscarriages." Her words hung in the air, the number nine hovering between us. Nine losses. Nine periods of mourning. "The last one was a stillbirth," Lala said. "Do you know what a stillbirth is?"

"I think so," I said. "It's when the baby is born, but it's dead."

"Yes," Lala said. "A stillbirth is when the baby dies in the uterus. It usually happens when a pregnancy is full-term. By the last trimester, a mother thinks she has passed that period of risk. That's what your mother thought when she met me."

"Wait," I said. "So you met my mother before I was born?"

"I met your mother almost a year before you were born," she said. "I was supposed to be the nanny to your older sister." I gulped down hard. "Everything was prepared. The nursery was painted. The crib was built. I was supposed to start work on the day she was born. When she came, your mother could hardly bear the pain. She was inconsolable. You have never seen your mother that way because she has shielded you from all her pain."

I suddenly felt sick to my stomach. I felt like everything I had ever thought about Sheila had been wrong. Her whole air of perfection wasn't just a way to keep up appearances, it was a way to cover up pain. And maybe she had shielded me from that pain for fifteen years, but now it hit me hard. "I wish she hadn't," I said. "I wish I had known all along. It's just all so dishonest."

"I know you like to think life is all about being authentic," Lala said. "But sometimes authenticity is a trap. Sometimes it just holds you captive, so you can't move on."

"I don't know," I said. "She can justify it however she wants, but she still should've told me."

"You're right. But if you want to blame someone, blame me," she said. "It was all my idea." She took a deep breath and then continued. "After the stillbirth, your mother told me she was done. She said she had tried too many times, and the universe had told her she wasn't meant to have another child. It was always her dream to have at least two children, and especially to have a girl, but some dreams had to be abandoned. What broke my heart most of all was how concerned she was about me. She knew I had given up another job to work for her. She assured me she would pay me my salary until I found another job. That's the kind of woman your mother is. Honorable. Generous. Maybe she made a big mistake in not telling you the truth, but you don't spend enough time appreciating all the things she did do right."

I gulped down hard again. I knew she was right about that.

"In any case," Lala continued, "I told her she shouldn't give up. I told her there were so many other options. And that's when I suggested adoption. I knew girls from my church who'd gotten pregnant and couldn't keep the babies. Your mother resisted the idea at first. And she paid my salary for weeks. And then after a few weeks, she called me one day. She said she had asked her lawyer to look into it, and that she would adopt a child. And she made me promise that when that child came into the world, I would be there to help raise her. And I promised. And less than a year later, you arrived." Lala took a *tres leches* cake out of the fridge, cut off a slice, and placed it in front of me. "Are you okay? Do you need a moment?"

I inhaled a mouthful of the cake, swallowed, and then said, "I don't know."

"What don't you know?" she asked.

"I don't know," I whispered. I could've repeated it a hundred times, because in that moment, I felt like I didn't know anything anymore.

"Look," Lala said. "I know how hard this is, but I want you to listen to your mother's side of the story. No story is a straight line. Stories have sides and angles. And if you try hard enough, you'll see that they usually fit together to create some kind of beautiful shape."

"Well, what about my side?" I asked. "What about all the times you all lied to me? What about the fact that you let me believe I was their daughter?"

"You *are* their daughter," she said.

"What about the fact that I'm not completely Iranian? You knew how important that was to me. I mean, what if you found out tomorrow that you weren't even Mexican? What if you found out you were, like, Afghani? How would you feel?"

"I would feel confused," she said. "But I would still be Mexican."

"Wouldn't you want to know your biological mother, though?" I asked.

"Of course I would," she said. "And I hope your biological mother will be open to knowing you. But that doesn't make her your *mother*. If you're so obsessed with authenticity, Daria, then you should know that your authentic mother is the one who raised you."

"You raised me," I cracked.

"No, my love," she said. "I supported your mother in raising you. You just can't see that yet."

"Did you know her?" I asked.

"Who?"

"Encarnación," I said. "You know, my biological mother."

Lala shook her head. "No," she said. "I never met her. I never even knew her name. I thought that was best, in case I knew her from church or something like that."

Suddenly, a screeching sound came from Rose's room. "Rose is awake," Lala said.

"Does she always wake up screaming like that?" I asked.

"That's normal," Lala said. "Babies go from zero to a hundred in a heartbeat. They can be laughing one second, crying the next, and laughing again one moment later. It's one of the most magical things about them. They haven't yet learned to control their emotions."

"So they have no secrets," I said.

Lala took my hand and led me toward Rose's room. "Exactly," she said. Once we reached Rose's room, Lala opened the curtain. Rose was in her crib, on her back. She had broken out of her swaddle, and she was violently shaking her arms and legs in the air. "Pick her up," Lala said.

I reached into the crib, cupped Rose's head under my right hand, rested her body on my right arm, and then gently raised her up into my chest. She looked up at me with her innocent baby eyes, those eyes that had no secrets yet, and within seconds her tears dried and her screams subsided. "She stopped crying," I said, proud of myself.

"See, you're an expert," Lala said. "You'll make a wonderful mother someday. And when you're a mother, you will start to understand your own mother. And as you understand her, you will probably forgive her too." Rose squealed in my arms, and for the first time since my hotel break-in, I laughed.

"But personally," Lala continued, "I think it would be sad if you waited that long to understand and forgive your mother. She deserves your forgiveness now."

I called home and told my parents I would be back as soon as Amir returned from lunch. They tried to act calm, but I could hear the concern in their voices.

For the next hour and a half, Lala led me through her routine with Rose. There was something mercifully absorbing about taking care of a baby. By the time Amir, Andrew, Meili, and Fang got home, I had changed a diaper, wiped a baby butt, learned how to use a Diaper Genie, swaddled, washed, rinsed, and bathed. It was hard, and it was bliss, and I felt so grateful to be an aunt.

Upon arrival, Meili made a beeline toward Rose, and took her from my arms. I immediately felt the loss of her. I wanted to hold her forever. Meili cradled her grandchild in her arms and greeted her by cooing, "Hello, my little beauty." Her whole face lit up when she looked at Rose.

But then she said something under her breath in Chinese, and Andrew sharply responded in Chinese, and quietly they argued. Now I knew how Sheila felt when Lala and I spoke Spanish in front of her. It really was awful not to understand what people were talking about. And I knew they were talking about me, because I heard my name sprinkled into the argument.

Caroline, Joy, and Kurt would always laugh about how when I spoke Persian with my parents, they would understand every tenth word. They would imitate our conversations, and Caroline would always say, "Nonsense, nonsense, nonsense, Disneyland, nonsense, nonsense."

But now I was the one who could only understand every tenth word, and that word was *Daria*.

"Nonsense, nonsense, nonsense, Daria, nonsense," Meili said angrily.

Amir approached me and put his arm around me. "I'm sorry," he said. "They're still arguing about the movie we saw."

"Um, was the movie called *Daria*?" I asked.

Amir took Rose from Meili's arms, then returned to my side. "Yeah," he said with a smile. "It was a small indie about a teenage girl who goes on a search for herself, and discovers there's no place like home."

"So it's the Iranian *Wizard of Oz*?" I joked.

"Exactly," he said. "Which, of course, means that the ruby slippers are a pair of Chanel pumps."

We laughed for a brief moment. Amir carried Rose back into her nursery, where he laid her on the changing table and checked her diaper. "Seriously, though," I said. "They're upset because they think I'm going to be a bad influence on their newborn granddaughter or something. Like she's going to become a slut by osmosis."

"Oh please," he said. "If sluttiness is hereditary, then my daughter will surely inherit it from me." I looked at him, surprised. "Someday, when you're old enough, I'll tell you all about my wild days. I was coming of age during the birth of Grindr, after all."

My eyes widened in shock. "I'm old enough now," I said. "Tell me everything."

"Another time," he said. "Over a drink."

"Ew," I said. "I'm never drinking again."

"That's what everyone says after their first hangover," he said with a smile.

Amir finished changing Rose's diaper and swaddled her again. It was nap time once more. She was in a constant cycle of eating and sleeping, that one. It seemed kind of nice. Amir held her swaddled body into his chest, rocking her. Then I realized Amir must have known all along I was adopted. He was twelve when I was born, after all.

"You knew?" I asked in a hushed whisper, and he just nodded. "Would you ever have told me?"

"Daria, it wasn't my secret to tell," he said. "Though, for

what it's worth, I plan on telling my daughter the truth about how she came into the world, surrogate and all."

"And for what it's worth," I said, "I think that's the right decision. You don't want Rose ever feeling as pissed at you as I am at Sheila and Baba."

"You know, I was pretty upset with them when I came out. All I wanted was for them to accept me, and they just couldn't. A lot of my American friends thought I should stop speaking to them, cut them out of my life entirely. But I could never do that. I forgave them by accepting their limitations, and by understanding the time and culture they were raised in. And eventually they came around and accepted me." I nodded, thinking about his words. Amir placed Rose down in her crib and spun her mobile until the little wooden fairies above her started swinging around to their tinny, optimistic sound track. "So, are you angry at me?" he asked. I shook my head. "You can be honest," he said.

I wanted to tell him I resented him a little bit for being the biological son, but instead I just said, "No." Then, to my surprise, I corrected myself. "Well . . ." And I told him exactly what I resented him for. It felt good to finally be authentic.

"You know," he said, "I always resented you a little too."

"Really?" I asked. "For what?"

"For getting such happy parents," he said. "For the first twelve years of my life, Sheila and Baba were stuck in an end-less cycle of hope and despair. There were weeks where Sheila wouldn't emerge from her room. And they never even told me why. I finally had to find out from Auntie Lida. After you, that all ended. I guess I always wanted your childhood."

I always knew that Amir hadn't had an easy time coming out to our parents, but I had thought it was the most difficult thing he had to do. Now I understood where he got his strength from. "Hey," I said. "I don't think I've ever thanked you for paving the way for me."

Amir smiled. "Paving what way?"

"The way to being yourself in an Iranian family," I said. "I know it wasn't easy for you." I looked at Rose, who had now drifted off into her innocent sleep. "And for what it's worth, I want Rose's childhood," I said. "She's really lucky to have you and Andrew."

Amir took my hand and squeezed it. "Thanks," he said softly. And then he led me out into the living room, where the argument had ended.

To my shock, Meili placed her hand on mine. "I'm sorry," she said. "I have been rude to you as a reaction to your parents, who were rude to me." Andrew glared at his mother. "I apologize once more," Meili continued. "Someone needs to break the vicious cycle, and it will be me. Please accept my apology, and tell your parents that I now understand they were not trying to get rid of me by putting me in some hotel room."

"Um, I will," I said.

"Another thing," Meili said, and I shivered a little bit, afraid of what was coming next.

"Mother, please," Andrew begged.

"Let me finish," Meili said. She looked me square in the eyes, like she could see into my soul or something, and my whole body froze. "When I was your age, my life was simple. I never dealt with anything as complicated as your situation. And you are handling it very well. If I had a daughter, and I always wanted one, I would be proud."

It took me a moment to let that wash over me. The thing about Meili is that she didn't say anything she didn't mean, so she really meant this. She was, I suddenly realized, entirely authentic.

"Thank you," I said, in disbelief.

And then, shocking myself even more, I hugged her.

When Lala and I entered my parents' apartment, we found them sitting on the couch, watching television. I thought that was kind of funny. They must have had so much to talk about, and yet they were escaping into some stupid comedy on the French satellite channel. To my mom's credit, she turned the TV off as soon as she heard me enter, and gave me a strong hug. I wanted so badly to melt into her arms, to become her little girl, but something held me back. I still had so many unresolved emotions toward her. Baba just hovered behind her, giving me a look that was equal parts support and consternation. I think he wanted to stand back and allow Sheila to have her moment with me. "I was so worried," she said. "Please don't do that again."

"I'm sorry," I said as I pulled away from her. There was a long silence as we stared at each other, taking each other in.

After I felt I had waited a sufficiently long time, I said, "Okay, it's your turn, Sheila."

"For what?" she asked, completely oblivious.

"To say you're sorry," I said. "Do I really have to spell it out for you?"

My mother flinched at my tone. She looked to Baba, who gave her a slight nod, then she turned back to me and managed to eke out a halfhearted "I'm sorry, Daria."

"Please, Sheila, sound like you mean it," I begged, suddenly wishing my mother were as transparent in her emotions as Meili. "I need you to mean it."

"Daria, give your mother a break," Baba said.

"She's not my mother." I regretted saying those words as soon as they escaped my lips, but there was no taking them back. They hit Sheila like a slap in the face, and caused my own chest to tighten with pain.

"What should I be sorry for?" Sheila exclaimed. "Should I be sorry for wanting another child? Should I be sorry for giving you a beautiful life? You love Iranian culture and Iranian rap, Daria, but you always seem to forget that your parents lived through Iranian *history*. We know what it's like to lose a home, to lose family members. And that was just the beginning. Tell her, Lala. Tell her what I went through. Tell her how much I wanted her. She'll listen to you."

"I told her," Lala said. "She knows everything."

"And I'm sorry, Sheila," I said. "I really am." I clenched my fists and then released them. "I don't want to be this person," I yelled. "I don't want to be angry or mean or . . . It's just . . . When Rose was born, all you and Baba would talk about is which one of you she looks like. 'She has your lips.' 'She has your eyes.' 'She looks just like her grandfather.' How do you think that made me feel?"

There was a long silence. I felt so vulnerable and small, like I was physically shrinking. Sheila and Baba looked at each other, and now Sheila did look truly sorry. "I didn't mean . . . ," she said. "I didn't think . . . well, I didn't think you knew."

"It doesn't matter," I said, struggling to control my trembling voice. "The point is you love me less, and now I know it."

"No," Sheila said desperately. "That's not true."

I took a deep breath, and finally asked the question that had been on my mind. "Do you sometimes wish . . . Do you sometimes wish I were her?"

"Who?" Sheila asked.

I couldn't even look at her as I said, "You know, the daughter you lost. The stillbirth."

I felt awful for saying those words to her, for bringing up a memory she had worked so hard to put behind her. I thought she might slap me, but instead she grabbed me by the shoulders. "Oh, Daria. My girl. You are the only daughter I ever wanted, and I never loved you less. If anything, I loved you more because I worked so hard to have you. And if you want to know the truth, I always *believed* you were my biological child. Sometimes I would turn to your father and I would say, 'Look, she has your eyes,' and he would agree. We both believed it, because that's how we felt. That you were ours."

"It's true," Baba said. "And you do have my eyes."

Now my eyes, which apparently were a version of Baba's eyes, started pouring out thick tears. I swallowed hard, trying to hold them back, but there was no controlling them anymore.

"There were so many times we wanted to tell you," Sheila said. "We knew we should. But we never did. Maybe because we didn't want to believe it."

"Or maybe because we were cowards," Baba added.

"And the more time passed," Sheila continued, "the harder it became to tell the truth."

Baba put an arm around me, and my head found his chest. I felt safe in his arms. Secure. His arms gave me that, and I let myself dissolve into them. I let myself be taken care of. "This will take time," Baba said, "but we will deal with it together. As a family."

Sheila nodded. "Yes," she said. "But our family is bigger now, isn't it?" I looked at her, confused. "Lida always accuses me of running away from Iran, running away from my country, from my problems. Well, I'm not running away from this. I called your birth mother, and I told her the situation. I asked her if she would like to meet us."

"And?" I said, anxious.

"We are expected at her home in thirty minutes," Sheila said. She stopped and took a long breath. She straightened her posture and composed herself, and then, finally, she added, "I'm truly sorry, Daria. I hope you will forgive us."

Chapter Fifteen

SHEILA, BABA, AND I SAT parked outside Encarnación Vargas's house for at least twenty minutes, the two of them immobilized just as I was the first time I drove up to the home. From the backseat, I could only imagine the thoughts running through the minds of my silent parents. Baba was biting his lip, and every few seconds he would swing his eyes toward Sheila. As for my mother's eyes, they were glued to the house as if it were a six-car pileup on the freeway. This did feel like a car wreck. Our lives and the life of Encarnación and her family had just crashed into one another, and now we had to pick up the pieces.

I tried to imagine what was happening inside the house. Were Encarnación, Fabio, and Iglesias immobilized like we were? Were they covertly watching us in the car, wondering what was taking us so long? Were they deciding what to wear, conscious of making a good impression? Were they excited, afraid, angry, annoyed?

Finally, Baba said, "*Shab shod*," which means, *it's night*. Of course, it wasn't night, not yet, but *"shab shod"* is one of those difficult-to-translate Persian expressions that basically means, *time's ticking*.

Baba gently placed a hand on Sheila's shoulder. She snapped out of her reverie and turned to me. "*Shab shod*," Sheila said, as if I were the one holding us up.

Baba knocked on the door, his free arm thrown protectively around my shoulder. When the door opened, Sheila took an anticipatory breath, only to be faced with Fabio, who smiled nervously.

"Hello," he said. "Welcome." Off Sheila's confusion, he said, "I'm Fabio. Encarnación's husband."

"Oh," Baba said. "It's a pleasure. It's a pleasure."

Baba always repeated himself when he was nervous, which was almost never. It had happened when Amir first came out of the closet, and it had happened when he first introduced them to Andrew. When Andrew said he was Chinese, Baba had said, "We love Chinese food. We love Chinese food." This had become a joke between Amir and me. Any time one of us wanted a laugh, we simply said, "We love Chinese food," twice, and it usually worked.

As Fabio led us into the home, Baba said, "Lovely home. Lovely home." Sheila said nothing.

Fabio led us into the living room and said, "Encarnación is cooking. She'll be right out." And then, as if he had been waiting since he opened the door to say this, he added, "I just want you to know that I am not Daria's father."

This forthright admission clearly shocked Sheila, because she broke out of her trance and emitted a hushed "Oh."

"Of course not," Baba said. "Of course not." And then, as if needing to explain himself, he added, "I am her father." And then he forced a smile in my direction.

"What I meant is," Fabio said, "I am not her biological father. Or birth father. Oh, I don't know what the right word is." Fabio sighed. "I think you already knew that, Daria, but in case your parents didn't, I thought they should know."

"Do you know who the, um, birth father is?" Sheila asked. "What I mean is . . . does she know who the father is?"

I cringed a little bit at the question, wishing my mother had asked anything but that. I tried hard to focus on the delicious smell of home-cooked food coming from the kitchen. How could a house smell so good and feel so tense?

From across the room came the sound of Encarnación's voice. "Of course I know who her father is. I'm not sure what you're implying." We all turned over, and there she was, holding a tray of homemade enchiladas.

"She wasn't implying anything," Baba said.

"Oh, don't answer for me, Pasha," Sheila said. "Obviously, I was."

"You could have asked me who her birth father was sixteen years ago," Encarnación said. "You could have asked me many things. But you barely said a word to me."

"I didn't want to know," Sheila said. "The more I knew about you, the more real you became, and the more I would remember you. And I wanted to forget you. To pretend you were just an illusion."

Encarnación nodded solemnly, and then she led us to her sofas and placed the tray of enchiladas on the coffee table. Plates, cutlery, and napkins had already been laid out. "I wasn't sure what the proper protocol was for meeting your daughter's adoptive family," she said.

Before she could continue, Sheila interrupted with, "She is *our* daughter."

"I know that," Encarnación said. "I just meant . . ." She trailed off for a moment and then caught herself and said, "Well, in any case, I didn't think it was right not to offer you something, so I made enchiladas. If any of you are vegetarians, the ones on the right are just cheese."

"Oh, we all eat meat," Baba said. "We all eat meat." I wished for a moment that Amir were with us, because surely we would have laughed, and that would have felt nice.

"Where's Iglesias?" I asked. "I mean, Enrique."

"Under the circumstances," Encarnación said, "I thought it best that he not be here." I imagined Iglesias banished from the house, perhaps on some deserted street with Stuey, spray-painting his heart out. Then Encarnación added, "He's in his room."

"Oh," I said with a small laugh. "Well, then he's probably listening."

"He can't hear us," Encarnación said. "He always has his headphones on anyway."

My phone *ding*ed. It was a text from Iglesias: **Of course I'm listening.** I recognized this for what it was: a small peace offering.

"Is that from him?" Encarnación asked.

"It's from a friend," I said, which was, after all, the truth.

Encarnación took a breath and said, "I want this to be about us, Daria. Not about Enrique."

"I'm sorry," I said. "I'm sorry for lying to you when we met. For letting you think I was his girlfriend."

"But you are his girlfriend," she said. "Aren't you?"

"Yes," I said as I watched Baba's fingers curl and tense, his knuckles betraying his anger. "No," I corrected myself. And then, finally, I said, "I don't know."

"I know it must have been scary to tell me the truth," Encarnación said. "I'm not upset you didn't. But I don't want this discussion to be about Enrique. I don't think it's appropriate for you and Enrique to be in a romantic relationship. He knows that. You now know that. And that's the end of that discussion. I'm sure your parents agree."

"Of course we agree," Baba said. "Of course we agree. He's her brother."

"Technically not," Encarnación corrected. "He is Fabio's son. He and Daria are not related by blood. But still, I don't think it's right for them to be involved. It's emotionally complicated, and our son is emotionally complicated enough as it is . . ."

"I thought he wasn't your son," Sheila said, itching for combat.

"I didn't give birth to him," Encarnación said. "But he is still my son. You of all people should understand that."

Sheila's lips tightened. Anxious to busy herself, Sheila grabbed an enchilada and forked a small bite into her mouth. She swallowed it and said, "Not bad."

"Are you a connoisseur of enchiladas?" Encarnación asked.

"Daria had a Mexican nanny," Sheila said, matter-of-fact, and I cringed a little inside.

"I see," Encarnación said. "I'm sure you raised her to believe that Mexicans make the very best hired help."

"Do you think I'm a horrible person?" Sheila asked, defiant.

"No." Encarnación sighed. "Just a slightly oblivious one."

I sat on the sofa listening to the two of them trade insults back and forth, and my mind started to go fuzzy, like it was filled with cotton candy. I couldn't hear the specifics of what they were saying anymore, just echoes. Sheila accused Encarnación of judging her, and Encarnación accused Sheila of the same. Their voices became more acute as the battle raged on, until finally, my mind cleared and I heard Sheila announce, "I've had enough of this. I came here because I thought it would bring my daughter peace, but clearly it won't do any such thing."

Sheila glared at my father, silently urging him to follow her as she headed to the door. But before she could reach the threshold, I yelled, "Enough!"

All eyes were on me. I stood up tall and pushed my shoulders back, puffing my chest out. I thought that by assuming a powerful pose, I would *feel* confident. But I didn't. I had no idea what I was about to say, but I knew I had to say something.

"This is not about you," I said quietly, to nobody in particular. "This is about me. This is my moment." Now I turned to Sheila, addressing her directly. "This is *my* life."

"I know that, Daria," Sheila said. "But . . ."

"Stop talking, Sheila," I begged. "Stop making excuses. Why can't you just focus on me for a little while? Why is it so hard for you to just ask me how I'm feeling? Why is it impossible for you to ask me what I want, what I need, who I am?"

Sheila was stunned into silence. Baba stood up and positioned himself between us. He placed a hand on each of our shoulders, careful not to pick a side. "Go ahead, Sheila," he said. "Ask her."

Sheila whispered, "How are you feeling?"

I'd wanted her to ask the question, and yet I couldn't bring myself to answer.

"What do you need?" Sheila asked, each word struggling to escape her lips, as if she were speaking a foreign language.

I took a deep breath and then unleashed my needs. "I need you to stop trying to control who I am, and what I become. Stop making my life all about you. And just sit down and listen to Encarnación without fighting, without arguing. Just listen. I want to know everything."

Sheila finally nodded and sat back down. Baba gave my shoulder a squeeze and sat down next to Sheila, who gently said, "I'm listening now."

I was the only one left standing, and all eyes were on me. I turned to Encarnación. "I want to know everything," I said. "I want to know where I was born, and when I was adopted, and how it happened, and who my birth father is."

Encarnación looked to Sheila and Baba. "Do you want to start, or should I?" she asked.

"Go ahead," Baba said. "Go ahead. The story starts with you."

Encarnación adjusted herself into a comfortable position on the sofa. "So," she said, "I was working in a clothing factory."

"Local," I said, and she nodded. "You know, that's how I

found you," I continued. "I Googled you and found a picture of you in the paper at the factory, so I went there and got your address from the head of the company."

"Wow," Baba said, impressed. "That's very resourceful, *aziz*."

"So you met Seth Nijensen?" Encarnación asked.

"Yeah," I said. "He gave me your address."

"Well," Encarnación said. "Then you've met your biological father."

The world stopped for a moment. It felt like everyone in the room disappeared, and I was alone. If Seth Nijensen was my biological father, wouldn't I have felt something when I met him? Wouldn't I have looked into his eyes and felt some connection?

Then my thoughts turned to Baba, and how it must have felt for him to hear another man referred to as my father. A pain in my chest seized me. The thought of Baba doubting his role in my life hurt me that much. I tried to read Baba's face for clues to his thoughts. He was biting his lip again. Perhaps this posed a new challenge for him. Perhaps he imagined my biological father was bound to be dead, or in prison, or in Mexico. Now here was a new twist: my biological father was alive, right down the street, and a CEO of a major company.

Once I got over trying to read Baba's mood, I let my own mind reel. It replayed the moment I'd met Seth, trying hard to find meaning in the encounter, to give significance to his handshake, to locate the deep pool of expression behind his horn-rimmed glasses. And then I wondered aloud, "Wait, so I'm Jewish?"

"Half," Encarnación said.

"Not technically," Sheila said. "Jewishness is passed on through the mother." She turned to Encarnación and added, "Iran had a vibrant Jewish community before the revolution. Most Persians in Los Angeles are Jewish, although our family is agnostic."

"You don't say," Encarnación said sarcastically.

"I'm sorry," Sheila said. "I'm listening. Only listening." And she pretended to zip her lips up, a gesture I had never seen her use before.

"Does he know?" I asked. "I mean, I went to his office and told him I was your biological daughter. Did he know who I was?"

Encarnación leaned forward, taking my hand in hers. "I don't think so."

But I knew he suspected it. Why else would he have helped me? Why else would he have gifted me clothes, as if that would make up for his actions sixteen years ago?

"Did you love him?" I asked.

"I thought I did."

"Did you tell him about me?"

Now she took a big breath, like she was going to need extra oxygen to get through this. "I was very young when you were born. Like many young people, I confused infatuation with love. Seth was like no one else I had ever met. He was a gringo who spoke Spanish like a Mexican, who knew how to make perfect mole sauce, who seemed to believe more than anyone I had ever met in equality. Back then, Local wasn't the big company it is now."

I saw Baba flinch again. My biological father's success really seemed to bother him.

"It was only a dream," Encarnación continued. "And I believed in the dream. So when he first asked me out, I couldn't believe my luck. I thought my life was set. I thought I had been chosen. We spent a lot of time together outside of the factory. He was so interested in Mexican culture. I taught him my secret recipes, and read him my favorite Mexican poetry, and played him my favorite Mexican singers."

"Chavela Vargas?" I asked, somehow desperate to prove my own street cred.

"Yes," she said. "Among others. And in turn, he exposed me to his favorite things. He gave me books by Philip Roth and Norman Mailer and John Updike. And he played me Tom Waits and Lou Reed and Nick Cave and Leonard Cohen. He was teaching me, and I was teaching him." She smiled at the memory. "I suppose I have him to thank for my life in many ways. He was such a dreamer, and he made me remember my own dreams. He helped me to see that I wanted to be a teacher. I worshipped him, so you can imagine how happy I was when I realized I was pregnant. I thought we would be a family."

Sheila swung her left leg over her right, the small motion drawing all our attention momentarily. Sheila had a hard time with emotional conversations, and I could only imagine how hard this one was for her to hear. She was listening, though. She remained quiet. And her silence spoke volumes.

"I didn't want to tell him at the office," Encarnación continued. "I wanted the moment to be special. So I cooked dinner for him. *Carne asada, platanos, flan*, the works. I remember it so well. Some days you forget, and others are engraved in your memory forever, no matter how hard you try to forget them. And I wanted to forget that day. I have tried to forget it. And maybe some days, I've succeeded in pushing that memory back. Fabio helped, and Enrique helped. They gave me the family I wanted long ago."

Sheila's face softened. I could see her wanting to comfort Encarnación, but she didn't.

"But wait," I said. "You skipped over so much. You told him you were pregnant, so he obviously knows about me."

"Yes and no," she said. She gulped hard. "That night, I discovered that sometimes the most dynamic, inspiring, loving people can let you down. He didn't want a child. Certainly not with me. He already had a child, and it was his company. So he wrote me a check, and I agreed to get an abortion. I couldn't go back to work after that. It was the last time I saw him. I never told him I kept you."

There was a long silence in the room. We all wanted to honor Encarnación's painful memory. Finally, Baba said, "This man is dishonorable."

To my surprise, I felt a desire to defend Seth. He was my biological father, after all, and if it weren't for him, I wouldn't even exist.

"No," Encarnación said. "It's not that simple. He didn't want to bring a child into the world, but that doesn't make him a bad person. I know that now. He is still all of those things that made me care for him. Passionate, ambitious. He dreams big. I think you do too, Daria."

"Well, I'd still like to punch him in the face," Baba said. These were the most aggressive words I had ever heard him speak. I backed away from him a little. Baba was like my teddy bear, my soft blanket. He wasn't supposed to sound this bitter.

"We can't judge a person by an isolated action," Encarnación said to Baba. "What if you and your wife were judged solely on your decision to keep this secret from your daughter? Wouldn't that reduce you to far less than who you are?"

"I suppose . . . ," Baba said, drifting off into thought.

"I should've told Seth about my decision," Encarnación said. "I thought about getting in touch with him many times through the years. But the more time passed, the harder it became. Now I think it's up to you, Daria, to decide whether you'd like to tell him."

I nodded. "Did you consider keeping me yourself?" I asked.

Sheila's legs didn't swing this time. She froze, awaiting Encarnación's response.

"No," Encarnación said. "I knew I couldn't raise a child on my own. I wasn't even close to ready. So I contacted an adoption lawyer, and he told me about your parents. They sounded so wonderful. I liked that they already had a son. I liked the idea of you having an older brother. And I liked that even though they weren't Mexican, they were immigrants. I wanted you to have a culture, with its own sounds and scents and flavors and traditions. I guess you can take over the story from here," she said, eyeing Sheila.

"Oh," Sheila said, her restless leg syndrome finally letting up as she sat up tall. "I'm only here to listen."

"Don't be so literal," I said. "I want to hear everything."

"But you know the rest," Sheila said. "Lala told you the whole story."

"Lala is our nanny," Baba explained.

"So you even outsource your intimacy?" Encarnación asked, not cruelly, but rather as a challenge to Sheila. I think Encarnación could see how much I craved this story, how deeply I longed for the truth.

My mother turned to me, her eyes moist. "I don't want to talk about the miscarriages, Daria. There were too many of them, and each one was worse. The pain of them was exponential. And then there was . . ." She drifted off, and I knew she was thinking about the stillbirth.

"It's okay," I said. "Really. You don't have to talk about it."

"I always thought that protecting you from all the ugliness in my life was a gift to you," she said. "There was so much pain in my life. So much death. So much sadness." My mother paused, and Encarnación gave her a gentle nod, urging her to go on. "And I didn't want that for you. But I was wrong. I should have just told you everything. Maybe by trying to protect you, I caused even more sadness."

I tried to replay my childhood with a different mother, a version of the mother Amir had described to me, who would hole herself up in her room for days at a time, who would wallow in memories of her difficult past, who mourned her father and brother day and night. It was a more honest childhood, and yet a far more painful one as well. And suddenly, I was overtaken with a deep sense of gratitude. It finally hit me how hard they had worked to give me a good life.

"No," I said. "I had a great childhood." I took a breath and then said, "I guess maybe things happen when they're supposed to. I wouldn't have been ready to process all this as a kid. But I'm ready now. It took me almost sixteen years, I guess."

"And it took me forty-nine," Sheila said.

And Baba and I laughed, because of course we knew it really took her fifty-two years. But that's one secret we wouldn't have dared reveal.

Once our laughter died down, Encarnación said, "I always

felt I made the right decision, Daria, and now that I see what a strong woman you've become, I know it with certainty. I guess what I'm saying is, this is the way it was supposed to be. I wasn't meant to be your mother. But perhaps I was meant to come in your life now. And if that's what you want, I'm here. Things fall into place in their own way."

My mother, antsy from having ceded the floor to Encarnación, gently butted in. "The day we got the call about you, I knew everything would fall into place. I'll never forget it. It was February nineteenth. We waited outside the delivery room for news."

"Wait, you weren't in the delivery room?" I asked.

"No," Sheila said. "I couldn't . . . I didn't . . . I wanted not to see you," she said to Encarnación. "I know it may have seemed cruel, but I didn't want to remember you."

"It's not cruel," Encarnación said.

"We were in the waiting room, and then we got news that you were born. Eleven eleven a.m. I always thought that was lucky."

"In the spirit of honesty," Encarnación said, "there's something I can tell you now. You were actually born at nine eleven a.m."

"What?" I asked.

"I wanted to hold you for a little while. Just to look in your eyes, and to explain things to you, and to say I loved you. I knew your parents were waiting, but the doctor let me hold you. He said it wouldn't hurt anybody."

"But my birth certificate says eleven eleven a.m.," I said.

Sheila shrugged. "Oh well, what difference does two hours make?"

"I think the last two hours have made a huge difference," I said. "Don't you? I mean, we're, like, friends with my biological mother now."

"Do we have to use that word?" Sheila asked.

"Your mother's right," Encarnación said. "You shouldn't think of me as your mother in any way."

"Well, what should I think of you as?" I asked.

"Just think of me as your . . . as your . . . Encarnación," she offered.

Sheila smiled. She clearly did not want to share the privilege (and, if I have to be honest, the pain) that comes with her designation as my mother.

"Thank you," Baba said. I waited for him to say it again, but he didn't. He must not have felt nervous anymore. And neither was I. Somehow, sitting here with my parents, across from my Encarnación and her husband, eating enchiladas as my nonstepbrother listened from his room, seemed totally natural.

When the conversation between my parents, Encarnación, and Fabio came to its natural end, Sheila and Baba stood up and announced it was getting late. Baba put his arm around me. I was about to ask if I could go up to see Iglesias, but I decided I didn't need to ask for permission. "I'm going to talk to Iglesias," I stated. And then, not wanting to appear too defiant, I added, "I hope that's okay."

Encarnación invited my parents to stay while Iglesias and I talked upstairs. She even offered them homemade blue corn ice cream. Unsurprisingly, Sheila and Baba rejected the offer. From what I could tell, this was the longest stretch of time they had spent out of their comfort zone since the Iranian Revolution, and I didn't begrudge them their desire to return to the comfort of home.

"I'll drop her off," Encarnación told them. "And don't worry, the door to his room will be open at all times."

"Thank you," Sheila said. "We appreciate it." And with a half smile, Sheila pulled something wrapped in tissue paper from her purse. "I almost forgot," she said. "It's a little gift. It's nothing, really."

Encarnación took the gift from Sheila's hand and unwrapped it. It was an ashtray, hand-painted by Auntie Lida with an image of an Iranian woman, wrapped in a bright blue shawl, holding a pomegranate. "It's lovely," Encarnación said.

"My sister, Lida, paints these," Sheila explained. "It's from Iran."

"This was very thoughtful," Encarnación said. "I'll bring you a little piece of Mexico next time I come over."

"You already gave them a little piece of Mexico," Fabio

cracked. It was practically the first time he had spoken since the conversation began. But the way Encarnación laughed made me get what she saw in him, and made me happy that she had found her own family in him and Iglesias.

"You're right," Baba said. "You did give us a very precious gift, but I'd say this ashtray is about on par with it." Baba winked at me.

"One more thing," Sheila said. I was nervous about what she was going to say. "Daria's sweet sixteen party is coming up," Sheila began. "I've invited many people she doesn't want there, and I think I should invite a few people she might like to have there as well. So would it be okay if I sent you an invitation?"

Encarnación's face opened up into a huge smile. "We would be honored," she said. To my shock, Sheila hugged Encarnación, and then my parents left.

I headed up to Iglesias's room and knocked on the door. "Yup," he said.

I opened the door and found him on his bed, a laptop in front of him, papers strewn about him. "That went well," he said.

"Yeah," I said, beaming a little. "Better than I thought."

I was still standing up. I didn't feel comfortable enough to sit. I wasn't sure how long I would be there, or if he was still mad at me, or what we even were to each other anymore.

"Hey, I'm sorry," he said, not looking me in the eye.

"For what?" I asked.

"It's my shit I'm angry about," he said. "Not your shit."

"Okay," I said. "Well, I'm sorry too. I should've stood up for you in front of my parents."

"It's cool," he said. "They're pretty intimidating, especially your mom. That woman's a baller."

"Yeah," I said with a laugh. "I guess she is."

There was a long silence, which was broken when, from downstairs, Encarnación shouted, "What's going on up there?"

"Jesus, Mom," Iglesias yelled back. "There was a natural lull in the conversation."

"Keep talking," Encarnación shouted back. "*Just* talking."

Iglesias rolled his eyes. "She was a lot more pissed at me than she was at you," he said. "I got *a lot* of shit. Almost as much as when I got arrested."

"And your dad?"

"I don't know. I think he's just rolling with it, you know. I mean, he knew you existed and all. I just get the sense that he's supporting whatever she wants. Like he's not allowed to have an opinion 'cause this is her drama."

"Well, I'm sorry you got reamed out 'cause of me," I said.

"It wasn't your fault," he said. "It was mine. We make our own decisions. And they have consequences. I think I finally get that now."

"Can I sit?" I asked.

Iglesias nodded. Sitting on his bed, he was a far cry from the towering and sexy giant he seemed to be when we first met. Sure, he was still beautiful, with his muscular arms covered in tattoos. And sure, he was still huge. His legs dangled off his single bed, which he must have outgrown years ago. But now he seemed less like a sexy giant and more like a sweet boy. I sat at the edge of the bed and glanced at the papers strewn about. There were some sketches and some scribbled writing. "What's all this?" I said.

"I'm working on a portfolio," he said.

"A portfolio, huh?" I replied with a smile. "That sounds like something someone works on when they have plans that go beyond spray-painting city walls and copying my mother's handbags."

"Yeah," he said, looking me in the eye, "I'm applying to art school." He gave it a beat for the news to sink in, and then he added, "In San Francisco."

"Oh," I said. And although I was really happy for him, sadness washed over me as well. I liked sitting on a bed with him, being close to him. "I guess you don't want to stay here, then. 'Cause there are great art schools right here."

"I think I need to get a fresh start," he said. "But I'll visit my friends often."

"Friends," I repeated. I felt hollow, like the part of me that still thought Iglesias and I could be romantic had been ripped out of me.

"Aw, come on," he said. "It's not like I'm applying to school in Reykjavik."

"Reykjavik!" I said with a laugh. "Where did you pull that one from? Why not Abu Dhabi?"

"Or Kuala Lumpur," he said. "I hear they have great art schools there."

"The very best ones are actually at the very top of Machu Picchu," I said. This was what I loved most about Iglesias. These moments when it felt like we could finish each other's sentences. "There's no internet or cell phone service up there, but that steep mountain air apparently does wonders for one's artistic voice."

"I'll look into it," he said. "But the school in Reykjavik is still really appealing. It's inside a volcano. Mad inspiring."

"I don't know," I said. "Do they have air-conditioning inside volcanoes? I bet it gets superhot."

Iglesias laughed, and then he stopped the banter and said with complete seriousness, "I really was considering Reykjavik. There's a really cool program there Stuey told me about."

From downstairs, the booming sound of Encarnación's voice traveled up toward us. "You are not going to school in Iceland!"

Iglesias shrugged. "And that was the end of that."

"So why San Francisco?" I asked.

"I don't know," he said. And then, because he did know, he continued, "Because it's near, but far. Because I want to be able to see all the people I love, but also go somewhere new. Somewhere where I can just figure out who I am as an artist, you know? Stop copying other people's shit and make my own."

"Am I one of those people you love?" I asked.

"Yeah," he said.

"Yeah?" I asked, giggling.

I inched closer to him. He shifted closer to me. And when our bodies couldn't move any nearer to each other, our heads started finding their way toward each other, our lips pulled together by a mysterious force, like magnets.

I closed my eyes.

I felt his hot breath against my face.

I remembered that first kiss on the Ferris wheel, the magic of it flooding through me.

Then, in an instant, the magic wore off, the mysterious magnetic force evaporated, and we both laughed.

Our lips were still hovering perilously close to each other, but we both knew we weren't going to kiss again. Ever.

"What's going on up there?" Encarnación bellowed from below.

"I farted!" Iglesias screamed back.

"You're disgusting," she responded.

Now I knew whatever romance existed between us was definitely over. No guy talked about farting in front of the girl he liked.

"Can I be totally honest about something?" he asked.

"Of course," I said. "Hit me with some honesty."

"I'm really glad we didn't sleep together," he said. "I mean, what were we thinking?"

I laughed nervously, and then I thought about it, and I said, "I guess that would've ruined everything, right?"

"Right," he said. "Because now we still have a chance to be friends."

"More than friends," I said. "We're nonsiblings."

Iglesias nodded, then pushed his laptop toward me. "Here," he said. "It's the essay I want to submit with my application. It's still a little rough. Tell me what you think."

I started reading, and to my surprise, the essay was about me. It was about how I had knocked on his door with a clear sense of purpose, although he hadn't yet known what that purpose was. He wrote about my search for my identity, and about how I'd questioned his art, and told him he didn't make anything original. He said he wanted the chance to go search for his own identity, and that I had inspired this mission. I caught some missing punctuation and fixed it.

"What are you doing?" he said.

"You were missing a comma," I said.

"That's it?" he asked. "That's all you have to say?"

"Yeah," I said. "I mean, that's the only thing wrong with it. You were just missing a comma. The rest is perfect."

"So I was missing a comma," he said with a smile.

"Also, thank you," I said.

"For what?" he asked.

"You've inspired me to finally finish an essay I've had due for a little while," I said, thinking of my genealogy assignment.

"So we inspired each other," he said. Then he leaped off his bed and towered over me. "Come on," he said. "We need to go."

"WHERE?" Encarnación shouted from below.

Iglesias took my hand and led me downstairs to face his parents. "We need to go photograph my work for my portfolio," he said. "You're welcome to come chaperone us."

"You bet your ass we're chaperoning you," Fabio said. "We're not letting you get arrested again."

And off we went, the four of us, like a family. Iglesias took us on a tour of the walls he had tagged. Some of them had been painted over, but some were still there. There was the *Girl with a Big-Ass Hoop Earring*. There was Marilyn with pills coming out of her mouth. There was Botticelli's Venus in a G-string. There was a replica of a Chanel handbag with a pet lion peeking out of it. There was *The Last Hipster Supper*. And then, of course, there was *Daria Lisa*. There were also all his different tags: Karne, Rico, Hoopla, and, finally, Iglesias.

By the time we got to *Daria Lisa*, Encarnación said, "They arrested you for making something this beautiful?" Iglesias nodded, and she turned to him with regret and pride in her eyes. "I am so sorry, Enrique. We should have been more supportive of you."

"After you got arrested for spray-painting, we just wanted to keep you out of trouble," Fabio added.

"But we never thought to come look at the work first," Encarnación continued, her eyes wide with wonder. "These are beautiful."

"Beautiful," Fabio echoed.

"They're not beautiful," Iglesias countered. "The whole point is that I have no voice as an artist. I don't know who I am. That's why I wanna go to school."

"You have so much time to develop a *voice*," Encarnación said, sounding very much like a teacher. "You have talent. That's all you need at your age."

She pulled Iglesias close to her and gave him a kiss on the cheek. Iglesias smiled, turning into a little boy in her arms. Then he pulled away and said to me, "Hey, pose in front of it!"

"No," I said, my cheeks blushing red.

"Come on, my whole essay's about you. Let's give 'em a visual."

I acquiesced and stood in front of the *Daria Lisa*. I tried to give the same smirk and searing gaze that made her such a force. Then I realized I didn't need to try because I *was* the *Daria Lisa*. I was the force.

Chapter Sixteen

ON TUESDAY MORNING, I GOT up earlier than usual for school and asked Sheila to drop me off outside Kurt's house. His mom lived superclose to school, and he walked to school in the mornings. I sat on his stoop and stared at his front door until finally it opened. Kurt emerged in a checkered shirt, red jeans, and his signature fedora. His mom was next to him, in a pair of wrinkled gray pajamas.

"Hey, Daria," Kurt's mom said.

"Hey, Mrs. Sanderson," I said, standing up to hug her.

"Seriously," she said. "Call me Susanne."

"Sorry. It's good to see you, Susanne. You look good," I said.

I tried to get Kurt's attention, but he was wearing sunglasses. With his eyes covered, I couldn't tell what he was feeling, or even where he was looking. The first thing he said was, "Okay, bye, Mom."

Kurt's mom gave him a hug, and way too many kisses on the cheek. "Have a beautiful day at school," she said.

"Every day is a *beautiful day* at school," Kurt said with a smile, then he started to walk away.

I rushed to catch up with him. "Hey," I said. "Wait up." Kurt stopped and waited for me. "Would it be okay if we walked to school together?" He nodded, then started walking again. We walked in silence for a few steps, and then I spoke again. "I've been through a lot lately. And the thing that felt worst were the moments when I felt forgotten. I guess that's how you must have felt, maybe. I mean, I'm not trying to tell you how you felt. I'm just trying . . . to be a friend."

"I didn't feel forgotten," he said.

"Okay," I said.

I waited a long time for him to speak again, then finally he said, "I just felt like, I don't know, like *what's wrong with me?* Why did you just stick me in the friend zone without even considering me? Am I not a guy?" Then he took his sunglasses off and looked at me for the first time.

I paused for a moment. "Kurt, I have to be honest. Your crush on me didn't feel serious. It's like you were trying to make me feel better or something . . ."

"Why would I need to make you feel better?" he asked. "You're awesome."

And there he was. The sweet Kurt I missed.

"In a way, you're right," he added. "It's just that I thought I *should* like you."

"Why?" I asked.

"High school is half over and I haven't even had a girl-friend." He started walking a little faster. "And the only three girls I get along with are you guys, and Caroline is a lesbian, and Joy is out of my league."

"And also a lesbian," I said. I almost walked into oncoming traffic.

Kurt grabbed my arm and pulled me back. "I know! I mean, can we take a moment to acknowledge the fact that Caroline and Joy are officially the strangest couple ever?"

"Acknowledged," I said.

"I'm happy for them," he said. "Not to sound like one of my mom's favorite movies, but I feel like they complete each other."

"Do you think Caroline and Joy had each other at hello?" I asked, and we laughed. "You know, I think you're the greatest Authentic of all."

"Why?"

"Think about it," I said, and I reached my hand out to hold his. "I kept a secret, and so did Caroline and Joy. You're the only one of us who was authentic all along. You never let us down."

Kurt nodded. "That's fine and all, but is every girl I ever meet only going to see me as a friend?"

"I will bet you that you'll have a girlfriend by the time we graduate high school," I said. "If I win, you can take me to dinner at Katsu-Ya."

"Betting on my love life might be the most Persian thing you've ever done," he said with a smile.

"What can I say? I am my father's daughter."

"Did you just quote another one of my mom's favorite movies?" he asked.

We walked the rest of the way to school holding hands, and laughing. The morning clouds parted and the sun hit my face, warming me.

The first class of the day was Mr. Farrell's, and he began by picking a name from the hat. Joy, Caroline, Kurt, and I all looked to each other nervously. "Here we go. Today's presenter will be none other than the one and only Kurt Sanderson."

Kurt stood up nervously. "Mr. Farrell, I'm totally willing to present today, but the thing is, I'm still waiting to find out the birthdays of a few of my distant relatives, and in order for my presentation to be wholly exhaustive and astrologically exact, I'm going to require about one more week."

"I'm sorry, Kurt," Mr. Farrell said. "The system is arbitrary."

"I understand," Kurt said, clearly disappointed.

As Kurt made his way to the front of the class, I stood up. "Mr. Farrell, if it's allowed, I'd like to volunteer." I wanted to help Kurt, but I also really wanted to present. I had a lot I wanted to get off my chest.

"Oh my God," Kimmy said. "This is so *Hunger Games*. She's volunteering as tribute."

"Well," Mr. Farrell said, "if no one objects, I don't see any reason not to allow Daria to present today."

"Thank you," Kurt whispered to me.

"Get ready for a Persian sermon," Heidi cracked as I stepped up to the front of the class, and the Nose Jobs laughed.

I stood in front of the class for a long, awkward beat. "I didn't bring a prop or a piece of art or anything like that," I started. "I just thought I'd draw a family tree for you guys, and tell you my story." I picked up a red marker, wrote my name on the dry-erase board, and then circled it. "So," I said. "That's me. Daria Esfandyar."

"This is such a compelling presentation," Heidi whispered to her sycophants.

I drew in circles for my mother, father, and Amir. "And these are my parents and my brother. My parents were born in Iran, and my brother is, um, gay." I swallowed hard. I knew my presentation was going horribly so far. I looked to Mr. Farrell, who gazed at me with rapt attention, willing me to do better by the sheer force of his belief. I drew in circles for Auntie Lida and all the ancestors she'd told me about. When I was done, I said, "A few weeks ago, this would have been my entire family tree. But now it's different. And not just because my brother and his husband had a baby." I drew in circles for Andrew and Rose.

I cracked my knuckles and gritted my teeth, and then I picked up the red marker again, and I drew in another circle above my name, and inside it I wrote the words *Encarnación Vargas*. I could see the confusion on the faces of my classmates. Even Heidi was quiet.

"See, the thing is," I said, "I found out recently that I'm adopted." Now there were a few gasps. "I could've just omitted that from my family tree. I mean, my family is the one that raised me, right?"

I glanced at Mr. Farrell. He looked concerned, like he was ready to step in any second.

"I've always prided myself on being authentic," I continued, gaining confidence. "I guess that's why I was so proud of being Iranian. I thought that being proud of my heritage was being authentic. But then I found out that my genes aren't Iranian at all. And that kind of threw me into an existential tailspin."

I drew in circles for Meili and Fang. "And then I thought about how my niece is half-Chinese," I said. "And I realized that my family tree is kind of like a map of the world. It has all these branches and they don't just point up and down. They point left and right, and in all kinds of diagonals." I took a breath. "I don't know what I'm trying to say," I said. "And I know I'm not exactly being articulate. But I guess my point is that I'm really happy I discovered all this. Because the way I see it, the more family you have, the better. It just means there's more love in your life."

I thought I was done, but then I surprised myself by drawing three more circles next to my name. I wrote in the names of Caroline, Joy, and Kurt. "And one more thing. I realized that friends can sometimes feel like family. And if they feel like family, then they *are* family. And that's a good thing too. 'Cause that's even more love."

Caroline, Joy, and Kurt all smiled, misty-eyed.

I put the marker down. "So I guess what I'm ultimately trying to say is that I'm superproud to be a part of an Iranian, Mexican, Chinese, American, Muslim, Jewish, and agnostic family. How authentic is that?"

In my head, I had imagined this rousing closing line would have been met with wild applause. I had imagined the Nose Jobs cheering me, and the jocks fist-bumping me, and the Latin Quarter giving me a standing ovation. But instead there was just an interminable, awkward silence, which was broken when Betty Powell said, "I've always known I was adopted. The only part of it that was ever weird was when my birth mother became a superfamous singer." *Only at Beverly Hills High*, I thought to myself, *is adoption a competitive sport.* And then, Betty added, "Well, you can talk to me about it anytime, Daria. I mean, if you have questions or anything."

I thanked her, and then handed Mr. Farrell my essay. He

finally stood up and said, "Thank you, Daria. That was moving. I thought this assignment would be thought-provoking, but I don't think I was prepared for just *how* thought-provoking. It reminds me of the fact that teachers often learn more from students than the other way around."

I gulped down hard, and I had a brief moment of thinking that being a teacher would be a really fun job to have. Someday.

At lunch, I heaped some food onto my tray and approached the Authentics' table. I thought a few people would stop me and say something about my presentation, but no one did. In fact, everything was status quo. The cliques were all at their designated tables, and nothing had changed. When I plunked down my tray, Caroline, Joy, and Kurt were midconversation. "What are you talking about?" I asked.

"How proud we are of you," Caroline said. "That was awesome."

I blushed a little.

"Seriously," Joy said. "We were just saying we should've given you a standing ovation, but we were all too moved to . . . move."

"Thanks," I said, laughing. "Hey, guys, can we make a pact that we won't have any more secrets among us?"

"That's fine," Joy said. "But I'm not ready for anyone outside the Authentics to know about me and Caroline. Okay?"

Caroline rolled her eyes. "My girlfriend is such a closet case."

"I just don't want to break my parents' hearts," Joy said. "Yet."

"So are we going to wait till they die to tell them?" Caroline asked.

"How can you even say that? It's like you're wishing for my parents to die," Joy said.

Caroline almost put a hand on Joy's knee, and then stopped herself. "Of course not. I just think you need to come out."

"But I don't even know if I'm gay," Joy said. "I think maybe I'm bisexual."

"Then come out as bisexual," Caroline insisted. "Or just come out as being with me, so I can kiss you right here in this cafeteria."

"Don't you dare," Joy exclaimed.

"Taurus Rising in action," Kurt said, shaking his head. "One more stubborn than the other."

"Speaking of astrology," I said. "I have a question, Kurt." Kurt looked at me, curious. "It turns out I was born two hours earlier than I thought I was."

"Wait," Kurt said. "You were *not* born at eleven eleven a.m.?"

"No," I said, amazed that Kurt remembered the exact time of my birth.

"You realize that totally changes your chart," Kurt said.

"Really?" I asked.

"Wow," he said, as if he'd just discovered there was life on Mars or something. "Everything makes sense now."

"You know what doesn't make sense?" I said, looking toward Caroline and Joy. "Calling ourselves the Authentics. I mean, it's too much to live up to, you know."

"I agree," Caroline said. "No one can be all authentic all the time."

"I actually think it's a little weird to have a clique name," I said. "I mean, we're almost sixteen. We're practically adults. Adults don't have clique names."

"Um, the Ya-Ya Sisterhood," Joy said.

"The Rat Pack," Caroline added.

"Okay," Kurt said. "Let's call ourselves the Inauthentics, then."

"But it's not like we're inauthentic," Joy said. "We're just selective about who we tell the truth to. We can be the Selectives."

"I don't know," Kurt said. "Maybe we don't need to define ourselves based on how authentic or inauthentic we are at all. Daria said we were like family, right? Maybe we're the Family."

"Ooh, like the mob," Caroline said.

"You know what the rest of the school calls us behind our backs, right?" I asked. And they all looked at me with questioning glances. "They call us the Island of Misfit Toys. Heidi told me during our tender heart-to-heart last week."

"Wait, that's hilarious," Kurt said.

"I love it," Joy said.

"Joy's my toy," Caroline said, and then, enjoying the rhyme, she added, "And I would love her even if she were a boy."

"But what if she were as mean as Lucius Malfoy?" Kurt asked.

"Oy," Joy said, with a dramatic roll of the eyes, and we all laughed.

Caroline stood up on the table and announced loudly to the whole school, "Hey, everyone, from now on, me and my friends can publicly be referred to as the Island of Misfit Toys. We're an island, we're misfits, we're toys, and we're damn proud."

Our classmates gave Caroline a moment of their attention before going back to their own conversations. And so the Authentics became the Island of Misfit Toys, the irony being that in finding each other, we were no longer misfits. We fit just fine.

Chapter Seventeen

ON THE ONLY RAINY NIGHT Los Angeles saw all winter, my mother and I sat across from our dinner table, with Baba and Amir as our impartial mediators. Slowly, we hammered out the details of my sweet sixteen party using the one skill we all shared: negotiation.

"I will concede to your venue selection," I said.

"Concede?" Sheila echoed. "The venue is beautiful."

"It's the banquet hall of a garish Persian restaurant," I scoffed.

"Daria, we agreed to keep all communication positive." This was Amir, holding me to one of our ground rules.

"Okay, fine," I said. "I will accept the beautiful choice of venue if you allow me to choose my own beautiful outfit."

"I will consider your proposal," my mother said. "But I

will need to see this beautiful outfit first."

I pulled up a picture of the body-hugging zebra-print Halston dress Joy had bought for me as an early birthday present. She was adamant I wear it to the party, and I finally had the confidence to do just that. "It's Halston," I said to Sheila, because now I knew who he was, and because Sheila loved a brand name.

"Do we have an agreement?" Baba asked.

"What shoes will you be wearing?" Sheila asked.

"Mom, come on," Amir said. "We agreed not to nitpick."

"Fine," my mother said. "We have an agreement. Now I'd like to discuss the guest list."

"As a reminder," Amir said, "we have agreed not to *disinvite* anyone."

"The thing is that the Malikis have some family visiting from Israel, and the Javadis have some family visiting from London, and . . ."

"Oh my God, Mom!" I yelled.

"Daria, we agreed to keep our voices calm," Baba said.

I took a deep breath, and saw this for what it was: an opportunity. "Fine," I said. "You can invite the distant relatives of all your friends, if we skip the requisite boring slide show."

"Skip the slide show?" Sheila looked to Baba. "We've spent months going through old photos, and she wants us to—"

"Sheila, we agreed that Amir and I are impartial," Baba said, and I loved him for that.

"I'm not done," I said. "Instead of a boring slide show chronicling my journey from adorable baby to pug-nosed, awkward teenager . . ."

"You do not have a pug nose," my mother said. "That's just a false—"

"As I was saying," I cut her off. "Instead of the slide show, I would like the banquet hall to be turned into an art gallery for the night. And it will be Iglesias's first show."

"What does his art look like?" Sheila asked.

"It's beautiful," I said. "And I'm not done. I want to sell his art at the party. And I want you guys to encourage all your friends to buy pieces."

"I don't know," Sheila said, biting her lip. "Every guest will already be giving you a gift. I don't want them to feel obligated to buy a work of art as well."

"Obligated?!" I asked incredulously.

"Daria, tone," Baba said flatly.

"Do you think the lucky people who bought Warhol's first pieces felt obligated? Do you think Picasso's first buyers felt obligated? It's a privilege!"

"Fine," Sheila finally said. "Fine. Let's just move on to the menu. Persian food, obviously."

"Sure," I said. "But I thought it would be fun if each course represented a different part of my identity. Like Chinese appetizers, Persian main course, Lala's *tres leches* cake for dessert . . ."

It went on like that for a few hours. I think we went through three pots of cardamom tea before every detail, from the flowers to the lighting to the décor, was planned.

No matter how hard we worked to plan the party, there were bound to be some surprises. Like, for example, I was dancing with Caroline and Joy when we saw Kurt approach Heidi by the buffet table. Heidi looked disgusted that he would deign to speak to her. We all inched closer to them to hear what they were saying.

"You know what's missing at this party?" Kurt asked Heidi. And before she could answer, he said, "Pink fondue. Oh, and pink goldfish."

And to our shock, Heidi laughed. "I'll have you know the fondue was my crazy mother's idea."

"But the goldfish were all you," Kurt said.

Heidi shrugged. "Guilty as charged. I thought they'd be cute, but they were creepy."

"Just a little creepy," Kurt said, and Heidi laughed again.

"Hey," Heidi said to Kurt, "do you always wear that hat 'cause you're prematurely balding? Because there's a pill for that."

Kurt took his fedora off, revealing his thick head of hair. "Nope," he said. "I've got newscaster hair. I just like fedoras."

"I'm gonna make you a T-shirt that says 'I Heart Fedoras,'" Heidi said. "Then you can stop wearing that hat."

Kurt laughed, and then a classic Leila Forouhar song came on the playlist my mother had made for the party, and Heidi screamed, "Oh my God, this is my jam!" And she pulled Kurt to the dance floor, and just like that, they were dancing. Heidi and Kurt, dancing together!

An hour later, Heidi approached me during a rare quiet moment, wearing Kurt's fedora, and asked, "Why didn't you tell me Kurt is bizarre but also totally charming?"

"Wait, are you acknowledging my existence again?" I asked.

"Yeah," she said. "I guess I am."

I smiled. "Kurt is totally charming. I just never thought you'd agree since we never agree on anything."

"True," she said. "But you know, we don't have to be the same person to be friends." As I took that in, she announced, "Kurt did my chart. He said I'm his astro–soul mate or something."

I smiled. Maybe it was a little odd that Kurt and Heidi were becoming an item, but I loved that Kurt had met someone who found him sexy. I couldn't wait to say *I told you so*. I was totally going to win that bet.

"It's a great party," Heidi said. And then, as if she couldn't end on a compliment, she added, "But seriously, Daria, that zebra dress is a little insane. You have to be Gisele to pull off a dress like that."

"You know, you don't *have* to be bitchy to me," I said. "You can just be nice."

Heidi smiled big. "I'm a Scorpio Rising," she said. "Cruel honesty is in my nature." And with that, she walked back over to Kurt.

At that moment, Sheila and Baba announced that a performer was about to take the stage. All the lights went out, and the guests, including me, wondered who it could be. Had my parents, in a desperate attempt to live up to the unreachable standards set by their peers, hired She-Reen to make a special appearance? To my delight, when the lights came back on, Caroline was onstage, wearing a white bodysuit. In broken Farsi, she sang a Persian version of "The Island of Misfit Toys" from *Rudolph the Red-Nosed Reindeer*. As she did, Iglesias spray-painted her bodysuit with the image of the *Daria Lisa*. It was epic performance art, and it was in my honor, and I couldn't have been more moved.

There were more surprises. Like the Skype message from Auntie Lida, who didn't just record some boring birthday message for me. She took me on a tour of life in Iran. "You seem so interested in your history," she said, "so I want to show you some of my Iran." And in the video, she showed me her home, and the city streets of Tehran, and her friends.

And then there was a Skype message from Meili and Fang, who wished me a happy birthday and told me I was welcome anytime in Beijing. "Of course," Meili said, "you will stay with us. In our home. Not in a hotel. And you will wake up bright and early because I am like a rooster." I laughed, reminded of how much I appreciated Meili's unique brand of opinionated humor.

Then there were the gifts—so many special, thoughtful gifts. Amir and Andrew gave me a framed picture of Rose and me that Andrew took covertly the first time I held her in my arms. "You're already the best aunt in the world," Amir said as he hugged me.

Caroline and Joy gave me a T-shirt and a hoodie, both of which read, "Misfit Toy." And they told me that they had them made for the three of us, and Kurt. Encarnación gave me a photo album, with photos of her childhood and her ancestors in them. When she gave it to me, she said, "All the people in this album are a part of me, and now they are a part of you." Lala gave me a leather journal, and on the first page, she wrote, "You have so many stories to tell, Daria. Write them down before you forget them." And I started almost right away. In fact, later that night, when I couldn't sleep from the buzz of energy still running through my veins, I filled up almost the entire journal.

But maybe the best gift of all came from Iglesias. "Almost all your pieces sold," I said to him as we drank sodas in a corner of the room.

"All but one," he said. And he must have seen my disappointment, because quickly he added, "It wasn't for sale."

"Oh," I said. "Which one?"

He pointed to one of the pieces on the wall. It was a mess

of colors, bright pinks and reds and oranges swirling around each other. It was beautiful. "This is the first piece I did for this show. The first piece I did that wasn't copying someone else's style. I don't really know if this is going to be my style, but it's the beginning of me at least trying to figure out who I am. And I thought . . ." He paused. "Wait, am I making you cry?"

I smiled through my tears. "Shut up."

"Look, I don't have to give it to you," he said.

"Hey, it's mine now," I joked. "What's it called?"

"*Ocean*," he said.

We looked at each other for a long beat, saying nothing.

Finally, he said, "Listen, Ocean, I gave you a memorable first kiss, and I just want to say that your first time had better be just as special. If I hear you gave it up to some gross guy at some lame high school party, I will haunt your dreams."

I wanted to say he would probably haunt my dreams regardless, because he was my first kiss, and my first love, and my family, but I just said, "Oh please, you lost your virginity to a girl with a fake tan and a septum piercing."

As we laughed, Sheila and Baba approached me with their gifts.

Baba handed me his gift. It was a big box, but it was pretty light, and I wondered what it could be. I opened the box, and to my surprise, there were clothes inside. It was unlike Baba to buy me clothes, so I eyed him with confusion. And then

I pulled out the clothes and realized they had all come from Local.

"I want you to know that if you ever want to see your biological father, I would support that decision," Baba said.

Tears formed in my eyes. I knew how hard this must be for Baba to say.

"We could even go see him together," Baba added. "If you want."

I looked up to Baba. "Thank you," I said.

I knew that someday, I would want to know Seth Nijensen better. But I also knew that day wasn't today or tomorrow.

Baba pulled me into a hug and said, "I love you, *aziz*."

I couldn't help it; I cried in his shoulder. Even though he was wearing a fancy suit that Sheila had picked out for him, and a red tie to match her dress, and even though she had doused him in cologne, I could still make out his unmistakable scent, which I smelled every time he held me close, and I was filled with such gratitude that the universe had conspired to make this man my father. Baba let me go, and placed his hands on my cheeks, and wiped away my tears.

And then it was Sheila's turn. She was, after all, the grande dame of the evening, and she was meant to give me the final present. With a sad smile, she handed me a box of her own, and she said, "This gift makes me very happy, and very sad."

I knew then what it was. I opened it, and unveiled it from the luxurious tissue paper it was entombed in. My very own

Chanel purse. I gasped as I held the purse tightly in my hands. It was so much more than a present. It was a rite of passage I wasn't ready for. "It's too early."

"No," she said. "You are a woman now."

She pulled me into a hug, and we didn't say a word, because I knew that this was a new day for us. I was no longer her little girl. I was my own person, and she knew that too. I could feel her letting go of one version of me and welcoming another. I suppose I was doing the same. Because this wasn't the Sheila I had known my whole life. This was a new Sheila, equally gorgeous on the outside, but less of a mystery on the inside. I understood her now, and I think perhaps she understood me too.

As she held me tightly, all I could think of to say was "Thank you." And then I paused and added, "Mommy."

She looked at me with so much love that it almost knocked me over. And then, as if unable to handle the emotions of the moment, she said, "Okay, let's move on. It's only a purse." But we both knew it was so much more than only a purse. It was a symbol. It was a torch being passed. And, c'mon, it was Chanel.

If you attended my sixteenth birthday party (and if you are Persian and live within a five-mile radius of Beverly Hills, or go to high school with me, you probably did, and rest assured your thank-you note is coming), then you probably had a blast. I mean, forget the Oscars, and the Emmys, and Taylor Swift's birthday party. This party outdid them all. I know you felt that way, because you didn't want to leave. I mean, it was a rager.

But when the party *finally* started to die down, and you exited the banquet hall, you might remember that my mother and father were standing atop the steps, bidding you good-bye and thanking you for coming. My mother was wearing a shiny red dress, her hair cascading down toward her shoulders, her entire presence singing "Don't You Wish Your Mother Was Hot Like Me?" And my father shook your hands and looked you deep in the eyes, and his gaze sang out, "Don't You Wish Your Father Was Kind Like Me?"

And then you probably turned around and took one last look at the room. The walls were lined with art that a rising artist named Iglesias made for the party. The art was colorful and unique: spray paint on cardboard. You had never seen anything like it, and maybe you bought a piece, not because you were obligated, but because it was a privilege.

In the back of the room, you saw the guest of honor still enjoying herself. I may not have been the most beautiful girl in the room, but I was certainly the happiest. In fact, I was beaming, because I was surrounded by just about everyone I loved. You didn't know most of them. You didn't know that the woman in green dancing with her family was in fact my birth mother. You didn't know that the old woman cooing at the baby was my grandmother, who had been released from her nursing home for the night. You didn't know that the man taking pictures was my brother-in-law. And that the baby being passed from my grandmother to me was my niece, Rose, who was up way past her bedtime for the occasion and who, yes, was dressed in couture.

But despite all you didn't know, you must have been thinking exactly what I was thinking: *This is the party of the century.*

Acknowledgments

This book wouldn't exist without the vision, encouragement, and support of Mitchell Waters and Holly Frederick at Curtis Brown. Mitchell, thank you for your patience and belief in me, and for seeing that there is (and always will be) a teenager living inside me. Holly, being your intern was my luckiest break ever. You have always inspired me to be true to myself and to follow my dreams. That we are still working together always puts a smile on my face. To the rest of the Curtis Brown team, especially Steven Salpeter, Anna Abreu, and Steve Kasdin, thank you for always making an agency feel so welcoming and fun.

To my brilliant and passionate editor, Alessandra Balzer, thank you for putting so much thought and care into this book, and for seeing something special in Daria and her world. I feel so lucky to have found a home with you and the amazing Balzer + Bray team.

I couldn't even begin to figure out how to live, let alone write, without the support of my family, and that begins with my incredible partner, Jonathon Aubry. You have taught me to love deeper and bigger than I ever thought possible. You are my partner, my best friend, and my Pally, and in the immortal words of Joan Crawford, we are *"a hell of a match!"*

My parents, Lili and Jahangir, have provided me with all the tools I've ever needed to build the life I want, along with love, support, and patience. I am forever grateful.

This book is a celebration of family, and I am so lucky to have a huge, beautiful family that I can always count on for dance parties, spades games, and so much love. To my cousins Maryam, Dara, Nina, Lila, Moh, Youssef, and Mandy, and my aunts and uncles, Shahla, Hushang, Azar, Djahanshah, and Parinaz, I feel so lucky to have you all in my life. To Brooke, John, Luis, and Mehrdad, thank you for joining our family and making it even more fun. To my nephews and nieces, Parker, Delilah, Rafa, Santi, and Tomio, I can't wait for you to continue the adventures of *la famille*. You guys have a lot to live up to! And to the Aubry clan—Jude, Susan, Kathy, Zu, Paul, Jamie, and company— thank you for welcoming me into your incredible family.

Two special *famille* shout-outs to my cousin Vida for sending me boxes of YA books and igniting my love for the genre. Reading Harry Potter books side by side with you is one of this muggle's favorite memories. And to my brother, Al, for teaching a stubborn quintuple Leo all about astrology. I hope this book's astrological forecast is bright.

To Tom Dolby, you are a collaborator who has made me a

better, more thoughtful writer. Your creative partnership and friendship always makes me feel like a young one.

To Melissa de la Cruz, thank you for your early support of this novel. It means the world to me. You are an inspiration to writers everywhere.

To Jennifer and Jazz Elia, there is no way I could get through life without your friendship. Thank you for always making me laugh, always showing up when I need a friend, and for being the best lesbian aunties the kids could ask for.

So many people have provided feedback on early drafts of this novel, support of my writing through the years, invaluable friendship, and most important, crucial help with child care, and a few that I must call out are Lauren Ambrose, Jamie Babbit, Fabio Blancarte, David Brind, Tom Collins, Mandy Fabian, Susanna Fogel, Nancy Himmel, Ted Huffman, Mandy Kaplan Klavens, Richard Kramer, Erica Kraus, Erin Lanahan, Gina B. Nahai, Busy Philipps, Melanie Samarasinghe, Micah Schraft, Sarah Shetter, John Shields, Lynn Shields, Mike Shields, Jeremy Tamanini, Amanda Tejeda, Serena Torrey Roosevelt, and Lila Azam Zanganeh.

Finally, to my children. I am grateful every day that I get to be your daddy. Watching you grow into the creative, hilarious, brilliant souls you are is without a doubt the greatest gift I will ever be given. I hope you read this book someday and ask your own questions about your beautiful, unconventional family, and that you always know how deeply you are loved.